MW01127072

The
Circuit
Riders

(Book One in the Circuit Rider series)

by
Bill Wood

Contents

Chapter One
THE MEETING..11

Chapter Two
THE RELATIONSHIP 22

Chapter Three
THE CONFRONTATION 30

Chapter Four
THE RETURN 38

Chapter Five
THE REJOICING..49

Chapter Six
THE HORRORS 58

Chapter Seven
THE HOLD-UP 70

Chapter Eight
THE REDEMPTION 84

Chapter Nine
THE ENTRANCE...96

Chapter Ten
THE HELPER 110

Chapter Eleven
THE FEELING 121

Chapter Twelve
THE TRICKSHOT...130

Chapter Thirteen
THE FIRE 139

Chapter Fourteen
THE CELEBRATION 151

Chapter Fifteen
THE COMMITMENT..157

Chapter Sixteen
THE CHALLENGE..164

Chapter Seventeen
THE SHOOTING 173

Chapter Eighteen
THE DECISION...181

Chapter Nineteen
THE MISSION 192

Chapter Twenty
THE PREPARATION 198

Chapter Twenty-one
THE JOURNEY 210

Contents

Chapter Twenty-two
THE LABOR 231

Chapter Twenty-three
THE FULL HOUSE 238

Chapter Twenty-four
THE NEW BEGINNING 247

Introduction

As the frontier of America began to expand westward, a group of brave, dedicated, itinerant preachers rode across the plains and mountains to spread the Christian faith. They endured heat and cold, rain and drought, despair and loneliness to fulfill their calling. They held services in saloons, schools, under tents, or in the open air depending on the receptiveness of their listeners.

These preachers became known as "circuit riders" because they were assigned specific territories within the backwoods areas. They traveled from town to town and from farm to farm or from stage-stop to stage-stop, anywhere a group of people had settled, preaching the Good News of Jesus Christ, carrying the Word of God to the fringes of civilization. Their travel was mostly performed on horseback, and the extent and duration of their territory was measured by their own endurance and that of their horses.

Danger lurked through every moment of their strenuous, lonely rounds. These preachers established new congregations in the wilderness areas, built new churches, and delivered sermons and Bible readings. Often times they would have to fight off disease and Indians and even unfriendly townsfolk who were not altogether thrilled with the idea of the circuit riders taming their villages. Still, these men knew no fear and were so outspoken as to be reckless in their condemnation of sin.

These saddlebag-preachers declared the Word of God to miners, gamblers, drunkards, and adventurers of every kind, women included. They preached to Whites, Blacks, Mexicans, Orientals, as well as Indians. Their message was for the world at large. Their sermons were delivered in barrooms, gambling halls, mining shacks, or wherever they could attract enough listeners to justify the effort. Arriving at a camp or new town, they would go from dwelling to dwelling announcing their purpose and appointing a meeting place. To summon their flock, they sometimes blew on a tin horn. If no one appeared, they scouted around for the largest group and began preaching anyway.

Between destinations, though, they were often caught by darkness and forced to spend the night in such shelter as they could make or find. Their rest was often taken in the saddle or, if they were lucky, in the barn or cabin of a believing family. They preached three times on Sunday and two or three times during the week. They crossed rivers, valleys, hills, and mountains to keep their schedule. They traveled through mud and swamps and were often forced to make long detours to cross or avoid the treacherous sloughs or flooding rivers.

Most of these circuit riders were single and lacked formal education, but were self-reliant, and courageous. They were rugged individuals who allowed neither rough terrain nor menacing weather to sway them from their appointed areas of service. They had to rely heavily on the hospitality of the settlers to get them from place to place. None of these men got rich doing what they were doing, so most were driven by a powerful dedication to the Gospel. And most never had a place to hang their hat for long, but these unsung heroes of the West helped bring true civilization to the plains, mountains, and valleys of the American frontier. There would be little or no reward beyond the spiritual.

This book is a fictionalized story of three such brave, country Gospel preachers on the frontier of Texas, and the problems they faced bringing the message of Christ to wilderness areas.

Chapter One

The Meeting

Brother Jeremiah stepped out of his elaborately decorated cabin after spending the early morning hours on his knees, onto the top deck of the *Delta Queen*. The aging circuit rider stood a few inches over six feet, blue-eyed and brown haired with patches of grey at his temples and streaked on top. He had a large nose set in a short-bearded, long face. This man of God was of Dutch ancestry on his father's side, but English on his mother's. He had inherited a stubborn streak from his father's side, which was sometimes noticeable in the square set of his jaw and the narrowing of his eyes. Those who knew him well knew that, at times like these, the aging preacher was thinking deeply about something. . . possible earthly. . . more likely heavenly.

Jeremiah breathed deeply of the cool, early-morning Louisiana air. This was the first time the fiftyish preacher had returned to his home state since he began riding the circuit for Jesus in central and eastern Texas more than thirty years before.

He had left his sister's house in Shreveport on the first day of August, the same day that Colorado, the Centennial State, added the thirty-eighth star to the grand old flag of 1876 United States. Brother Jeremiah was enjoying his trip down the muddy Red River, which would eventually lead to New Orleans on the mighty Mississippi where the old Bible-expositor planned on attending revival services led by the great Dwight L. Moody.

The tall, greying man-of-the cloth leaned against the white, elegantly decorated, iron railing of the riverboat and gazed dreamingly at the sandy tree-lined bank. As his mind recalled almost forgotten events of his youth, a sly grin crossed his lips the way it did when the old preacher was "settin' someone up for the kill."

"Hey, *Delta Queen!*" yelled the two young boys who were string-fishing from a homemade pirogue in a small cove. They both waved their arms furiously like they had never seen a riverboat before, despite the fact that this large, floating hotel frequently parted the waters of the Red.

"Hullo, lads!" answered Brother Jeremiah, returning the greeting of the boys with an enthusiastic wave. The scene passing in front of the old Bible-thumper caused him to recall one long, hot summer that he had spent with a friend of his shooting alligators along Alligator Creek just a few miles east of Bartlett, Texas. Back then, deer, wild turkeys, buffalo, wild horses, ducks, and wild hogs were plentiful on the rolling plains of central Texas, and the two pre-teenaged boys spent as much time as they could tracking, stalking, and shooting at whatever wild animal happened across their path. Luckily for the animals neither one of the boys was a particularly good shot at that age. The alligators were just slower than the others.

The old preacher recalled, too, how he and his friend, Benny, had helped Benny's grandpa hitch up his old wagon and ride on over to the lignite beds near Rockdale, Texas, the night before their summer fun ended. It took the better part of a day to get to their destination because the two old horses pulling the rickety wagon had to stop so many times to rest. Still, the three adventurers returned later that particular night with enough lignite to last Benny's grandparents through the winter. Those memories of more pleasant days brought a broad smile to the lips of the old Psalm-singer.

Then the broad smile on the thin, wrinkled face of the Circuit Rider changed slowly to an expression of deep reflection as the old Scripture-wrangler remembered the conversation he had had only a few days prior to his riverboat journey in which his widowed sister, Ruth, spoke about her only son, a young man named Philip whom

Brother Jeremiah had never seen. Letters seldom reached the old preacher with family news until months after events had taken place because of his constant travel from one small farm town in East Texas to another.

"Jeremiah, have you heard of the Custer Massacre at the Little Big Horn River?" Ruth asked the morning the old sermonizer shared breakfast with his only living relative. The former dark-haired beauty's eyes swelled with tears as she sat by her dormant fireplace in her favorite rocking chair, pretending to knit.

"Yes, of course," answered Brother Jeremiah. "I read about it in the Austin newspaper."

The *Statesman* had written a stirring account of the battle between the 265 men of the US 7th Cavalry led by Colonel George Armstrong Custer and some 2,500 Sioux and Cheyenne warriors led by Chiefs Sitting Bull and Crazy Horse on June 25, 1876. The article reported that Colonel Custer had ignored the orders of his commanding officer, General Alfred Terry, and decided not to wait for the main forces to arrive, but had, instead, attacked the warriors camped along the Little Big Horn River in eastern Montana. In the engagement every US soldier, including Colonel Custer, was killed. General Terry arrived in time to save some of the 7th Cavalry that had been ordered by Custer to attack the Indians upstream.

Ruth began playing with the thread on the knitting needles in her lap and said, "Philip was under Custer's command."

"But how could that be? Philip couldna been more than seventeen," responded the puzzled Scripture-slinger.

"Sixteen," answered Ruth, sobbing softly. "Philip was a lot like you. Tall, strong, big for his age, and full of adventure. He lied about how old he was and joined up before I could stop him. You shoulda seen him, Brother, the day he left. . . grinnin' like a baked possum he was. . . so handsome in his uniform."

Ruth's eyes began to fill with tears again as she relived that day in her mind. She sniffed a couple of times and toyed with her handkerchief. Then she continued her story.

"Philip volunteered for Injun fightin'. Oh, Jeremy, he was gonna come home for a few days around Christmas." Ruth looked up, tears streaming down her face now. "Those heathen savages cut him to pieces!" she almost growled the words in a savage tone herself.

The aging circuit rider had comforted his younger sister as best he could and prayed with her before he left. He had always had a little trouble finding the right words of wisdom to say to folks who had lost loved ones. Now, he felt like he could minister more effectively to the grieving survivors. True, the old preacher had never actually met his only nephew, but he had grown to love the young sandy-haired, blue-eyed boy about whom Ruth had often written. Brother Jeremiah clasped his hands together tightly and breathed a prayer of hope. He knew that he would see Philip one day if the boy had asked Christ to be his personal Savior. But if not,. . . the old sky-pilot's mind blocked out the thought of the pain and torture of what Jesus had described as being like the burning garbage dump of Jerusalem.

This frontier minister had made that decision himself over 35 years before this great adventure on the fabulous riverboat. Brother Jeremiah had grown up quick in the hills of north Louisiana. The son of a poor dirt farmer, the old hymn-singer had left his folks when he was only seventeen to seek his fortune. He soon found out that making a fortune took a lot of hard work.

Over the next seven years, the rebellious farm boy had cleaned stables and scrubbed spittoons in bars. He did a little trapping, hunting, and even some high ridding before trying his hand at wrestling and prize fighting. The old preacher was still solidly built and walked straight and tall despite having had his back broken once and his collar bone twice. The elderly saddlebag minister could still ride all day and never get tired. His hands were disproportionally large compared to his six foot-three inch height, but his pale blue eyes and square jaw had made him attract the women folk with ease.

The maturing circuit rider was not particularly proud of his life just before he had asked Jesus to be his Savior, and so, spoke about that dark time on very rare occasions. Instead, he focused his conversation, whenever possible, to the abundant blessings his Lord had poured out upon him in more recent days. Brother Jeremiah possessed a rare quality which had touched the hearts of the most hardened ranchers, farmers, businessmen, and even gunmen that central East Texas had ever seen. He was a man with a great strength of conviction and would go to any length to see that the Word of God was heard by those around him, whether that was a group or an individual.

As the stately sternwheeler churned through mid-channel, Brother Jeremiah, in his new sharply tailored frock coat, walked towards the stairs leading to the middle deck and the spacious social hall that dispensed fine food and drink and, of course, the tables where a man might play a friendly game of poker or faro. Gambling was a popular pastime aboard these slow-moving, waterborne palaces. Sometimes, the boat itself was the focus of a bet against another steamer's speed. Many a Captain found himself standing on the shore watching his floating bastion fade away around the bend of the river.

With a shrewd eye, the old churchman looked over the great hall of the sternwheeler. There were only about fifty or sixty passengers aboard the *Delta Queen* that included several European immigrants, an aristocratic English lord, a farmer from the colder regions of northern Wisconsin, a few local politicians, three graceless gamblers, and several rich merchants and land speculators heavily laden with gold and bank notes. Brother Jeremiah felt a little out of place on the fancy river cruiser, but the trip had been a gift from a wealthy central Texas rancher in appreciation for the old preacher's persistence in witnessing to the rancher's son. The boy was killed by a wild bull only a week after being born into God's family.

While a ceiling fan whirred lazily overhead in the steamer's cabin, Brother Jeremiah scanned the large room for an empty table where he might take a bite of grits, eggs, and bacon. A bald, black waiter carrying a tray with refreshments to a table of shirt-sleeved poker players approached the broad-shouldered religionist.

"Sorry, Mr. Preacher, Suh. Tables is all taken. There is some stools over to the bar," said the waiter in a gravelly apologetic tone.

"No thanks, Nick," answered Brother Jeremiah with his patented grin.

"You can sit here, Preacher," said a voice behind the circuit rider. "If you don't mind sharin' a table with a sin-filled, riverboat gambler."

Brother Jeremiah turned and gazed momentarily into the clear blue eyes of a young, lean but muscled, smartly-dressed, professional cardsharp. The old disciple-of-faith had asked his friend, Jesus, for an opportunity to talk to someone about his Savior, but the wiry Scripture-peddler had not figured the subject being a fancy-dressed con man.

"That's very kind of you, Sir," said Brother Jeremiah. "I'd be thrilled to 'share' with you," he added with a grin. "Folks call me Brother Jeremiah," he said as he offered his large, rough hand in friendship to the young man at the table.

"McKelroy. Tom McKelroy," answered the gambler as he firmly shook the preacher's hand. Tom, like most men of his day, sized up a man in the way that he shook hands as well as his grip. The young pasteboard-bender figured that the Scripture-slinger was a man of deep confidence in his calling and mission.

"Mighty proud to meet you, Tom," grinned the old Psalm-wrangler while sitting in the fancy, red-upholstered chair across from the fancy-dressed card-pusher.

John Thomas McKelroy was a tall and brawny twenty-seven year old professional gambler with jet-black hair and neatly-trimmed mustache. He carried himself straight, and his quiet assurance bespoke a masculine virility. The oldest of twelve children, the son of a poor Georgia potato farmer, Tom could, according to folks back home, chop a cord of wood in two hours. And he possessed a "stomach like that of an ostrich, which could digest anything." Tom had tired of the life of a farmer and dreamed of adventure and wealth. At sixteen, he left the farm and headed west to seek his fortune.

The lanky plow-boy had at first hooked up with a con-man who tricked folks into gladly handing him their money. Redding the Magnificent, as the fake magician was called, would come into a town and boldly announce in several well populated establishments that he had been given a unique gift, the gift of becoming invisible at will. Of course, his bragging would soon cause the folks in each small town he visited to "force him" to prove his allegations. Redding would arrange for a "demonstration" of his "gift" on a night towards the end of the week to help build up speculation as well as enhance local word of mouth advertisement. The cunning entertainer would arrange for a building, of course, and charge a measly two bits for adults, who had by the end of the week, increased their own inquisitiveness by arguing over the possibility of man's ability to perform this unusual trick, which of course, Redding kept hidden until the night of the performance. Tom McKelroy would collect the meager entertainment fee at the door and make sure that everyone either had a chair in which to sit or that they stood at the back of the building. Then when all spectators had paid, he would light strategically placed candles to give an eerie effect to the situation, and then vacate the "stage area".

There would always be a black curtain hung against one wall behind a small table that held a black tablecloth and a flickering candle. Finally, Redding would step partially out from behind the curtain with his arms raised to the heavens and announce that he would make himself "vanish into thin air". The old con-artist would then step behind the curtain again and mumble some made-up words as if he were praying while moving the curtain a bit and announcing that he would soon be walking amongst them totally invisible. Then there would be silence. At first, not anyone in the audience would say anything or even move a muscle for fear of messing up the trick. Some would move their eyes to various spots in the room, supposing that they had "seen" the magician "touch" something or someone in the room.

After several minutes of this "silence", most folks would become bored. Some would clear their throats, others might stomp their feet, but all eventually would start hissing and booing. And always someone in the crowd would get tired of waiting for something to happen and would rush the stage to pull back the curtain, revealing an open door which led to an alley.

The folks in the audience would sit dumb-founded for a handful of seconds until someone realized what had happened. Then someone would always start laughing loudly and clapping his or her hands, which would start the rest of the group to do the same as they all realized that Redding the Magnificent had indeed "vanished", never to be seen in that town again.

Tom assisted the fake escape artist for about a year before the blue-eyed, black-mustached giant took a job loading freight on a

Mississippi riverboat bound for St. Louis. It was there that he was struck by the glamour of the riverboat gambler. He spent every free moment watching the professional pasteboard-benders and asking questions about their methods. Within a few years, the former black-land farmer had become one of the best high stakes gambler to ride Old Man River.

Tom was known for his honesty and skills at the tables all along the river. He always played things "close to the vest", taking time to study his opponents. His facial expression seldom changed which made the other players only pretend to know his "tell". He was known to bluff once in awhile, and no one ever caught him cheating because he didn't have to. Of course, he didn't win every hand, but he usually came out ahead when bending the pasteboards.

The young cardsharp, on this August day, was dressed resplendently in a knee-length, black, broadcloth coat and a ruffled white shirt that sparkled with a huge diamond stud pin as his "headlight". His vest was black, decorated with hand-painted roses. On his nimble fingers he wore a giant diamond ring. His high-heeled boots were hand-made of the finest leather by a boot-maker in San Antone, and his white "gambler's hat" was enhanced with an extra wide, diamond-studded, leather hat band. Most impressive was the massive, European-made gold watch with a one-carat diamond set in its stem attached to a remarkably long, heavy gold chain. Tom's handsome, high-cheek-boned face and his pale, clear blue eyes showed pride and dignity.

Gamblers, whether on a riverboat or dry land, had to be quick-witted if they wished to ply their trade and stay alive. Like his comrades, Tom McKelroy had already experienced many adventures. He often had to jump from the deck of a moving riverboat to avoid a group of disgruntled losers who assumed his luck at the tables was due to his cheating. The powerfully-built, broad-shouldered, former corn-planter had to fight for his life using guns or his fists on a few occasions. Still Tom had never killed anyone and had no intention of doing so, especially over the turn of a card. Still, one or two men carried a bullet in their shoulder or hip from the silver-plated derringer the former Georgia dirt-stomper kept in his left vest pocket.

Brother Jeremiah ordered breakfast, and then turned his attention to starting a conversation with the young, expensively dressed river-boat gambler. Public resentment of the gambler was well known. . . not because they played games of chance, but because they almost always won by cheating or so most folks thought. The grey-haired Gospel-peddler didn't want to judge his new acquaintance by his looks, but it would have been hard to not at least consider that the young, professional hustler was more than just lucky. The old preacher looked across the table into the eyes of a troubled man.

"Been on the river long, Tom?" asked Brother Jeremiah.

"Seems like most of my life, Preacher," answered Tom with just a hint of sarcasm in his voice.

"Peers like you've had a winnin' stint," remarked the old preacher, indicating the gambler's fancy attire.

"It's a livin'," answered the young cardsharp with little feeling. "Course, I have been able to save a little." Tom grinned slyly.

"I'm sure you have saved, but have you been saved?" The old circuit rider was "settin' him up."

"Saved from what?"

"From the flames of eternal punishment for all the wrongs you've done," answered the old Heaven-chaser.

"You sound like my pa, Preacher," said the young gambler dryly. "Don't talk to me about repentin'. I ain't proud of what I've become, but I ain't ashamed neither. I play a straight game, and I play a smart game. I used to go to church back on the farm, but I enjoy what I'm doing and the way I'm living. I don't mean to sound harsh, Sir, but I would appreciate a change in the subject."

Brother Jeremiah's keen wit recognized that the Holy Spirit was already working on Tom McKelroy, so for now he was willing to back off. He knew he would have another chance to talk of Jesus during their long journey. And somehow he believed that young Tom's life would never be the same.

"We'll see what we can do about 'changing the subject'," said the old preacher with that special little grin of his.

The waiter, Nick, returned with a large steaming platter of eggs, grits, and bacon, expertly placing the feast in front of the preacher without spilling a single morsel of food.

"Here's yuh paper, Mr. Mac," said Nick.

"Thanks," said Tom. "Hope you don't mind, Preacher, if I catch up on what's happenin' while you eat. Please, eat to your heart's content and enjoy every bite." Tom smiled his "I-might-be-bluffin'-smile" while the old circuit rider scrapped a couple of eggs onto his plate.

Brother Jeremiah bowed his head to say grace for the food while Tom pretended to read the headlines of the front page of the *New York Sun*. His young eyes scanned the bold print of the usual stories about the Presidential campaign between the Democratic candidate, Samuel J. Tilden, and the Republican candidate, Rutherford B. Hayes, plus the continuing smaller stories about the new telephone, the typewriter, the refrigerator car, and the other different exhibits from some fifty countries at the Centennial Exposition at Fairmont Park in Philadelphia. There was also a small article about William "Boss" Tweed who had been convicted of fraud in New York, but was still a fugitive from justice. The tall gambler smiled at the political cartoon Thomas Nast had drawn concerning "Boss" Tweed, but his mind was occupied with far more important things than the daily news.

Tom had really hoped that the old soul-wrangler would pursue their discussion about changing. He was, in fact, miserable inside, but his strong Southern pride made him say things he didn't mean or know how to retract. He had thought many times about retiring and returning to Georgia, but he was afraid. . . afraid of being turned-out by his family.

Tom and his dad had been really close at one time, but the two had drifted apart as Tom got older and yearned for more independence. The former hay-shaker from Georgia knew that he had worried his pa something fierce when he had left his home in the middle of the night. The river-boat card shuffler had been thinking about his life back home in Paulding County more often in the last few weeks. He particularly thought about his ma, and brothers and sisters. . . and about a certain little girl who used to tag along after Tom and his brothers all the time. He wondered if that skinny little girl with all the freckles had changed much over the years. . . and he wondered if she had a family of her own now.

20

Tom had sent letters home for awhile, but the correspondence back to the family ceased about the time the former potato-wrangler had turned to the poker table for his living. Tom wasn't at all sure that his pa could ever forgive him. But for some reason, the former sod-buster felt stronger in the presence of the old circuit rider, but he did not want the aged Psalm-slinger to know. . . not just yet.

"Everythin' alright, Suh?" asked the black waiter.

"Everything's fine with me," answered the grinning Bible-thumper, "how's 'bout you, Tom?"

"Fine," the young gambler said with a solemn note as he gazed into the sparkling blue eyes of Brother Jeremiah, trying to 'read his hand'. "Just fine as frog hairs."

****

Chapter Two

The Relationship

R elationship. . . an important word to Brother Jeremiah. It was the kind of word that described the closeness that the old circuit rider felt towards his Lord and Savior. For almost thirty-five years the tall, sunbaked man-of-God had experienced a special, personal relationship with Jesus that just kept getting sweeter and deeper as Brother Jeremiah spent hours every day on his knees talking intimately with his friend. Then the old soul-merchant would read carefully in his large, worn-out Bible and listen attentively through Spiritual ears to what God had to say. Brother Jeremiah had spent the afternoon sitting comfortably on the elegantly decorated walkway enjoying the cool breeze, reading, and listening.

The big paddle-wheelers carried all kinds of supplies for the small pioneer towns located along the river. Farmers along the way shipped whatever goods they grew to markets up north or south. . . everything from cotton to produce and fruit to livestock. On the return trips, the farmers got seeds, plows, and other hardware needed to make their farms productive. Because of the riverboats, small towns that became ports-of-call grew quickly as even pre-fabricated build-ings and houses became a regular part of the transported cargo. And, of course, whenever the floating gambling establishment anchored in one of the small towns along the river for a short stay, folks from miles around were more than willing to try their luck at the various games of chance offered aboard the steamer.

The upper deck offered a commanding view of the river and the land, but the silver-laced-black-haired sermonizer looked past the beauty of the scenery into the visionary distance of the future. His instincts and experience told him that Tom McKelroy, the young gambler he had met at breakfast, was a troubled individual. . . the kind of man who allowed few people, if any, to establish a relationship with him. Brother Jeremiah had a habit of zeroing in on people like Tom during his "talks" with Jesus, and then allowing the Holy Spirit to open conversation that would lead to a close friendship. The circuit rider had prepared himself; now he was ready to casually encounter the young cardsharp again.

The social hall of the *Delta Queen* was crammed with high rollers in both top hats and slouch hats by the time Brother Jeremiah strolled into the gaming area. The well-proportioned floating saloon was brilliantly lit up by several very fine chandeliers. The velvet-papered walls were decorated with ornamental paintings, large mirrors and showy pictures that clashed with the plain, plank floor. The circuit rider's eyes searched the compact crowd of eager betters that surrounded each of the dozen or more gaming tables until he finally located his young friend.

Brother Jeremiah began elbowing his way between the tables in the room filled by men of all shapes and sizes and wealth with great difficulty. The atmosphere at Tom McKelroy's table matched the haze from the tobacco smoke of the rest of the room. The smoke itself was filled with the fumes of strong brandy. The old preacher took note of the patrons of the establishment which included men of every class from the highest to the lowest as well as an extraordinary variety of character and dress. Brother Jeremiah stood in the crowd carefully observing the poise and concentrated-control of a professional at work.

"Bets to you, Sir," said a gray-goateed man wearing a white colonel's hat who sat across from Tom.

Tom studied his hand. . . a pair of kings ten high, then pursed his lips, sighed, and threw his cards into the pile of money and chips in the center of the table.

"I apologize, Gentlemen. My mind seems to be occupied with other thoughts. If you'll excuse me, I think I'll step out for some fresh air."

With that, Tom pushed his chair back and began to push his way through the crowded room towards the exit leading to the deck. Brother Jeremiah stood and watched the country-boy-turned-river-boat-gambler slowly exit the ornate main cabin of the *Delta Queen* and wondered just how long Tom would resist the Holy Spirit. Then, like a moth drawn to a flickering camp fire, he followed the young cardsharp into the clear night air.

"Somethin' troublin' you, Son," asked the old preacher as he gently touched Tom's shoulder.

The young gambler turned and looked longingly into the clear blue eyes of the circuit rider. Somehow, Tom figured that he could trust this stranger with his story and with his most recent thoughts.

"Been thinkin' 'bout home. . . a little. Folks'd be beddin' down soon. Right after Pa reads from that book you been studyin' all afternoon," answered Tom as he turned back to stare into the river waters.

"When was the last time you seen your folks?" asked the old Scripture-beater.

"Nine. . . ten years. . . a lifetime. You know, I just lost more money than Pa makes in three years," said Tom.

"Why don't you go back now?" asked Brother Jeremiah.

"Can't. My folks could never accept what I am. Pa always said he wanted me to be a preacher. Said he dedicated me to the Lord when I was born," answered Tom.

Brother Jeremiah grinned. "Sounds to me like the Lord's got a hold of you, Boy. If'n He has, you might as well give in. He'll win you know."

"Maybe ," answered Tom, "but I ain't ready to fold my hand, Parson. Lady Luck's just turned her back on me for awhile. I ain't ready to turn in my deck of 52 for a book of 66. May never be ready!"

"What'll it take to get you ready?" asked the wise old preacher.

Tom stood tall and looked square into the sparkling eyes of the old Scripture-wrangler. He swallowed hard before answering that simple question.

"I don't know," he said after a long pause, "but don't start tellin' me what to do, Mister. This is my life, and I'll make my own decisions. If I wanna be a gambler, I'll be a gambler, and if I wanna be a soldier or a storekeeper or a rancher or even a preacher, I'll be one. . . but only if I want to. Understand?"

Brother Jeremiah understood Tom's rebellious attitude better than he knew. He had gone through the same thing some thirty-two years before. He also recognized a man being dealt with by the most powerful force in the universe. . . the Holy Spirit of God.

Tom didn't wait for an answer from the backwoods preacher. He just turned and walked briskly back into the social hall. Brother Jeremiah knew that God had to sometimes get rough with some folks in order to get through their stubbornness and pride. The old warrior whispered a silent prayer that God would not have to be too severe in order to get Tom's attention. . . unless that's what it would take to establish that special relationship with the young man.

****

The tobacco smoke hung heavy throughout the large, stylish social hall where most of the men aboard the *Delta Queen* had gathered to try their hand at simple games of chance on the unfinished boards of square table tops that were covered with heavy green cloth. All throughout the room could be heard the chinking of coins as men from all walks of society waited patiently to take their turn at the poker or faro tables. Others converged on the three-card monte table to try their luck at this slight variation of the old shell game that never gave its victim a chance.

Tom McKelroy had been playing draw poker for most of the night with a young, rich Englishman who was on his honeymoon, a cotton buyer from New York who wanted folks to think he was from the South, and a well-dressed one-eyed man who looked untrustworthy. Tom had developed an instinct over the years about the character of most hard-core pasteboard shufflers, and his gut gave him a real hard feeling for that fella with the eye-patch. The former-Georgia-plowboy thought the one-eyed man looked so crooked, he could swallow nails and spit out corkscrews.

The young professional gambler's mind had not totally been on the cards in front of him. Like the old itinerant preacher, Tom's occupation offered him no fixed abode, and the thought of the old family farm was laying heavy on his mind. The one-eyed man had been winning most of the hands which seemed to really bother the young Englishman.

"Bets to you, Earl," said the Yankee businessman.

Tom thought the fake-Southerner's mustache smelled like a mildewed saddle blanket after it had been ridden on a sore-back horse three-hundred miles under a Texas-August sun. Tom had already thrown in his pair of eights as the catch began to grow, and since then, had only partially paid attention to the two remaining men who continually raised one another while a small crowd of interested spectators gathered closely. The Englishman, sweating heavily, toyed with his chin whiskers.

"Gentlemen, I seem to be temporarily out of further resources," he said softly.

"Then you're out," answered the one-eyed man with a crooked smile.

That smile made Tom recall what his old pappy had said about the old man who ran the general store in the small town near the McKelroy's farm back in western Georgia.

"That fella tells lies so well a man would be a fool not to believe them," commented Pa McKelroy after the shopkeeper had complained of his bad back as an excuse to not help the farmers unload their baskets of corn one day.

"Wait! Please!" The loud interjection from the nervous Englishman jolted Tom back into the world of the present. "I'll sign a note for whatever amount you say," pleaded the visitor-from–across-the-pond.

"Sorry, Earl," said the man with the big smile. "I made it a practice years ago to never take notes from strangers."

"How about my land?" asked the desperate Brit. "I've got title to a beautiful country estate outside of Chelsea. I'll put that up against the pot. That's worth twenty times what's in there now!"

"If you don't mind me sayin' so, Earl," ventured the one-eyed cardsharp, "how do I know you really have this place? 'Sides, I don't think I'd like livin' in a furin country where folks talks so funny."

Several of the men standing near laughed loudly at the words of the well dressed gambler.

"Please! Look at this picture," answered the young, frustrated lord.

Tom felt the desperation in the voice of the Englishman and saw the look of a professional sharp who fleeced suckers at cards for a living sitting beside him. The one-eyed man had expertly played a cat-and-mouse game with this wooly little lamb, allowing the Englishman to win several times. Now, the victim was ready for the slaughter. If the Englishman had owned a whole herd of Texas longhorns, the one-eyed man could have still sold him a load of manure at that moment.

Tom looked deep into the eyes of the young Brit and saw a foolish, desperate young man addicted to winning "the big one". Then he looked at the fancy-dressed circuit-riding cardsharp to his left and saw. . . a reflection of himself. And he didn't like what he saw. Despite the fancy clothes and the other trappings, the former Georgia clod-buster was no better than Redding the Magnificent. . . a con man taking advantage of folks' feelings of insecurity. . . and their dream of "winning the hand that would set them up for life."

"Say, this is mighty pretty," said the smiling, one-eyed executioner of the pasteboards. "I always did dream of ownin' a castle. OK, Earl. I'll take a chance that you're tellin' the truth, and take your note."

The one-eyed gambler was grinnin' like a jack eatin' cactus as he watched the young Englishman sign the back of the deed to his ancestrial home in England.

The young lord's eyes sparkled with excitement as he laid down his hand. "Four kings," he announced proudly.

With a sly smile, the one-eyed gambler spread his cards in front of the foreigner. They showed four aces. Everyone within eyeshot murmured about the luck of the one-eyed man. . . or the stupidity of the Englishman.

The one-eyed cardsharp grinned from ear to ear as he pulled his winnings closer to himself and separated the hard cash from the cards. The pasteboard con-man examined the deed, too, and wondered how and when he could travel across the pond to take possession of the land.

"Sure am sorry about takin' your place in England, Fella," commented the professional paste-board bender, "but you ought not wager what you cain't afford to lose. Please give my sincere apologies to your missus."

And then the cunning card-wrangler started laughing. . . a wild, maniacal laugh that belied his courteous statement of one-upmanship.

Tom looked at the one-eyed gambler with contempt and then turned his gaze at the foolish Englishman who just sat in a stunned-stupor, sweating profusely and turning red with embarrassment at the laughter of the folks standing nearby.

"Yeah," thought Tom to himself, "the tinhorn is sincere alright. . . as sincere as an undertaker's grief at a five-dollar funeral."

The eyes of the young Englishman filled with despair as he realized that he had just lost his family inheritance. Then his chin dropped to his chest, and his hands went limp as the color left his tired, distraught face. Slowly, he rose from the chair. The news of the winnings spread quickly through the hall, and all movement and conversation ceased as hundreds of eyes stared at the pitiful, defeated figure of a man walking slower than a crippled turtle through the mass of wagerers.

For the first time, Tom saw the glamour of the riverboat gambler's life dissolve into a heap of wasted greed and unconcern for the human race. He felt sick to his stomach, and he hated what he had become. It was then that he remembered one of the stories his Pa used to read from the Bible, and like the Prodigal Son, he knew home was a better place even if that meant working as a hired-hand for his Pa. And once again Tom recalled some of his dad's sage advice. . . "if'n you wallow with pigs, expect to get dirty."

It was at that moment that Tom McKelroy decided that he would give up his life on the river and at least make an attempt to return to his Pa's small farm in Georgia. The young poker-player looked at the other men at the table who were having great sport at the Englishman's willingness to wager everything he had held dear to come out on top. The sounds of the laughter of the men throughout the room died as the sight before Tom changed these men into savage animals ready to destroy what little pride another human being had. . . just to win. . . win at any cost. Tom began to perspire himself, and he felt so uncomfortable and out of place. The plowboy-turned-gambler pushed his chair away from the table and walked slowly but deliberately out of this den of contemptible wolves who awaited their next victim with such glee.

Brother Jeremiah had been standing close to the floating saloon's bar, sipping a glass of cold milk. He had been praying silently for the young gambler he had already considered a friend. And the greying Bible-teacher noticed the change in Tom's face as the young high roller passed by. Tom stopped just for a few seconds to look the Heaven-salesman in the eye. Neither of the two men said a word. Then Tom turned his eyes to the floor as if ashamed to even be in the same room with the old sin-slayer. Without looking up again, the humbled poker-player exited the gambling hall into the warm Louisiana night.

****

Chapter Three

The Confrontation

Tom McKelroy stood on the top deck of the *Delta Queen* and leaned over the railing while gazing into the churning waters in the wake of the huge paddle wheel. The scene he had witnessed and, in fact, been a part of in the social hall that left a young Englishman willing to gamble his entire fortune on the turn of a few pieces of fancy, stiff paper had left him disgusted with everything he had prized for the past nine years. The Englishman was wrong, but then so was the one-eyed cardsharp, and Tom knew he, himself, had been wrong all this time. Perhaps he should have listened to his pa. Perhaps plain, old-fashioned, back-breaking work was far better than taking advantage of others dreams and greed.

Suddenly the stillness of the early morning was shattered by the sound of a gunshot and a woman's scream. As Tom turned towards the heart-stopping noises, a young, blonde-haired woman in a pink night-shirt ran shrieking from the passenger cabins right into his arms.

Hysterically she cried out, "He shot himself! Please help him! He's dying!"

Tom ran behind the young woman into a beautifully decorated room where a man lay face down on the floor in a pool of crimson-colored liquid. Tom knelt beside the lifeless body, afraid of what he would discover. Ever so gently, he turned the body over and stared into the bloodless face of the young Englishman with whom he had shared a table only a few hours before. Tom touched his neck hoping against hope that he would feel something. He didn't. The former Georgia haystacker slowly removed his coat, not taking his eyes off the face of the young Englishman, and laid his coat over the body so as to cover the head of the fellow on the floor. Then he ever so gently cradled the former-landlord from across the sea in his arms.

"I'm sorry, Ma'am," said the lanky former-dirt-jockey.

The young woman began to weep openly and slumped into a nearby chair. Tom, not knowing what to do, just continued holding the corpse of the young Brit. Finally, he stood and walked over to the young lady.

"Excuse me, Ma'am, but perhaps you should go someplace. . ."

The young widow rose, still crying, and Tom put his arm around her shoulders and led her to the door. Brother Jeremiah and the waiter, Nick, met them as they exited the death chamber.

"What hap'n, Suh? I thought I heard a shot!" exclaimed a wide-eyed Nick.

"You did, Nick. It's the young Englishman. You'd better go get the captain," answered Tom.

"Yes, Suh, Mr. Mac."

"Preacher. . . can you. . . uh. . ." stuttered the former Georgia plowboy who still held the weeping widow in his arms.

Brother Jeremiah could see the desperation and perhaps a sense of embarrassment in the eyes of the former farm-boy. The tired gambler looked so helpless and out of place. The traveling messenger of God almost laughed, but the situation kept him from doing so.

"Of course, Tom. Ma'am," he said taking the former-bride-turned widow's hands, "may I be of assistance. I am a preacher of the Gospel."

The young lady tried to control her crying enough to tell the two men what had happened. Between sobs and gasps of air, she related the final moments of her groom's life.

"Oh, Reverend, I don't understand. William came back from the social hall feeling so terribly wretched. He said that any man who would gamble away everything he owned did not deserve to live. And then he took a pistol, and he. . . he. . ." Again, she started crying while Brother Jeremiah comforted her.

For the first time in many years, Tom McKelroy's eyes began to fill with tears. A new determination covered his countenance.

"Why doncha take the lady to my cabin, Preacher. I won't be needin' it for awhile. Gotta run an errand for a friend," the Georgia native said ever so softly. Tom excused himself and walked quickly to the stairs leading to the social hall with but one thought flooding his mind. . . winning back that castle in England.

****

The games in the social hall continued without the faintest hint of interruption. No one had heard the gun blast or the scream from the young woman. Nor had they been disturbed by the quick exit of the ship's captain and the old black waiter. Each man was far too occupied with increasing their wealth at the games.

Tom McKelroy strolled purposefully across the room and took his usual chair at the table towards the eastern corner. The one-eyed man was still there as was the cotton buyer. A scroungy-looking old prospector occupied the chair at which the young Englishman had sat. The same scene that had taken place just a few hours before was expertly recreated, except that this time, Tom was paying complete attention to every move of the one-eyed gambler and the businessman. It took Tom only a few hands to discover the scam. The two crooks were obviously after the curly-bearded old man's claim. The problem was getting rid of Tom. Finally, Tom was ready to make his move.

"Let's get down to some serious gambling, Gentleman," he said raising one eyebrow. "No limit?"

The one-eyed cardsharp and the businessman eyed one another nervously. "Well, only if it's alright with Mr. Grim," answered the one-eyed dude.

"Sure, Sonny. Even if'n I lose it all I kin jest go dig up sum more," cackled the toothless prospector.

"Nick!" cried Tom. "New deck, please." The young gambler stared straight at the crooked cardsharp seated across from him.

"Mr. Grim, you deal," stated Tom in his matter-of-fact voice. "By the way, I've noticed someone cheating at this table. And while I don't want to accuse anyone just now, if he does it again, I'm gonna shoot his other eye out," said Tom while placing his four-barrel derringer onto the table.

Mr. Grim laughed and dealt the cards. The old prospector figured he was about to watch one heck-of-a-show. . . a challenge between two professionals that might leave one of them wishing he'd never met the other. The old man deliberately placed each card in front of the participants.

"I'll open for a thousand," said Tom without blinking an eye and only glancing at the cards in front of him.

"I reckon I'll just deal this hand," said Mr. Grim as he looked first at each of the other men sitting at the table. The old prospector could feel the tenseness in the air between the three gamblers who remained in the game. And the scene made the old man shirk his shoulders and cackle again.

"I'm in," said the businessman as he looked at his three tens.

"I'll see your thousand, Sir. And I'll raise you two thousand," said the one-eyed man glaring at his opponent.

Tom counted out the bet and tossed the large bills onto the middle of the table as did the crooked gambler's partner. The one-eyed gambler took one card, the businessman took two, while Tom played with what he had.

"Bets to you, Mac," announced the one-eyed man after re-arranging the cards in his hand.

"Three thousand dollars," said the former plow-pusher. By now, news had spread throughout the hall of the grudge match between the two cardsharps. Many eyes and ears were turned in the direction of the high stakes game.

"Too rich for my blood," said the businessman as he threw in his cards.

The one-eyed dude studied the cold stare of the young card player and decided he was bluffing. "Three thousand once. Three thousand twice," said the smiling con man.

"Let's not quibble over peanuts, Sir. I've got fifteen thousand in cash and another ten thousand in jewels," declared Tom.

"I don't have that kind of money with me, Mac," answered the one-eyed speculator.

"You do in the form of that land the Englishman lost," replied Tom. The land against my twenty-five thousand and the rest of your winnings."

The one-eyed professional wagerer smiled broadly and then reached into his coat for the piece of paper given him by the Englishman. Even if he lost, the one-eyed gambler figured he hadn't lost all that much for he had no attachment to the land. . . and he had to know if the Southern gentleman was bluffing.

"Sure, Mac," he said as he placed the paper and all his money on the table. "Can you beat a full house? Jacks and fours."

Tom glanced at the cards spread in front of his alter ego and then fixed his gaze on the smiling face of the man with one eye.

"Easily," answered Tom as he spread his cards on the table. "Four deuces. . . ace high."

The crowd murmured loudly as Tom gathered his winnings and rose to leave. The two crooks leaned back in their chairs and just grinned.

"Mr. Grim," said Tom, "if I were you, I'd find another game at another table. Good-evening. . . Gentlemen."

****

The early morning rays of the rising sun streamed through the pine trees that lined the banks of the muddy Red River as Tom McKelroy walked to his private room aboard the *Delta Queen*. Tom had spent the night thinking of home and playing what he had decided was to be his last game of poker. He paused momentarily in front of his door, not knowing whether he should walk in or knock. At that instant Brother Jeremiah opened the door and stepped outside.

"How's the little lady, Preacher?" asked the reformed gambler.

"Sleeping," answered the worn out circuit rider.

34

Brother Jeremiah had spent the night consoling the young English widow and reading precious Scriptures to the heart-broken young woman.

"It'll be a long time before she loses the sight of her husband killing himself in front of her. She never did quite understand why."

"It'll be a long time before I forget the sight, Preacher," said Tom turning his head so as not to look directly into the old soul-wrangler's piercing eyes. "Her husband killed himself because he lost his family's estate in a poker game last night. Only he didn't know that the game was crooked. I won the marker back for the lady early this morning. I'm quittin', Preacher. The smells, the life, the false friendships, the cheats. . . it's just not what life's all about. It took that young Englishman killing himself to make me see me as I really am."

"So what do you do now, Tom?" Brother Jeremiah walked over to the ornate railing where the young, former gambler stood.

"I'm not sure, Preacher. I know the first step is to go home and face my folks."

Brother Jeremiah grinned broadly, "You sure make it easy to get sermon illustrations."

"Yeh, I reckon I do," said Tom with a smile. "Anyway, I'm gettin' off the *Queen* at the next stop, so I'd appreciate you giving this envelope to the English lady. Tell her it's from a friend who owed it to her husband."

Tom gave Brother Jeremiah a large envelope stuffed with money and the deed to the lady's husband's family estate back in the Old Country.

"You've got a pastor's heart, Tom," commented the old saddlebag preacher. "I've got a feeling God's gonna use you in a big way to get the Gospel where it's needed."

"You're soundin' like my pa again," responded Tom with a smile. "Although I must admit that I kinda like the idea of helpin' folks. First, I'd like to plow the fields on my pa's farm for a bit."

"There's lots of fields that need plowin'," said the old Bible-thumper with his usual grin. "And sowin'. . . and harvestin'. . . You'd be surprised how few people want to work the fields."

"I know what you're gettin' at, Preacher," answered Tom, "but most folks don't trust riverboat gamblers. . . not even reformed riverboat gamblers."

"Most folks don't trust tax collectors, either, but that didn't stop the Apostle Matthew," countered Brother Jeremiah.

The former card-sharp raised one eye-brow and sighed heavily like a man trying to talk himself into something. . . or out of something.

"OK, Preacher, I'll admit that maybe God's been workin' on me. On the other hand, maybe I'm just homesick. But I promise if I ever start preachin' somewhere, I'll let you know," Tom said as he took the Bible-teacher's hand. "Thanks for helpin' me get straight."

Brother Jeremiah shook the young man's hand firmly and said, "Thank the Lord, Tom. You know, He's got everything under control. I'll be seein' you again." Then he smiled warmly. "I don't see how Dwight Moody can top this."

Tom returned the smile and then turned and walked towards the stairs leading to the bottom deck from where he would depart for Georgia and a new beginning. Tom stood in a relaxed manner as he watched a farmer plow a field about 50 yards from the Big Muddy's shore line. He wondered how many times that farmer had been flooded out but stuck to what he knew best. That farmer's life was much more reliable than his own. . . and he recalled what his pa had said the night Tom left in search of his fortune.

"You can always come home, Son," whispered the farmer while clasping Tom's hands in his own calloused mitts. "You've always been reliable. . . and that shows character. . . and a boy with character will always bring a heap of joy to his ma and pa."

Just as Tom's boot hit the lower deck, old Nick handed the former pasteboard shuffler his morning paper.

"Sorry to hear about your friend, Mr. Tom," said Nick as sincerely as he could. "Forgive me, Suh, for readin' the headlines. Reminded me of sumthin' my mammy used to say. She say, 'Nicholas, the road of life is hard and long, and ain't none of us gwan git out this alive'!"

Tom looked puzzled as he opened the newspaper, and then he grinned, shook his head, folded the paper neatly, and tossed it onto one of the deck chairs with the headline starring up at anyone who passed by: "Wild Bill Hickock Buried in Deadwood", "Famous

Lawman Shot From Behind During Poker Game", "Murderer Jack McCall Caught".

The tall card-sharp took out his big watch and began to wind the stem, all the while thinking about his folks back on the family farm.

"Everything's gonna be fine," he said half aloud, "finer than a fine watch." He placed his treasure back into his vest pocket, leaned on the railing of the floating gambling house, and grinned.

From what seemed out of nowhere, the rain started pouring. Tom stepped back under the porch and noticed that the sun was shining on the shoreline. The former card-hustler smiled as he recalled his pa speak of the refreshing, early morning showers that made everything smell fresh and clean. And for the first time in many a year, the former Georgian dirt-scrapper felt clean.

The old circuit rider watched the shower, too, and thought deeply about his meeting the young paste-board-slinger and the events of the past 24 hours. Brother Jeremiah had come home to Louisiana for a visit and now was ready to leave renewed and refreshed. . . returning to a life in the saddle and the small towns of east Texas. Preaching was his life. He would never achieve the fame of Moody or R. A. Torrey, but his life would touch many like Tom McKelroy who would heed the message God had given, despite the road blocks the Enemy might construct. For Brother Jeremiah knew the "cards" were stacked in His favor.

****

Chapter Four

The Return

A s was his custom, Brother Jeremiah was up at the crack of dawn. He had spent the night in the east Texas woods on a short detour from his regular route to help out an old friend who had taken ill with pneumonia. The old circuit rider stretched and yawned. As he looked in the direction of the sunrise he recalled the reason he had traveled so far off his normal route after his return to the pines of east Texas.

"I hate to ask you to look in on some of my flock, Jeremiah," Ben Toller had explained one unusually warm afternoon in mid-October of 1876, "but I'm just too weak to ride over to Banner and Horse Shoe."

Ben Toller had been one of the first preachers to accept Jeremiah's conversion to Jesus just over thirty years before. Toller had been a lawman when he first met Brother Jeremiah in Alexandria, Louisiana, but had himself come to know Jesus in a personal manner while awaiting death from a back-shooting ambush near Coleton, Tennessee. The white-haired man of the cloth from the hills of Davy Crockett's country stood just under six-foot and was still broad-shouldered, but walked with a limp and a bit stooped over. Toller wore wire-framed glasses "just fer readin'", but actually needed them more than he admitted. Brother Ben had been caught in a cloudburst during the first part of October, but had not seen a doctor 'til almost a week later. By that time, his sniffle and cough had turned into pneumonia. Neither of the two men had given much thought to the former Tennessean not recovering.

"It's quite alright, Ben," answered Brother Jeremiah, "at least now those folks will hear a real preacher for a change."

The old circuit rider grinned to let his fallen colleague know that he was just ribbing his fellow saddle-bag minister. Both men snickered a bit before Toller started coughing deeply. Toller's wife came with a cool, wet cloth to soothe her husband's forehead as best she could. She looked up into the eyes of the stronger of the two black-coats and pleaded with Brother Jeremiah to end the visit. . . without saying a word. Brother Jeremiah took the hint.

"I'd best be on my way, Ben," said the tall Bible-teacher. "I got some new ground to cover, but I'll find them places and give your folks your love. Reckon you'll be back on your feet by the time I return this way in a couple of weeks. Take care, my Friend. . . and let this little lady of yours spoil you for a while. You deserve some time off."

The two comrades of the Word shook hands and each said their "good-byes" while staring into the windows of the soul of the other. Both knew that the sickness that had sent Toller to bed was more severe than either let on. . . but both knew that they would see each other again someday in a place far beyond the skies.

****

Tom McKelroy wiped the sweat from his brow and sat upon the stump where he had been chopping firewood for an hour. The tall farmer closed his eyes and breathed deeply of the fresh October air. He drank a full dipper of cool spring water as he awaited the arrival of his cousin, Mark McClure, with the small wagon which the two men would load down, eventually stacking the wood next to the lanky former-cardsharp's folks' home. Tom surveyed the scene before him, looked at his calloused hands, and recalled the morning some six weeks earlier when he had ridden a young bay mare into the yard belonging to the McKelroy farm in northwestern Georgia, just south of what would eventually be the small town of Braswell.

"Somebody's comin', Pa!" shouted young Franklin McKelroy. "Cain't quite make out who 'tis. . . sun's right at his back. . . but he's got a mighty purdy horse!"

Jamieson McKelroy opened the door to the five-room cabin he had built with his own hands to see if he could identify the stranger. The McKelroys didn't get too many folks just passing by their place, mostly because the farmhouse sat a mite fair distance off the main road and around a curve. Visitors pretty much had to be headed down their road on purpose to ride up to their front door. Pa, as most folks around Paulding County called him, was tall, muscled, but just a mite skinny. He had a corn-cob pipe protruding from his mouth which itself was almost completely covered by a bushy mustache. The old man's eyes were cold blue, but strong and surrounded by crow's feet that dug deep into his sun-scorched skin. . . except for the white patch that covered half of his forehead. . . a sign that he was used to wearing a hat when outdoors. For a sixty-five year old farmer, Pa stood straight and strong.

"Why Heavens to Betsy!" exclaimed the shirtless sod-buster as he pulled up his suspenders. "That's my boy! Frankie, that there's your brother, Thomas! He's done come home!"

The tall farmer turned to holler back inside the comfy little house to his wife and the two other remaining young'uns he had sired. Franklin, who was just a tadpole when Tom had left home over ten years earlier, didn't wait for verification from his ma. Instead, he ran as fast as he could the thirty yards to the front gate to greet his long lost brother.

"Ma!" cried the elder McKelroy, "Ma! Come quick! It's Tom! He's done returned home! Billy! You and Martha come see who's here!"

The whole family crowded the porch of the little farmhouse. . . Ma in her apron, wiping her hands; twenty-four-year-old Billy brushing back a shock of straight, black hair from his eyes; and an eight-year-old Martha who had never met her big brother. Frank walked beside his brother, leading the mare, and trying to match Tom's stride. The former pasteboard-bender walked up to his ma, a slightly pudgy, fiftyish woman not much over five feet tall, and grabbed the diminutive lady in a bear-hug. Billy slapped his brother on the back, and even little Martha joined in the family welcoming committee.

Pa just waited a spell on the porch, his eyes filling with tears at the sight before him. Tom had not written a letter to the family in a month of Sundays, and the aging head of the McKelroy clan in northwestern Georgia had begun to imagine that he might not see his oldest boy again. The old plow-pusher had heard rumors in town about Tom and his loose moral habits, but dismissed the stories as idle gossip from individuals who were just jealous. Now the stories didn't matter because Tom was home.

After several moments, the welcoming subsided enough for Pa to say his piece. "Welcome home, Son," said the old dirt stomper in a cracked voice while extending his big, sun-baked hand.

Tom looked at his pa's huge hand in front of him and then into the wrinkled old face of the one man on this earth that he wanted most to impress. The former gambler grabbed his pa's hand in both of his own and shook it firmly, then he threw both arms around the old man, and the two men embraced for the first time in more years than either could count. The whole family had tears of joy streaming down their faces.

"Pa," started Tom in his serious tone, "I don't know if or what you've heard about what I've been doing over the past few years, but I want you to know that I never intended to do anything to bring shame to you or the family. I reckon I don't deserve no consideration, but I'd appreciate you lettin' me work here on the farm for you for a spell to earn my keep. I'd be proud to be your farmhand and sleep there in the barn if'n you'd let me."

Tom had rehearsed his little speech for days while riding across Mississippi and Alabama, and he felt like he had mastered the presentation. It actually wasn't what he had meant to say, but it was what came out of his mouth.

"Don't reckon I can let you be a hired-hand, Son," answered Pa with a stern voice and furrowed brow. "But I reckon I can welcome you back as a partner, just like Billy and Frankie are. There's plenty to keep all of us workin' from sun-up to sun-down, Tom, so you'll earn your keep alright. You don't need to tell us nuthin' 'bout what you been up to, Son. We's just mighty proud that you're back!"

And with that pronouncement, the family hugging session resumed, and the tears flowed freely, especially from Ma and little Martha.

The next day, Pa sent Franklin around to all the neighbors inviting them to a barbecue and dance at the McKelroy farm on the next Saturday night. The old hay-stacker killed a young calf, and he and Billy started cooking the critter over an open pit between the house and the barn. Ma and Martha started baking pies because that was Tom's favorite dessert. News of the return of Pa's prodigal son spread quickly around the countryside, and every single gal for twenty miles around started getting all gussied-up for the doin's and dancing to Pa's fiddle music and the banjo pickin' and guitar strummin' of the Tritt family and the singin' of that Lovelace girl, hoping all the while that each and every single man in the county would be attending that little shindig. And all did just that!

But the greatest surprise came when Tom's younger cousin, Mark, arrived back on the McKelroy farm after taking a load of pota-toes to market in the nearby farming community of Dallas. Mark hadn't seen Tom in more years than the rest of the family, and had, himself, only been back on the farm for only a handful of years. . . ever since his folks had been massacred by Indians out near the Texas-New Mexico border. Mark reined up the mules in front of the weather-beaten old barn. The tall, red-haired, muscled, twenty-one-year-old dirt scratcher hadn't noticed an extra face standing on the porch of the farmhouse, but had paid attention to the two men cooking over the open pit. Mark truly enjoyed Pa's outdoor, fire-pit cooking.

Pa McKelroy stopped brushing the slab of meat, took off his gloves, and walked over to meet his young clean-shaven nephew.

"Got a surprise fer ya, Mark," said Pa with a face-full of grin. "My boy, Tom, returned home yesterday. And he's gonna be stayin' 'round here fer a spell. Reckon y'all ain't seed each other in a mighty long time. I'll put up the mules, Boy, and you go on over to the house and get re-acquainted."

Mark stood dumb-founded for a moment or two. Tom McKelroy had always been his "hero" of sorts. . . mostly because Tom had had the courage to escape life on the farm and had explored the world. Or at least that's what Mark had imagined that Tom had been doing during the previous ten years or so. Tom's young cousin had heard the rumors of the oldest of the McKelroy boys being a gambler, but he never believed them. In fact, Mark had busted his knuckles on two or three young fellas who had insisted one night that the rumors were true.

Mark took extra-long strides from the wagon to the porch while brushing off the dust that had accumulated on his clothes from the ride back from town. The well-proportioned young farmer stopped short of the porch by a few feet. And a grin wider than the Mississippi crossed his chiseled features.

"Tom?" Mark managed to say, "is that really you? Are you really gonna be stayin'?"

The former cardsharp stepped off the porch to meet his younger cousin. He grabbed Mark's rough hand and pulled him close.

"It's me, Mark," answered the tall Georgian, "and I reckon I'm gonna be 'round for quite awhile. . . at least 'til I get my mind made up as to what the Lord wants me to do with my life. It sure is good to see you! How's your folks been?"

The six-foot, two-hundred-pound crop-wrangler's countenance changed, and he dropped his head. Mark tried his best to not let Tom's question spoil the reunion as he realized that his older cousin must not have heard of the massacre at Fort Harrison.

"They's all dead, Tom," replied Mark. "Murdered by Injuns in '67 back when we was livin' in New Mexico Territory."

"I'm so sorry, Mark," stated Tom as he looked squarely into his cousin's eyes. "I didn't know. Reckon there's a lot of news about the family that I need to catch up on."

"Well, you two young'uns just need to come on inside and sit a spell," interjected Ma McKelroy in an effort to change the subject and the atmosphere. "Y'all kin jaw some over a cup of coffee and some of my doughnuts while Pa and Billy work on that calf fer tomorrow's hoedown!"

"Ma's doughnuts?" said Mark with a gleam in his eyes.

"Those doughnuts are ten times better than what I remember," added Tom with a grin. "I'd sware they must come straight from one of Heaven's recipes. . . it'd be a mortal sin to let 'em go to waste."

The two young men whupped each other on the back and sauntered into the kitchen to "sample" Ma's tantalizing pastries. They stopped momentarily at the door of the farmhouse, contemplating inviting the other two men to their impromptu feast. Then they looked each other in the eye, laughed out loud at an unspoken joke, and trudged onward to the prize awaiting them on the kitchen table.

****

Brother Jeremiah rode his big Appaloosa into the small town of Horse Shoe, Texas, just four days after leaving his friend, Ben Toller, on what would become his old friend's death-bed before the month was out. It was a bright, sunshiny Wednesday, but the presence of the old circuit rider made it a Sunday. . . at least for an hour or two. The townsfolk had made a "gentleman's agreement" with each other to declare whatever day the traveling parson came to town a Sunday.

And as soon as one of the boys playing in the school yard on the edge of town spotted the old Psalm-singer riding past, he high-tailed it down the street to announce the arrival of the mobile minister.

All the stores in the little village of less than a hundred folks hurried their customers out the doors so that they could get themselves and their families ready to attend the meetin' at the town's only saloon. Bev's Beverage Barn was the only building in town large enough to hold all the folks who regularly showed up for the gathering and eating afterwards.

Hank Esterling, the bartender at the Triple B, as some folks referred to the saloon, began hanging drapes over the pictures of the naked women that hung on three of the walls. Gus Evans, the saloon's piano-player, hustled into the back room for a box of old hymn-books for the worshipers to sing from, and Stinky Wallace, the town drunk, pulled out a make-shift pulpit of sorts from the storage room and placed it on the small stage for the preacher. Then Old Stinky stacked the tables and arranged the chairs for the folks to sit in. He was rewarded with a swallow of whiskey for his efforts. . .

usually the last drink served to anyone until the "Sunday" services were finished.

Within an hour of Brother Jeremiah's arrival, folks began to gather for their monthly dose of singing and sermonizing. Several ladies came in together, each sporting an outrageous hat purchased from the local general store and guaranteed to be the latest fashion trend straight from New York City. The old Bible-thumper sat over in the corner by the stage and the piano, awaiting his cue from Mr. Evans that all who could come to the meetin' was indeed there. Gus played "Rock of Ages" so many times, that the saddlebag preacher was sure it was the only song the man knew.

Two cowboys who were just passing through the small community bellied up to the bar, slapped down their dimes and loudly ordered a "tall glass of Dutch courage". Hank, the bartender, politely explained why the bar was closed and told them they would just have to wait. . . or ride on to the next town. One of the cowhands grabbed Hank by his vest and tried to pull him over the counter. But Hank was a rather large man, about twice the size of the bewhiskered cowpuncher, and he didn't move very far. Neither of the two "gentlemen" had noticed that the bar-swamper's hands were not resting on the top of the bar. . . until they heard the distinctive "click" of the hammers of Hank's double-barreled, sawed-off shotgun.

"Don't wanna turn this here meetin' into a funeral," whispered the big man with the big gun, "but I will if that's what you two gents want. Either way, you're not gettin' no shot of whiskey 'til that preacher man's through tellin' us all how to be good Christians. You understand. . . Gentlemen?"

Both of the doggie herders gulped loudly and slowly backed away from the bar, nodding their understanding. It was about that time that a very pretty, tall, red-headed lady walked in the converted saloon with a five or six-year-old little blonde girl. The little girl wore an outfit that matched that of the older woman. Each was dressed rather conservatively with simple bonnets. They took seats near the front primarily because that was all that was left.

"The nerve of that woman," whispered one of the ladies with a particularly ugly hat, "dragging that brush colt of hers in here. . . and sittin' right up front where that nice lookin' preacher can see her!"

"I'm sure she only came because Brother Ben's not here!" added one of the lady's companions. "He'd know what kind of woman she is!"

"Momma," whispered the little girl, "if those two old hags are the kind of folks that are goin' to Heaven. . . let's us go some place else."

"Shhhh, Charlotte," answered the red-headed woman, "you can't judge all Christians by the mouths of a few."

The younger of the two cowboys elbowed his companion and said, "Maybe we ought to hang around a mite longer and listen to what the preacher says. . . just wish there was an empty seat next to that redhead yonder!"

Some of the men in the congregation, who overheard the cowboy's remark, snickered a bit just as their wives elbowed them. Gus looked over his shoulder at the "crowd", smiled really big, and nodded at Brother Jeremiah that it was time to start.

The old Bible-wrangler walked slowly up the three steps to the little stage where the pulpit stood. He placed his worn-out Bible on the podium and looked out over the group assembled there, stopping at each person long enough to give an unspoken greeting. He grinned special for the little blonde girl and her mother. They all looked pretty much like Ben Toller had described them.

"Sure glad all you fine folks could make it today," stated the maturing Psalm-singer. "And I'm grateful for the two visitors who have joined us and pray that they'll get over their head-colds soon. . . that must be why they still have their hats covering their heads."

The two cowboys looked incredulously at the circuit rider, then at each other, and then at the bartender who placed his shotgun on the counter. They removed their hats quickly while a few of the church-goers snickered.

The old sin-buster led the group in a couple of songs and a prayer. But the two cowhands were getting restless and even more thirsty by the minute. Finally, the tall one in the mangy-looking buffalo robe pulled his .44 from his holster.

"OK, Preacher-man," he growled, "that's enough foolin' around. . . read a Scripture and close the service so's we can all have a drink!"

Brother Jeremiah sighed deeply and just stared at the man whose partner had pulled his six-shooter and aimed it at Big Hank. The crowd showed extreme nervousness. The red-haired lady got up and walked straight to the man in the buffalo robe and slapped him hard across the face. The man was momentarily stunned by her actions. He most certainly had not expected that.

"What the blazes do you think you're doin', Woman?" yelled the smelly cowboy. And she slapped him again. The cowpoke was about to back-hand the women across the room when the old Satan-basher interrupted.

"Hold it, Mister!" yelled Brother Jeremiah. The circuit rider motioned for Gus to pitch him the piano player's side-arm, which the keyboard specialist did as if the two had practiced the maneuver before. "You ever see what a .45 slug does to the barrel of a .44?" continued the preacher.

The red-headed woman slowly backed away from the befuddled drover. His gun was still leveled in the direction of the old sin-stomper, but it wasn't cocked.

"Put that hogleg of yours back into your holster. . . very slowly, Mister," said Brother Jeremiah calmly. "If you say one more word, I'm gonna put a bullet down the barrel of your pistol, and you'll never fire it again."

"You're. . ." was all the rough-lookin' cowhand got out of his mouth before he heard the explosion from the revolver the preacher held and saw his own gun flying through the air into the waiting hands of Old Stinky. The suddenly sobered saloon swamper examined the cowboy's Smith and Wesson.

"Well I'll be dad-burned if'n that preacher didn't put a slug right down the barrel of thet feller's gun. . . plugged it up. . . and peeled the barrel like a banana!" commented the old barfly. "I ain't never seen shootin' like thet afore! You fellas gonna hang around for the ending of the sermon?"

"I told you not to say another word," said the preacher with a grin.

The cowboys looked at the ruined weapon in the hands of the town's drunk, and then slowly turned to gaze in amazement at the old Bible-teacher. The younger one gagged on a fly that had found its way into his open mouth, and the two men ran through the doors, jumped on their horses and lit out for parts unknown never to be seen in Horse Shoe again.

Gus Evans played "Rock of Ages" again to get the group refocused on the reason each one had come to the meetin' that "Sunday". . . a task that wasn't easy, for all in the group speculated about what the man who stood before them had been before he became a preacher. Brother Jeremiah led the congregation in another hymn while the three ladies with the ghastly hats discussed amongst themselves his previous occupation. When the song ended, the old circuit rider picked up his Bible and turned to a specific page.

"If you kind folks have your copy of the Scriptures," started Brother Jeremiah, "let's us take a look at one of my favorite passages. . . found in the Gospel of John, Chapter 8, beginning at verse 1."

Over the next hour, the old frock-coat masterfully told the story of the woman taken in adultery who was forgiven by Jesus himself. He spoke of the real intent of the Pharisees who wanted to feel superior to the woman as well as to Jesus. He pointed out that the accusers of the woman had failed to implicate the man who was just as guilty, since she was "caught in the very act". He stooped down and wrote in the dust on the floor, "gossiping". . . "spreading rumors without knowing the facts". . . "not showing love and forgiveness". . . and other sins that most all of the folks, including the over-dressed ladies in the audience, had probably committed. Then he spoke of Jesus' forgiveness and took them all to the cross and eventually the empty tomb. By the end of his message, the mourning bench that Old Stinky had set up near the front of the small stage was full of people repenting of the wrongs done to others. Even the ladies with the despicable hats were on their knees beside the red-haired woman and her daughter, praying for forgiveness.

It took a while for all the folks to regain their composure, but the covered-dish meal shared that "Sunday" morning was among the very best that the old circuit rider had ever eaten. The saddlebag clergyman would know many spiritual victories before the Lord called him home to receive his vast rewards, but none was sweeter than the victory in the lives of the folks of Horse Shoe, Texas.

****

Chapter Five

The Rejoicing

Christmas of 1876 had turned out to be one of the most memorable holiday celebrations that Tom McKelroy could recollect. He had been back home with his folks on their farm in Georgia for just over two months, had led his cousin, Mark McClure to a saving knowledge of Jesus, and had gotten re-acquainted with a young brown-haired, brown-eyed lass who had been all elbows and knees when he had last seen her just a day or two before he had abandoned the plow-hazer's life in search of excitement and adventure. The former pasteboard-shuffler had experienced more excitement than he cared to remember as a gambler aboard some of the fanciest riverboats that ever sailed the Mississippi. And Tom smiled as he recalled his meeting Brother Jeremiah just a few months prior on the *Delta Queen*.

The former riverboat gambler fondly remembered how the old circuit rider had made such a difference in his life. . . and how the words of that old preacher had made him start thinking about surrendering to the Gospel ministry himself. And he chuckled to himself as he heard in his mind the voices of his poker-playing "friends" trying to discourage him from leaving the life of chance that depended on luck and the turn of a card.

Tom had sold all of his jewels, except for the large watch that was his most prized possession, to those former friends who thought they were taking advantage of some kind of "illness" they believed the tall Georgian to be going through. He had banked the money, hoping to use his winnings to help his pa turn a profit on what Tom had remembered to be the rock-filled soil that had one time been his home. But Pa McKelroy's hard work and persistence had turned his 180 acres into the showplace of Paulding County. The McKelroys were not rich by the standards of the world, but the Lord had provided their every need and made them successful enough to help their neighbors during rough times.

As Tom watched the snowflakes fall gently from the skies, the former chip-hustler recalled that afternoon just a month ago when he thought he was alone in the woods, reading from Pa's old Bible. . . and practicing a sermon he had been asked to deliver in the absence of the local pastor.

"A new commandment I give unto you," read Tom, "that you love one another."

The young plow-pusher closed the worn Book and hugged it close to his heart the way he had seen Brother Jeremiah do and continued talking to the trees.

"Love is the most powerful force in the world," he said as if the trees were actually listening. "Love can overcome any obstacle. . . make a raging river seem like a quiet stream. . . turn an unclimbable mountain into an ant hill. . . melt the coldest heart . . . change the hardest mind. . . love can do anything!"

"Can love change the kind of anger that leads to hate?" asked a familiar voice behind the young Bible-expositor.

Tom turned quickly, startled by the voice, to look into the green eyes of his red-headed cousin. But Tom had never seen the look on Mark's face that he saw at that moment, and he prayed that God would give him the words that his younger cousin needed to hear.

"Why yes, Mark," began the would-be preacher, "love can change hate. . . least wise the love of Christ can overcome hate. . . no matter how deep. . . of course, we have to let Him love through us."

"What if a person doesn't really know who it is that he's hating?" asked the younger of the two men. "I mean I used to. . . think. . . I knew who I was hatin'. . . but since you've come home, now I'm not quite so sure."

"You wanna tell me about it, Cuz?" asked Tom.

The gambler-turned-farmer-turned preacher had a sincere, caring quality in his voice recognized by anyone who talked with him at any length. Mark had always admired that characteristic of his older cousin. He recalled that sometimes complete strangers would meet Tom at a barn dance or at a celebration in town, and after talking to him for just a few minutes, tell him their life-stories and open up about inner pains and fears.

"It started back when my folks were killed at Fort Harrison," replied Mark as he straddled a fallen pine tree.

The young carrot-top plowboy picked at the bark on the log as Tom meandered over to where Mark was sitting. Though inexperienced in offering spiritual help to folks, Tom felt like he needed to at least listen to what was troubling his younger kinsman. Silently he prayed that God would put Scriptures in his head from those he had become most familiar with over the past few months. Mark looked up into the face of this man whom he trusted above all others to be honest with him as Tom placed Pa's Bible between them.

"When I woke up in the hospital after the raid," began Mark, "I was angry with God, and I hated God because I blamed Him for the massacre. I mean. . . if He was as strong as my ma always said, then He could have stopped those renegades from storming the fort. . . and my family would still be alive. Ain't He got that kind of control over things? Ain't He supposed to have the power to stop bad folks from slaughtering good folks like my ma and pa. . . and my brothers?"

Mark's eyes began to fill with tears as he recalled the deaths of his family in his mind. Tom didn't really know how to answer his younger cousin, but he knew that the young man's questions came from a broken heart.

"God is all powerful, Mark," answered the more worldly of the two men as he thought of that horrible night on board the *Delta Queen* when the young Englishman took his own life. "But why He doesn't interfere with our lives every time something bad happens. . . I don't know. I wish Brother Jeremiah was here. . . he knows this Book better than any fella I've ever known. If he was here, he'd probably tell you that God has a plan for you. . . as He did for your folks. . . and no matter what, He loves you, Cuz. . . He wants you to know that love. . . feel that love. . . and live in that love."

"God don't love me, Tom," stated Mark in an ashamed tone. "He couldn't. . . not after all the mean things I've said to Him. . . and about Him to anybody that would listen. We ain't seen each other in quite a spell. . . but I noticed somethin' different 'bout your eyes. . . and your smile. . . and I thought maybe you had found the answers. . . to everything."

Tom grinned, not unlike the grin he saw come over Brother Jeremiah's face a time or two. The seasoned former-gambler leaned back against a big limb on the fallen log.

"I have found the answers, Mark," declared Tom, "Or rather, I found the One who knows the answers. . . and I know where those answers are located."

The soon-to-be preacher picked up the Bible and looked at the worn cover like it was worth a fortune. Then he continued sharing what he knew to be true.

"God does love you, Mark," affirmed Tom. "It says here that God proved His love for us by sending His Son to die in our place when we all were bad folks. If you can accept that as a fact, and ask Him to come into your heart. . . He will do just that. . . and His love will replace the hate. . . scrub it all out of your heart and your mind. . . and make you brand new."

For the next thirty minutes or so, Mark asked question after question. And each time Tom brought the answer back to the love of Christ, even though the young Bible-teacher couldn't quote Scripture and Verse. Tom didn't tell his younger cousin, but passages that his ma had quoted or read years ago came to mind. . . verses that the future circuit rider had long forgotten. . . as if Someone was whispering those verses into his ear so silently, that only Tom could hear.

"Do I have to wait 'til Sunday to ask Christ to come into my heart, Tom?" asked the muscular hay-shaker when he couldn't think of any more questions.

"Don't reckon you do, Mark," answered Tom with that new grin of his. "You can ask Christ to come into your heart anywhere. . . anytime. . . even right here."

Mark slid off the log and dropped to his knees. And there beneath a canopy of pines stretching their branches to the skies as if in praise to their Creator, another soul was flooded with the peace that comes when the burdens of the world are lifted from one's shoulders. And Tom felt his inner self overcome with an unexplainable joy. And they went on their way rejoicing!

****

Brother Jeremiah had never liked trains because trains moved too fast. But here he was. . . riding the rails from Buffalo, New York, back to his territory in East Texas. The old Bible-slinger had ridden the train to Buffalo to talk to a publisher who had enclosed a round-trip ticket for the old circuit rider in a letter that sounded urgent. The trip back to "civilization" was much slower than the trip to the big city, mostly because of the snow and wind. It was powerful cold way up north, but Brother Jeremiah kept his mind set on his return to the piney woods, and that thought made his heart rejoice.

The old Bible-teacher had preached about the birth of Christ to one of his congregations in Elysian Fields, Texas, on Christmas Eve morning in 1876. It was the first time he had used a hymn like "O Little Town of Bethlehem" as the basis for his text supported by Scripture. Brother Jeremiah had since decided that he would explore the possibility of using another hymn from time to time as the basis for his message.

As soon as he could after that inspiring message, the old preacher rode the short distance to the boom-town of Marshall, Texas, and boarded a Texas and Pacific Railroad car for the journey to Yankee land to discuss with representatives of Beadle and Adams the possibility of him being featured in a series of dime novels to be called the "Old Circuit Rider Library". At first, the idea sounded silly to the experienced sin-buster and perhaps even a bit repulsive. But then he thought about the possibility of thousands of folks reading about his adventures in the forests and towns of east Texas, which might just lead some of those readers giving their lives to the Lord.

As the train the old Bible-thumper now rode, *The Pacific Express*, slowed down to take on more passengers in Rome, Pennsylvania, Brother Jeremiah's thoughts turned to the meeting with the northern publishers that had taken place earlier that day.

"Good morning, Sir," stated a tall, skinny man with bushy sideburns that almost met at his severely dimpled chin. "My name is Roscoe Thornberry. I am head of the Creative Department for Beadle and Adams, the foremost publishers of dime novels. I trust you had a delightful trip from the wilderness."

Mr. Thornberry offered his hand to the old Psalm-singer, but only slightly shook the fingers of the Texas black-coat. No one but a woman had ever shaken Brother Jeremiah's hand in that manner, so he was a bit taken back by the gesture.

"The trip was fine, Mr. Thornberry," answered the aging saddlebag-parson. "But I didn't come from the wilderness. . . the towns are small, especially compared to Buffalo, and the area is surrounded by tall trees, but it's home to a bunch of mighty fine folks who might think that your city, with its tall buildings, is a wilderness of sorts." Brother Jeremiah grinned to try and set a more friendly mood for the meeting.

"Yes. . . quite," replied the book-man, who Brother Jeremiah thought looked an awful lot like Washington Irving's description of his character Ichabod Crane in *The Headless Horseman*.

The skinny publisher sat behind a large desk that made him look even more comical to the "wilderness-minister" and began rummaging through some papers in a folder. He read a piece of paper for a few seconds after placing what appeared to be a copy of one his dime novels face-down on the desk.

"As we said in our letter of last month," began the Ichabod-look-alike, "we are prepared to offer you a contract to publish no less than six of your books each year for exclusive access to your stories. We will provide the cover illustrations as well as the inside illustrations, of course."

With that declaration, Mr. Thornberry slid what looked like a very wordy contract across the desk for the small-town pastor to sign. He then walked around the desk with an ink well and a pen. Brother Jeremiah leaned back in the chair and looked questioningly at the man standing to his left holding the pen.

"Before I read and sign this paper," said the old soul-wrangler, "I've got a couple of questions I need answered. First off, why me?. . . I mean. . . why me instead of somebody like Dwight Moody, for instance? And secondly. . . since I spend a great deal of time in the saddle, when I am I supposed to find the time to do all this writing?. . . I mean. . .what am I supposed to write about?"

The skinny Northerner took a deep breath and held it for several seconds before finally letting it out. He blinked his eye-lids about a million times to suggest that the old preacher should not be asking these questions. Then, he cleared his throat a couple of times like he hadn't had a drop of water in two days, placed the pen back into the ink well, and started pacing to the other side of the room where he stood facing the wall for a handful of seconds before turning to answer Brother Jeremiah's annoying questions.

"I suppose you are entitled to some sort of explanation," stated Mr. Thornberry in his don't-you-know-your-wasting-my-time tone of voice. "Beadle and Adams has been working on this project idea for several months. We had originally thought about using stories by Mr. Moody or others of his stature, but we decided that his stories would be too dull to publish. We wanted something more adventurous. . . real-life stories that our readers would follow. . . convincing stories that the public could hardly wait to read in each installment."

The skeleton-like figure walked to the back window of his fourth-floor office and peered outside like he was talking to one of the pigeons resting on the flag pole that extended from the building.

"Several weeks ago," continued the bookseller, "one of our employees visited a cousin who lives in your wilderness area. . . and that employee heard you tell one of your tall tales about your run-in with a posse looking for a horse thief. . . and the resulting display of marksmanship that freed you." Thornberry turned to look at the circuit rider as he continued his story. "Mr. Beadle decided that your all-American adventures of a frontier preacher was just what we were looking for to bolster our readership."

"Bolstering your readership means more sales. . . more money for the company. Is that it, Mr. Thornberry?" asked Brother Jeremiah as a real question.

"Yes. . . quite," answered the publisher's assistant. "You won't actually have to write anything, Sir,. . . just send in ideas of your escapades from time to time. Our staff writers will take care of the details."

Thornberry walked back to the desk and picked up the 100-page booklet, and then tossed the dime novel in the general direction of the old pulpiteer.

"We've already got the first issue in the 'Old Circuit Rider Library' ready to hit the stands as soon as you sign the contract," declared the skinny Yankee.

Brother Jeremiah picked up the book and examined the black and white illustration on the cover that proclaimed in large letters 'Frontier Preacher Meets Jesse James', then he opened the book randomly and read some of the contents. He closed the book and placed it back onto the desk, shoving it back across to the Creative Department head.

"I hope you haven't printed very many copies of this trashy pack of lies," stated Brother Jeremiah rather calmly.

"Do you find something not to your liking, Mr. Jeremiah?" asked Thornberry.

"Nothing's to my liking, Mr. Thornberry," pronounced the preacher. "In the first place, I don't wear a backwards collar underneath a set of buckskins. . . and in the second place, I've never met Jesse James. . . and in the third place, I don't preach with a Bible in one hand and a Colt .45 in the other. . . and finally, I've never done anything like what I read on just those two pages in the middle of the book!"

"It's called using poetic license, my Friend," countered the skinny New Yorker. "Editors and publishers do it all the time. Most authors don't mind if a phrase or two is changed to enhance the storyline. It's done all the time!"

"Well. . . it won't be done this time, Mister," answered a distraught Brother Jeremiah as he rose and walked towards the door of the publisher's office. He reached for his hat as he continued his exit. "I'm normally a very reserve individual, Mr. Thornberry. . . but if I ever hear of Beadle and Adams publishing that piece of hogwash using my name. . . I'll come back without my Bible. . . but with a lawyer and my Colt. . . and that's no poetic license. . . that's a hard, cold fact! Good day. . . Mr. Thornberry."

On his exit, the old Bible-wrangler shut the door hard enough to shatter the glass on the top half of the door. He stopped momentarily, peaked in at the astonished bookseller, and grinned. Then he put his hat on before leaving the outer-office, tipped his hat to the secretary, and strode down the hallway to the stairs, whistling "Rock of Ages".

****

Chapter Six

The Horrors

*T*he *Pacific Express* had only stopped in Rome, Pennsylvania, long enough to take on just a few passengers before trudging through the snowstorm towards Chicago, Illinois, where Brother Jeremiah would change back to a train owned by the Texas and Pacific line. That connection would take the old circuit rider back to Marshall, Texas, and his home area. The old Bible-thumper had decided to brave the cold winds of the north to get some fresh air before settling in for the evening. He was still a bit upset over the meeting that morning in the Buffalo offices of Beadle and Adams, but Brother Jeremiah hoped the crisp, cold air would clear his mind. He had tried praying that the Lord would allow him to meet someone aboard the train with whom he could talk about Jesus.

"Allllll aboard!!" yelled the conductor.

Brother Jeremiah peeked around the corner of the parlor car to see the conductor wave the lamp signaling the engineer that the passengers were all safe and sound aboard the cars. The old Gospel-peddler reached for the doorknob of the car he had called home for the past several hours and walked back into the warm surroundings. He noticed a man and his wife taking a place of rest across from the bench he had been sitting upon just before the train had pulled into the Rome station.

"Excuse me, Folks," said Brother Jeremiah as he tipped his hat to the strangers. "Would you mind if I kept you company for just a bit? I don't want to disturb you none, but I was sitting here just a while ago."

"You won't be disturbing us in the least," answered the bearded gentleman accompanying the lovely lady who sat next to the window.

The gentleman arose, and the lady smiled graciously as the old traveling parson scooted into the opposite seat. Brother Jeremiah removed his hat, copying the gentleman with the baritone voice. The old Gospel-pusher tried not to stare at the couple, but the man's face seemed rather familiar.

"Pardon my staring, Sir," said the old preacher, "but you look very familiar. Have we met before?"

"That's possible, Sir," replied the smooth-voiced man. "My name is Philip Bliss. . . and this is my wife, Lucy." Again the quiet, attractive lady at his side smiled and nodded her head.

"Philip Bliss. . . the Gospel singer and song writer?" asked the old sermonizer from Texas.

"The very same, Sir," answered the hymnist with a broad smile.

"Brother Buck Whittle introduced us at the Preacher's Conference in New 'Rleans a few months back," stated Brother Jeremiah while extending his hand. "You sang just before Dwight Moody preached. Brother Moody could have given an invitation without preaching a word. . . you mesmerized the entire audience that night."

"You flatter me, Sir," answered the Gospel singer.

"Oh. . . I'm so sorry," blushed the old preacher. "Folks call me Brother Jeremiah. I'm on my way back home to Texas. . . been up this way for. . . an interval. It's really grand to meet you again and your charming wife."

"There's no point in all the formalities, Jeremiah.. do you mind me calling you Jeremiah?" asked the solidly built singer. "You can call me Philip."

"You can call me anything you want, Philip," answered the star-struck preacher. "I really like your songs. . . they preach! I often use 'Almost Persuaded' as an invitation for folks to come to Christ."

What a time the three Christian travelers had as they shared stories about their adventures presenting the Gospel. Bliss and his wife talked about the opportunities in the big cities where violence and poverty seemed to permeate every aspect of society. Brother Jeremiah shared the hardships of trying to pastor four churches in developing areas where folks longed for the Gospel message, but had few worldly goods to share with anyone, much less a traveling clergyman. The trio didn't even notice that the train had slowed to just 10 miles per hour in the blinding snowstorm.

Brother Jeremiah shared his story of why he had journeyed to Buffalo, and Mr. Bliss explained that he and his wife had spent Christmas with his mother and sister in Rome, Pennsylvania. The singing couple had not planned on returning to Chicago until January, but had received a telegram from D.L. Moody encouraging them to return for a special New Year's Eve service. So, they had sent their luggage on to Chicago, left their two boys with his mother in Rome, and boarded *The Pacific Express* the evening of the 29th.

"Ashtabula Station. . . next stop!" yelled the conductor while looking at his watch and walking down the aisle. "One minute to Ashtabula Station!"

Both Brother Jeremiah and Philip Bliss looked at their watches instinctively. It was 7:38 p.m. . . the train was three hours late but crossing the bridge that spanned the icy creek below. Suddenly, something in the supporting beams of the bridge snapped. For an instant, there was a confused crackling of beams and girders as the eleven cars in the train pitched the passengers to and fro, ending with a tremendous crash, as the whole train, but the leading engine, broke through the framework, and fell 75 feet into a heap of entangled iron, wood, and humans at the bottom.

For a moment there was silence. The survivors of the fall lay in stunned amazement among friends and family members, some dying, some dead, but all in various stages of mutilation, piled on top of one another. Then arose the screams of the maimed and suffering in the darkness. The few who remained unhurt hastened to escape from the splintered wreckage.

Brother Jeremiah and Philip Bliss crawled out of the windows closest to them into freezing water waist-deep. Others who weren't maimed or injured too much crawled out other windows. One nameless man struggled to aid a woman near by the two evangelists. Brother Jeremiah, with a cut across his face, watched two other men pull a pregnant woman from the car to his left. Her left foot had been crushed, and they laid her in the snow. The old preacher crawled to her to offer her comfort, but decided to try and carry her up the steep, snow-covered hill to the closest house he could find. It was obvious that the woman had gone into labor.

Bliss had been trying to free his wife, who was screaming from pain. Lucy was trapped, entangled in the ironwork of the seats. He looked at his new-found friend, pleading for help, but discovered that the old circuit rider, stumbling and slipping half-way up the embankment, literally had his arms full. At that instant, Brother Jeremiah turned to look at the carnage and caught the look of desperation in the eyes of the great song writer. Then Bliss returned to the inside of the twisted car from which he had escaped. And about that time, the cars caught fire from the kerosene lanterns and stoves that had lit and heated the cars. Despite the cold winds, the falling snows, and the freezing waters from the little creek in which most of the cars lay, the fires spread quickly.

Crowds of people from the town of Ashtabula, who had heard the noise of the crash, ran to aid the folks aboard the train. The fire department arrived, but the order was given to try and save the survivors. Bursts of flames kept most rescuers away from the tangled mass of machinery and people. The scene was one of sheer horror.

Men, women, and children, with limbs severely bruised or broken, trapped between timbers and pierced by pointed splinters, begged with their last breath for aid that no human power could give.

Though completely exhausted, Brother Jeremiah got the woman he was carrying safely to the top of the hill. There he was met by two railroad workers who hurriedly took the woman to the hotel where a make-shift hospital had been set up. Another woman from the town tried her best to minister to the head wound of the old preacher. As she did, Brother Jeremiah turned to look at the valley below.

The surviving wounded from the accident were lying in the snow. Some were strapped to stretchers or hoisted onto the backs of rescue workers and carried up the bluff to the hotel. The spectacle was turning more frightful by the minute, but those who had gone to assist, worked steadily in spite of the intense heat. They carried away all who could be rescued, and then waited tearfully for the flames to die down, so that bodies might be taken out. Within thirty minutes after the collapse of the bridge, it was impossible to get near the wreckage because of the heat from the fire.

Brother Jeremiah staggered down the way to the hotel with the aid of one of the townsmen. The folks of Ashtabula supplied a willing hand, and all that human skill could do to save life or ease pain was done. The two hotels nearest the train station housed a majority of the wounded. They were scattered about on temporary beds or cots or pallets in the dining-rooms, parlors, and offices. Both doctors of the community worked frantically throughout the night to save lives, mend bones, sew up cuts, and even deliver a baby.

By midnight, the fires that had cremated so many died down. The snowstorm had let up, but the wind still blew a fierceness that cut to the bone, and the cold was more extreme. When morning came, all that remained of the *Pacific Express* was a charred collection of twisted metal lying in a black pool at the bottom of the gorge. The wood had burned completely away, and the ruins were covered with white ashes. Here and there could be seen a mass of a scorched material that sent up a little cloud of sickening vapor, an indication which hinted that it had at one time been a human being that slowly yielded to the destruction of the fires.

None of the remains would ever be identified, including those of Philip and Lucy Bliss. Altogether, some ninety-two men, women, and children perished in the wreck and fires of the Ashtabula Horror, as it came to be called.

Brother Jeremiah left the next day for Cleveland aboard the train which carried those who were among the worst wounded to the hospital there. He made the connection to Chicago and then back to Texas. But he would carry the memory of the night the bridge gave way for the rest of his life. . . especially every time he sang or heard one of Philip Bliss' songs, like the manuscript that was found in his trunk containing the words to his last song, "My Redeemer".

****

The last night of 1876 was one of celebration for the McKelroy family of Paulding County, Georgia, with their friends and neighbors, which included a barn dance and covered dish supper. Pa McKelroy once again "set the barn afire" with his fiddle playing. Folks would come from miles around just to hear him play and watch him dance a jig at the same time.

Pa was backed up well by the Tritt family. . . Austin on the guitar, Bowie on the banjo, and Lamar on the harmonica. These boys originally moved to Paulding County from the hills around Chattanooga, Tennessee, just after the War of Northern Aggression. Their grandpa's favorite brother was killed with a bunch of those Texas boys at the Alamo, so their dad, Houston Tritt, named all his young'uns after some of the folks who became famous for leading the fight for Texas Independence. Old man Tritt even named his daughter after Susannah Dickinson, the only lady to live to tell about the battle.

Tom McKelroy had not been to a country-style, down-home kind of New Year's Eve celebration since he had left the farm some ten years earlier. And he was having the time of his life. . . eating and dancing and swapping yarns with old friends. The party had been going on for about an hour when Susannah Tritt walked into the barn.

Susannah was only eight years old when Tom had run away from home to seek his fortune. He remembered her as wearing overalls, buck-toothed, a face full of freckles, and skinny as a rail. The only thing about her that was half-way promising was those big, brown eyes with unbelievably long eye-lashes. She used to tag along after Tom and his brothers whenever they'd go fishing down to the little creek that ran close to the McKelroy farm. And Tom recalled, too, how that skinny little girl would get riled so easily and start chunking rocks at the boys. But the most annoying thing of all was how little Susannah would tell folks how she was "gonna marry up with Tom when she growed up".

And Susannah did grow up, turning into the prettiest gal in three counties. She had been blessed with the kind of curves that drive most men and other women crazy. Her teeth straightened out on their own, and the freckles disappeared, and she wasn't at all skinny. Susannah no longer dressed or acted like one of the boys. Her brown hair was long and soft and tied oh so pretty with a bow that matched her dress. And Tom noticed, as did all the young men in that part of Georgia, that her eyes were still just as big and brown as they were ten years before.

Susannah stood just inside the doorway of Barnes' Livery Stable, the site of the celebration in Dallas that was ushering in 1877. She wore a high-necked lacey blouse and a floor-length bright blue skirt with a large black belt around her 19-inch waist, and she fanned herself with a black hand-fan that had come all the way from Atlanta. Susannah surveyed the dancers and those who watched from the sides for Tom McKelroy.

Tom was holding a plate of food when he noticed the young brunette sashaying towards him. She was trying to hide a slight grin with her fan. The former-card player had been awe-struck by the young woman ever since the two of them had gotten re-acquainted during the party Pa had thrown just a few days after Tom's home-coming. Susannah was no longer a nuisance, and Tom found her presence a joy. The two of them had spent most of that evening talking about the past, laughing, and hinting about the future.

"Good evening, Tom," said Susannah from behind her fan. Only her big, brown eyes showed just above the edge of the fan.

"Good evening, Miss Susannah," answered the tall farmer, his hands still holding the plate of food. "And may I be the first to wish you a happy New Year."

Tom grinned from ear to ear as he slightly bowed. Susannah returned his greeting with a slight curtsey. Then the two laughed just a little. Ma and Jenny Lovelace, a cousin to Susannah, noticed the young couple as they stood in the shadows gossiping about their neighbors.

"Don't they make a lovely couple?" asked Jenny as she leaned close to Ma.

"They always did," answered Ma. "I just knew that one day they'd be together. . . just like Susannah said."

Tom and Susannah ate together and danced together and laughed together like they were the only two people in the barn that night. And at midnight, as was the tradition in those hills, the two kissed while dancing midst a crowd of people to a waltz played by the Tritt brothers. The young sod-buster drove the pretty lady home that night, followed by her dad and brothers, of course. And under a full moon, just one mile from Susannah's house, the former high-roller took the biggest chance of his life and asked the young woman to be his life partner.

There was never any chance in Susannah's mind that she would say "no". She had dreamed of this moment most of her life, and not even the sharp pain in her side could erase her joy. Despite the pain, which had been coming and going for the past year, she smiled bigger than she ever thought she could. And when her menfolk drove up, the beautiful lass jumped off the wagon and ran to tell the boys her good news. Tom followed close behind her. He had fully intended to ask her pa for her hand in marriage before they made any kind of public announcement.

"Is what Suzie says true, Boy?" asked a stern-faced Houston Tritt.

The former poker-player gulped, put his arm around his young love, and answered sheepishly, "Yes, Sir. I'd be mighty proud to make her my wife. I like her more than any other woman I've ever met. . . and I love her more than I've ever loved anyone I've ever known."

The Tritt boys were all grinning like treed possums. Susannah moved closer to Tom and held her breath that her pa would give his consent. Mr. Tritt milked the moment for all it was worth. He glared at the young couple standing below him, and then looked over his shoulder into the faces of his boys. Finally he breathed deeply and grinned a crooked grin.

"Well, Boy," said the elderly Tritt, "then I'd be right proud to have Pa McKelroy's son a part of my family."

The aging farmer descended the wagon seat in one leap and stuck out his callused hand as a sign of welcome to his future son-in-law. Tom gripped the old hay-stacker's hand firmly as the boys jumped out of the wagon, hugged their little sister and slapped Tom and their pa on their respective backs, all the time hootin' and hollerin' to beat the bands. This was turning out to be the best New Year that anyone in both families had experienced in quite some time.

****

Two weeks into 1877 and Tom McKelroy had the framework of a small cabin completed on a section of land that came from both the McKelroy and Tritt farms. His younger brother, Billy, and his cousin, Mark, had been helping the former-cardsharp build a new home for him and Susannah. The two had set the wedding date for Valentine's Day. So far, the weather had been holding out. . . there had been some snow, as usual, but the skies had been clear for the past 10 days and the temperature hovered in the mid-50s. And if the rain held off, the McKelroy boys and the Tritt boys were planning a roof-raisin' party for Saturday, the 13th of January.

Tom had stopped work on the little house about noon on Thursday. He was to go with Susannah to town where the young farmer would transfer the funds he had in a bank in St. Louis, Missouri, to the little bank in Dallas, Georgia. The former-pasteboard shuffler had decided that the Lord just wanted him to be a farmer and maybe a deacon in the little country church on the edge of Braswell, and he was in the process of buying some more land adjacent to that the young couple had been given as a wedding present by their families.

As the tall dirt-scraper drove his bride-to-be into the county seat of Paulding County, he noticed that his beloved had turned a bit pale. She hadn't said much on their little trip because Tom had done most of the talking. . . talking about finishing the house and what he planned for the extra 100 acres or so that he was trying to buy from the Riley homestead.

"You feelin' poorly today, Darlin'?" asked the farmboy.

Susannah tried her best to smile despite the pain in her side. The pains had become more frequent over the last few days and more severe. But they always went away in a minute or two, and the young beauty wasn't a complaining kind of person. She always tried to make everyone else laugh. . . or at least smile.

"Oh. . . it's just meanness breakin' out," replied the future bride with her sweet grin. "I'll be fine."

"There ain't an ounce of meanness in your entire body, Darlin'," quipped Tom as he bent over to give his girl a kiss while reining in the horses.

"Tom!" blushed the brown-eyed young lady. "What will folks think?"

She looked around quickly to see if anyone had been watching. She didn't really care what folks thought, but she had to act like she did. Even if anyone had noticed, they wouldn't have said anything. Everyone in the county knew of the upcoming nuptials.

"They'll think 'what a lucky guy! Gettin' to kiss the prettiest gal anywhere's around here'," answered Tom. "And they'd be right as rain during growin' season!" Susannah blushed and smiled and deliberately blinked her long eye-lashes at her hayseed sweetheart.

Tom jumped down from the wagon seat, tied the horses to the rail outside the bank, and returned to the wagon to help his beloved to the ground. Susannah winced in pain but covered her reaction to his touch with a little giggle while checking to see if anyone were watching. Then she stood on her tip-toes to give her plowboy a tender kiss on the lips, which almost caught Tom off-guard. Other than New Year's Eve at midnight, Susannah had never done that before. . . at least not in public.

The young couple walked hand-in-hand to the door of the Paulding County Bank. Tom stepped ahead of Susannah and reached for the doorknob. Suddenly, Susannah collapsed in a life-less heap at his feet. Two other women who were walking down the wooden sidewalk just a few feet away screamed as the bride-to-be apparently fainted. Tom picked her up and carried his beloved into the bank and gently laid her on the small couch in the lobby. Several customers almost tripped over themselves to satisfy their curiosity, and a crowd of folks blocked the entrance to the door.

"Somebody get Doc Hayes! Fast!" yelled the perplexed dirt-digger. "Bring me some water! Stand back, folks! Give her some air!"

Isaiah Hughes, the banker, brought the distraught young farmer a cool, wet cloth from the water fountain near his office. One of the tellers brought a pillow he sometimes sat on to put beneath her head. Tom could hear the murmurs from the folks nearby who questioned each other about what had happened. All Tom knew to do was pat her hand gently.

Doc Hayes had a difficult time getting through the crowd gathered outside the bank, but pushed his way through and took charge of the situation. He gently brushed Tom to the side as he quickly examined the young lady's eyes, felt her pulse, and listened to her heart. Then he commandeered four men to carry her, couch and all, across the street to his office.

"What happened, Tom?" asked the doctor as he placed his stethoscope back into his little black bag and stood to let the men pick up the couch with the young lady still lying unconscious upon the pillows.

"I don't know, Doc," answered Tom. "She wasn't feelin' too well on the ride over here, but you know Susannah. . . she never really complains about anything. She just collapsed as we were entering the bank."

"Well. . . you come on over to my office, Son," replied the old sawbones, "and we'll see if we can't figure out what's goin' on. Come on now. . . come on!"

Tom hadn't felt this helpless since the night of the shooting aboard the *Delta Queen* when the young English woman ran into his arms after her husband shot himself. Doc Hayes, who stood only about 5'3" grabbed Tom's arm and practically dragged him across the street. Tom wanted to go, but his feet felt like they were in cement blocks and weighed a ton each. His mind would not let him think past the horror of seeing his lady-love lying so limp at his feet.

****

About a half an hour had passed before old Doc Hayes walked out of the room where he had been attending Susannah Tritt. He gently closed the door and walked to where Tom McKelroy waited. The look on the old physician's face was grave.

"Tom," began the aging doctor, "I'd like to run a few tests on Susannah that might take the rest of the afternoon to get the results. She's resting comfortably now. . . but I'd like to keep her here for tonight anyway."

"What's wrong, Doc?" asked the teary-eyed plow-pusher. "What made her faint like that? Is she gonna be all right?"

Like everyone else in the small, northwestern Georgia county, Doc Hayes knew that Tom and Susannah had planned on getting married in just a few weeks. His mind flashed back in time to seeing the young Susannah growing up and how she told the old sawbones on several occasions that she was going to marry Tom McKelroy, despite the fact that no one knew where he was at the time.

Doc wanted to relieve Tom's worries, but he didn't have all the right answers just yet. And the maturing pill-pusher didn't want to add to Tom's concerns by a wrong diagnosis.

"I'm just not sure, Tom," responded the kindly medicine man as calmly as he could. "That's. . . that's why I want to run a couple of tests. She seems strong and healthy on the outside, but something caused her to black-out the way she did. . . maybe stress about the wedding and starting a home with you. . . could be any number of things or nothing at all. We'll just have to wait and see. You can get a room over at the hotel. . . or go on home. . . I've sent a rider out to the Tritt farm. . . but I'll take good care of her tonight. . . I gave her something to help her to sleep. . . so. . . so there's no use in you sittin' up here and worryin'. Just go on home. . . come back in the mornin'. . . but go on home."

Doc Hayes could be quite persistent when he wanted to be, and Tom knew that the old medical practioner would take good care of his beloved, but he hated being away from her right now. The tall farmer walked out of the doctor's office to the little hotel down the street. He took a room and once inside did the only thing he could think to do. . . what he figured Brother Jeremiah would do at a time like this. . . sink to his knees and pray.

****

Chapter Seven

The Hold-up

B rother Jeremiah did not enjoy leaving his churches. He did not enjoy being away from the pulpit on Sundays. He was very seldom absent from the pulpit, but had, during the last year or so, done just that. He had missed his first Sunday in almost 30 years when he had traveled to New Orleans to the Preacher's Conference featuring Dwight L. Moody. Then there was the two Sundays that he had missed after the Ashtabula Horror, and now he would miss at least one Sunday as he traveled by stage coach to carry a bag full of money to an old friend in Van Horn, Texas.

The little church pastored by one of the old circuit rider's early converts, Thaddeaus Hood, had burned the previous winter, and the folks of Brother Jeremiah's four churches had raised some $3,000 to donate to the folks out in far West Texas to rebuild their little structure. This had been a major mission project for the small congregations of the East Texas Piney Woods, but they wanted to do the best they could. The folks in Brother Jeremiah's congregations had contacted other churches within a 150 mile radius, telling the other Christians in the area of the plight of their sister church in Van Horn. And even though most of those churches were in rural, farm areas, the people had worked together much like the Gentile churches did in the days of the Apostle Paul, and gathered a generous offering to help their even poorer brothers and sisters out in the far west. Each of Brother Jeremiah's churches insisted that he personally take the gift to their fellow Christians.

But by the middle of July of 1877, the road was hot and dusty. And the ride itself was most uncomfortable for the aging preacher as well as the two passengers who had caught the stage in Sweetwater. There wasn't much to do on the journey but talk. Brother Jeremiah was not fond of this part of the trip past Fort Stockton. There were hardly any trees. . . lots of rocks and sand. . . and cactus and more sand. A few head of cattle grazed in a handful of pastures that were scattered along the way.

The young lady of Oriental ancestry who sat in the seat beside the old Psalm-singer was named China Jones. She was quite small and dainty; in fact, the old Heaven-salesman thought at first that she was just a young girl. The attractive blue-eyed lady was only about 4'5" tall and couldn't have weighed more than 70 pounds dripping wet. Miss Jones did not dress in Oriental clothing nor did she have an Oriental accent. She wore a skirt made from blue-jean material, a beige blouse under a dark brown vest and a pair of expensive, custom-made, brown boots that she admitted was made by a family friend in Ft. Worth. She looked every bit a Westerner complete with a Texas-drawl.

"Have you been out West long, Miss Jones?" inquired the old Bible-pusher, trying to just make polite conversation.

"All my life, Brother Jeremiah," answered the young lady politely. "I suppose you're wondering why I don't speak like a normal Chinese. It's probably because I was born in Texas and am only half Chinese. . . what some might call a half-breed."

The young lady smiled as if she understood the preacher's questions before they had even been asked. She was a joy to talk to. . . so honest, so straight-forward, and not at all intimidated by folks staring at her. . . and asking questions. Miss Jones was quite comfortable in the body the Lord had provided for her and quite proud to be a Texan. Brother Jeremiah learned later that she had majored in American history at the University of Texas in Austin and had even worked as a tour-guide at the Capitol.

The two continued prying into each other's background in a conversational way while the scruffy-looking gentleman who sat across from Brother Jeremiah pretended to be sleeping. But the ride was actually too rough for anyone to really sleep or rest for that matter. The old preacher had considered taking the train, but decided he had had enough of trains for the rest of his life. Miss Jones laughed out loud at one of the old Bible-teacher's stories, which roused the sleeping cowboy, who shifted his position a little, pulled his hat down over his face, and once again pretended to sleep.

"My daddy was Colonel Washington Jones," said the lovely young lady as she continued her story. "He fought in the Mexican-American War in '48, but retired shortly after the close of the hostilities. He dearly loved Texas. So, he bought a spread just southwest of Coleman and started raising cattle. But that was still Comanche territory back then, and some of Nocona's men attacked my pa's ranch, stealing about a 100 head of cattle and killing his wife. This grieved my daddy so much. . . he blamed himself, of course, and sold off the remaining herd and went off on a world tour."

The petite young woman shifted herself so that she could look into the face of the traveling pulpit-pounder as she continued her story. "When the Colonel got to Hong Kong about 1851, he met a beautiful Chinese woman who stole his heart almost 'overnight'. Her name was Marabelle, and the two of them were married in a mission church the following spring. She wanted to see his ranch, so my daddy took his bride to Coleman County. Marabelle loved the house and the ranch and talked my daddy into starting over, using her dowry money."

Miss Jones fidgeted with her purse a little and grinned just a mite. "I was born a year later in that same room where my daddy's first wife had been murdered by the Comanch. My mother died from consumption when I was twelve just before my daddy returned from fightin' Yankees in the War. He had been severely wounded at Gettysburg and never fully recovered. Daddy died just before my 17th birthday. . . the day I enrolled at UT," her voice cracked just a bit as she recalled getting the news that day back in 1869.

"I still have the ranch," continued the half-Oriental beauty. "I live there most of the time, but I've always wanted to see America. So,

I'm on my way to explore the Grand Canyon and eventually visit some cousins in San Francisco."

The dusty cowboy raised his hat and sat up straight during the last part of China's dialogue. Zac Westerfield, as the man in the homemade buckskin vest had introduced himself at the beginning of the journey, looked at the preacher and the young lady in a squinting manner as if he were sizing them up. Brother Jeremiah returned the stare.

There was nothing particularly outstanding about the man who appeared to be more of a gunslinger than a ranch hand. His hazel eyes were cold as if he had known too much sorrow in his fortysomething years. His curly, black hair was covered with dirt as were his clothes, and old Zac had not scrapped the whiskers off his face in probably a week or more. Westerfield wore a bracelet on his left wrist made of braids of blonde hair that had belonged to his wife.

China Jones thought her fellow traveler might be quite handsome if he ever took a bath. Brother Jeremiah thought the man looked mean. . . mean enough to pick his teeth with a Bowie knife.

"Well, Mr. Westerfield," stated the old Bible-teacher. "hope you had a restful nap."

"Kinda hard to nap," stated the gunman coldly, "what with that driver up there trying to hit as many chug-holes as possible. . . and you two jawin' like you been doin'."

The young ranchin' lady raised her eyebrows and giggled and then turned her head to look out the coach's window. It was a lady's prerogative to change her opinion as often as she changed her clothes. . . and she did just that. No amount of water, thought Miss China, could ever get him clean from the filth of his rudeness.

Brother Jeremiah believed that the Lord might be opening an opportunity to tell the man about Jesus. "I'm mighty sorry that our conversation kept you awake, Mr. Westerfield," said the old saddlebag preacher, "but I am glad you're eyes are open now. Perhaps we can swap stories to help pass the time."

Westerfield looked at the watch he carried in a shirt pocket. Brother Jeremiah noticed that the cover of the timepiece contained a picture of a light-haired woman and a young boy. The watch also played a sweet tune when opened. The gunman only glanced at the hands, sighed, and placed the time-recorder back into his pocket.

"I don't think you two'd be interested in none of my stories, Parson," answered the gunslinger as he squinted at the old Bible-expositor.

"You been makin' you're livin' with a gun long, Mr. Westerfield?" asked China.

Zac looked instinctively at the pistol strapped to his thigh, crossed his arms, and stared at the young woman with his best it's-none-of-your-business look.

"What makes you think I make my livin' with a gun?" asked the gunman.

"Your attitude," answered the pretty rancher with little hesitation. "The way you carry that Colt. . . tied down even when you're sitting. . . your right hand always being close to the butt of that six-shooter. . . your arrogance. . . the scowl on your face like you haven't got a friend in the world. . . your fear of trusting anyone long enough to carry on a descent conversation because they might get the upper hand. . . the smell of death about you. Shall I go on?"

Westerfield swallowed hard. How could this young woman know him so well when they had only met a few hours earlier? The gun-hand looked at the old preacher, who was grinning like he was watching someone reeling in a big fish. Then Zac relaxed some.

"Reckon you're right, Missy," stated Westerfield still just a bit coldly. "I've been makin' my livin' with a gun since before the War. Joined the Army in '55 to fight Injuns. . . was stationed at Fort Phantom Hill for a couple of years just after it was re-opened to protect folks in that area from the A-patch and the Ka-manch. Then I got myself transferred to Fort Mason with General Albert Sidney Johnston, Kirby Smith, John Hood, and Bobby Lee. I remember your pa's ranch. . . know right where it 'tis. . . it was on our patrol. . . had a couple of scrapes with Kiowas and Ka-manch protectin' that ranch and his cattle."

Westerfield studied the eyes of Miss Jones to see if she perhaps remembered those scrapes. Even though she was just a little girl, she could still recall the tense days of those confrontations with the Indians. Her eyes softened while she returned the gunman's stare as if to say 'thanks' for the security he and his fellow soldiers had offered during those days and during the War. Brother Jeremiah seemed to notice a slight change in the eyes of the gunslinger.

"When the War of Northern Aggression broke out," continued the sloppily dressed traveler, "I joined up with Captain John Hood and the 4th Texas Infantry. The Captain was later promoted to General and the 4th Texas became known as Hood's Texas Brigade. We was in a mess of battles durin' that awful war, includin' Gettysburg. I can't say as I ever met your pa, but there was a lot of men on both sides that didn't make it out of those hills and woods up there in Pennsylvania. Sorry about your pa gettin' shot-up that way. . . I lost a brother and two cousins during that fight." Westerfield's voice almost cracked, but he regained his tough veneer.

"I am truly sorry for your loss, Mr. Westerfield," said China softly.

Brother Jeremiah decided to let the big man finish his story. . . at least as much as he wanted to tell. All the time the old sin-killer prayed for his fellow passengers. Both seemed to be changing before his eyes.

Westerfield lit a cigar, but hung the burning weed out the window at this side and continued his story. "After that, I was transferred to General Sterling Price's cavalry under General Kirby Smith out around the Shreveport area. Went to a tent-meetin' out close to Mansfield not long after whippin' the Yankees there. . . heard you preachin' that night, Parson. . . almost walked down to the mournin' bench, but figured I didn't have no right to even try and get into that place you talked about. . . not with all the killin' I'd done. . . and not with all the killin' I figured we'd have to do before that War was over."

Westerfield took a drag on his cigar, and looked the old sin-slayer right in the eyes. Brother Jeremiah seemed to be at a loss for words momentarily, and the gunslinger continued.

"And we did a heap of killin'," continued Zac. "When the fightin' was finally over, I headed back to Texas. . . and my home town of Austin. Became the sheriff of a little town east of there called Brushy Creek. . . settled down. . . got married to a beautiful young lady named Rebecca Jordan, daughter of the town's banker. . . had a young'un I named Jacob. . . and had a real good life for the next five or six years. Then Jacob died of diphtheria in '72. . . Rebecca

75

went plumb crazy. . . ran off with a fellow. I stayed drunk for most near a year,. . . then I tracked 'em down and killed 'em."

Westerfield again studied the faces of the passengers sitting across from him to see if either was shocked by his story. Neither of them appeared to be.

"That's when I turned to outlawin'," declared the gunman as he threw his cigar out the window and drew his pistol in one, smooth motion. "Started robbin' banks, stagecoaches, kidnappin' rich folks, shootin' folks for money. . . anything that needed to be done. . . for money. Picked up a nickname along the way. . . folks call me Cottonmouth Zac. Mebbe you heard of me. . . my gang's waitin' about five minutes up the road. We're gonna rob the stage and relieve both of you of all your possessions. . . then most likely kill you, Parson, and the driver. . . take Miss Jones here with us. . . try and get some money from her ranch. . . and probably let the boys have their way with her after we get the money. . . then she'll have a fatal accident on her way home. . . don't need no witnesses. Now, just sit back and enjoy the scenery for the next few minutes. You two wanna swap stories to help you pass the time?"

****

Tom McKelroy stared into the flames of the campfire that his cousin Mark McClure had built. Mark was busy warming a can of beans and frying up some bacon in an old iron skillet as the two pilgrims took time to eat just before noon. The men had been on the trail for about a week, heading west from Paulding County, Georgia. The flames seemed to put Tom into a kind of trance as he re-lived the worst six months of his life.

"I've got some bad news for you, Tom," said a saddened Doc Hayes the day after Susannah Tritt had collapsed in front of the bank in Dallas, Georgia. "Susannah has a cancer. . . advanced. . . in her stomach and intestines."

"What does that mean, Doc?. . . 'advanced'," asked Tom, whose breath suddenly became quite heavy and uneasy.

"It means that the cancer is too far along, Son," stated the old sawbones while wiping his glasses with a stained handkerchief. "An operation won't do any good. I can give her some medicine to help ease the pain. . . but that's about all."

"Are you tellin' me that Susannah's. . . gonna die?" inquired Tom as his eyes began to fill with tears. Doc Hayes nodded and turned his head towards the floor so that he didn't have to look Tom square in the face.

"How long does she have, Doc?" asked Tom, trying to retain his composure.

"A month. . . six months. . . a year at the most. . . it's hard to tell," stated the old medicine man. "The pain will get worse. . . toward the end she won't feel like gettin' out of bed. . . even the slightest touch or movement will cause her discomfort. She'll get to the point where she'll drink laudanum like it was water."

Tom sank down into a small wooden chair and put his hands over his face. Doc Hayes walked over to the young farmer and put his hand on Tom's shoulder.

"Does Susannah know. . . about the cancer?" asked the former card-sharp.

"Yes," said the old doctor, "I told her early this morning. She took it hard. . . so I gave her something to help her to rest. She's sleeping now. You can go sit with her if you like. I think she'd want to see you when she opens her eyes."

The tall sod-wrangler walked carefully across the old squeaky floor of Doc's office to the little room that served as a hospital. He slowly opened the door and entered the room where his true-love lay. Looking around, Tom pulled up a chair, placing it close to Susannah's bedside. After sitting down, he took his bride-to-be's left hand in both of his, then bowed his head and began to pray for a miracle to take place.

Only a few minutes had elapsed when Susannah opened her eyes. At first she said nothing, then she slowly moved her right hand across her body to gently touch Tom's head. Tom looked longingly into those big, brown eyes of the beautiful girl lying on the bed. She smiled as best she could, and her farmer smiled back despite the fact that a tear trickled down his cheek.

"I reckon Doc told you, huh?" asked the farmer's daughter bravely.

"Yes, My Love," whispered Tom, "he told me."

"Tom," stated Susannah after a few seconds of just holding her beloved's head. "I want you to promise three things. Been thinkin' 'bout each one, and I know you can do 'em. Will you promise me?. . . before I tell you what they are?"

"For you, Darlin'," said Tom softly, "I'd do anything in my power to do whatever you request. I promise."

Susannah momentarily shut her eyes and sighed deeply. Then she opened her eyes to look square into Tom's. "First off," she said calmly, "I don't want you to pity me which also includes grieving while I'm still around."

Tom gently squeezed her hand to let her know that he understood.

"Secondly," continued the brown-haired beauty with a big smile, "I want you to marry me as soon as possible. . . not wait until Valentine's Day. . . 'cause I might not see that day."

Again Tom squeezed Susannah's hand and matched her smile with his own. He had actually thought of the same thing just moments after Doc had explained his betrothed's illness. He raised her hand to his lips and kissed it ever so gently.

"Done," replied Tom with a wink. "What else can I do for you?"

"Before the year is out," answered Susannah in her 'stern' voice, "I want you to find out what you have to do to become an ordained preacher of the Gospel. You're not cut out to be a farmer, Tom. You've got some special talents that have been loaned to you by the Lord, and I want you to use them for Him. I wanna look down from Heaven while I'm talkin' with some of the Saints and say, 'you see that tall, good-lookin' preacher right there. . . that's my Tom McKelroy!'"

Tom wasn't real sure that he could fulfill that last request, but if it was that important to the little freckled-face girl from long ago, he'd give it a try. The tears returned, but the young clod-breaker shook his head in agreement with Susannah's request.

Suddenly one of the limbs in the small cook fire popped, and Tom was brought back into the present.

"Grub's pert near ready!" said Mark with a grin on his face. The want-to-be cowhand wasn't the best cook in the world, but he was much better than his older cousin. While most folks figured that it was a difficult task to mess up beans over an open campfire, the former card-player had developed the skill of doing just that. So Mark had "volunteered" to be the camp-cook while the two rode together, mostly out of survival.

"Mmmmm, Cuz!" said Tom, "you sure 'nough have a way with a skillet! Maybe you ought to think about openin' up an eatin' joint out there in the Panhandle instead of punchin' cows! Maybe we ought to find us a cabin out here in the Mississippi hills and just hold up awhile. . . get fat off'n your cookin'."

****

"Hold on, Folks," cried the stage driver, "looks like we may have some trouble up ahead!"

"That'd be my boys," said Westerfield calmly. "So jest sit back and think about the stories you could have told your grandchildren. . . about the time you was robbed by Cottonmouth Zac's gang."

Suddenly, the stage driver whipped the horses hard and screamed at them, calling each one by name. The resulting jolt sent all three passengers sprawling onto the floor of the coach. Westerfield momentarily lost control of his .45, but regained it again in the confusion. Brother Jeremiah had held onto the satchel he was carrying and both men assisted the young ranching lady back to her seat.

The ride became more like a ride on a roller coaster when the stage took a sudden turn to the left. The chug-holes and rocks bounced the occupants of the stage higher and higher into the air while slinging them from side to side. And all the while the coach was being pursued by a trio of outlaws, all of whom were shooting at the coach and the driver.

Brother Jeremiah was trying to help Miss Jones to have as safe a ride as possible when the latch on the satchel he carried gave way. While none of the money fell out of the little bag, the other two passengers looked at the clergyman as if he might be a crook. Preachers, especially circuit ridin' preachers, weren't supposed to carry that kind of money. The old saddlebag-preacher hurriedly shut the bag and fixed the latch.

"Looks like me and the boys are gonna get an extra bonus out of this hold-up!" stated the hardened-law-breaker while trying to hold onto the seat and the window of the coach as best he could and maintain his drop on the other two.

Then the three passengers heard a loud scream coming from the driver as he fell off the seat of the coach. The horses did not slow down. In fact the loosening of the reins made them seem to run faster.

Westerfield and the old puddle-jumpin' parson looked out the windows at the same time to notice that the coach was on the edge of a cliff. Both men tried to shift their weight to the right side of the coach at the same time, but their actions were just a bit too late. The wheels slid off the side of the cliff, and the coach began its descent. The tongue broke just as the coach began an end over end tumble some 100 feet into a tree-filled, rock-encrusted ravine below. Each passenger heard a shot, but was unable to determine where it came from while being tossed around the inside of the coach like a man might jiggle coins in his pocket. Finally, the coach, or what was left of it, hit bottom, landing on its top with the folks inside piled on top of one another against the roof.

The robbers stopped their horses at the top of the ravine and watched the coach's crashing through the trees and bouncing off the rocks until it came to rest with only one wheel still intact. They could not see any movement in the coach itself. They, too, had heard the gunshot, but they knew it had not come from any of them.

"Reckon anybody's survived that?" asked Rafe del Rio, an Irish-Mexican known for his meanness towards victims and even friends. Del Rio spit a mouth-ful of tobacco juice as he evaluated his compadres opinions.

"Don't see how nobody could survive that fall, Rafe," replied Nate Martin, a small man of 4' 10" who looked like a possum complete with beady eyes and stoop-shoulders and no front teeth.

"Can't be so, Rafe," added Odie Gibson, the oldest of the bunch, a man of average height but about 45 pounds overweight. He had been hung 10 years earlier, but had survived the ordeal, and so spoke with a gravelly voice.

"Too bad," said del Rio, "I'm gonna miss ol' Cottonmouth."

The other two bad men looked at each other and then at the mean-spirited half-breed, who had never voiced a concern for the safety of anyone before. Del Rio spit again and started laughing which caused the other two men to laugh cautiously.

"Just means that the loot will only be split three ways, now," conjectured Rafe, "Let's us go on down there and see what we've inherited from them poor, misfortunate folks."

"We can't get down there from here, Rafe," offered Odie, "and it'll take us the rest of the day and part of the night to ride down the trail to that ol' river-bottom and back to here."

"Then, I reckon we'd best get started, Boys," countered del Rio. "I don't reckon none of them folks is goin' nowheres. C'mon. . . let's get to ridin'."

****

Night time was one of the loneliest of times for Tom McKelroy ever since that awful night when the Angels came for his beloved Susannah. In mid-January, he had married the little girl who bragged to everyone that she would one day be the wife of the tall farmer from Georgia. Susannah was such a beautiful bride, and Tom had held back the tears because he wanted that afternoon to be so memorable to his darlin'. The wedding was perfect, even though Tom couldn't find Brother Jeremiah to either perform the wedding or be his best man. And the party afterwards rivaled the New Year's Eve celebration just three weeks before. Her family put on a good act and played lively music for hours as practically the entire county celebrated the nuptials.

And their wedding night, spent in the little three-room house that Tom, Billy, Mark, and the Tritt boys had finished just three days before the ceremony, was as perfect as it could be. The young couple simply held each other close while sitting on a bear-skin rug in front of romantic flames from the rock fireplace. They fell asleep that way and awoke to the crowing of Pa's prize-winning rooster the next morning.

Susannah seemed so very happy over the next few weeks. The young bride hid her pains very well, and Paulding County's newly-weds languished in each other's love. She spent her days canning the fruits and veggies her folks had given to them, making a small quilt patterned after the larger one that Ma McKelroy had sewed for the couple, and reading from the Family Bible that Pa McKelroy had passed along to them. Tom spent his days clearing the land and plowing portions for spring planting. He'd come home most nights exhausted and filthy. Susannah would meet him at the door, throw her arms around him, and kiss him tenderly. . . then. . .

"Don't you even think about comin' into my house and sittin' at my table as dirty as an old hog, Tom McKelroy," Susannah would say playfully while pushing her young farmer back onto the porch. "Jest you git on out back and clean yourself up presentable if'n you want to share vittles with me!"

Tom recalled how she would stand at the doorway in her apron, left hand on her hip, and a stew-ladle in her right hand and seem to dare him to come inside. But he never did. He played the game, kissed her on the forehead, grabbed the towel hung outside the door, and went off to wash up, whistling some tune every time.

Evenings were spent on the front porch when the weather permitted, Tom gently strumming his guitar, and Susannah rocking in her chair while mending something.

Then came that day in the early spring. Tom headed off to town to pick up some supplies and a package of flower seeds. Susannah seemed to want to plant the entire yard in flowers of every sort and color. The young farmer could still hear the robins singing so merrily that morning as he drove off, his beloved standing on the edge of the porch waving enthusiastically and blowing him kisses.

The journey took a little longer than expected, for Tom had spent a short time talking to Doc Hayes. The young farmer had arrived home to a dark house about sundown. He had stopped along the way and picked some flowers for his young bride. Susannah loved flowers so. Tom found his beloved in her rocking chair close to the fireplace where she sat when she knitted. She was asleep, so the tall dirt-scratcher walked as silently as an Indian to where she sat, leaned down, raised her chin, and kissed her gently on her lips. But this time, she didn't respond with that big smile of hers and the fluttering of her long eyelashes. There was no response at all. Her eyes didn't open, and her hands fell to her side as the ball of twine fell from her lap.

Tom clutched her lifeless body to himself. . . let out an awful moan. . . and cried openly. After several minutes, he picked up his bride, carried her to their room, and gently placed her on the four-poster bed that had once belonged to his grandma. Then he went back into the main room, sat in her rocking chair, and stared at the fire for the rest of the night.

Pa and young Frank McKelroy found Tom that way the next morning. Pa recognized the look on his son's face and could see Susannah's bare feet through the door going into their bedroom.

"Frankie," stated Pa in a calm tone. "Run back to the house. . . tell your ma to get out here now. Then go over to the Tritt farm and tell Mr. Houston and his boys that they need to get here, too."

"Why, Pa?" asked the youngest of the McKelroy boys. "What's wrong with Tom? What's goin' on?"

"Never mind about that now, Boy," said Pa as his eyes filled with tears. "Just you do as I tell ya to do. . . and do it now, Boy. . . do it now!"

Pa walked over to Tom, who seemed to be comatose, and placed his big, rough hand on his boy's shoulder. Frank glanced into the bedroom and saw the same thing Pa had seen. His eyes were overrun with tears, and the young boy turned and bolted through the front door and down the steps, running as fast as he could to tell Ma.

The howl of a pack of coyotes on the chase for some varmint jolted Tom back to the ebbing campfire where he and Mark had decided to spend the night. The former card-sharp picked a small log and pitched it onto the fire, splashing glowing embers every-where. He could hear Mark snoring softly, so the former sod-buster laid his head on his saddle and tried to sleep.

****

Chapter Eight

The Redemption

China Jones, who was sandwiched between Brother Jeremiah and Zac Westerfield, was the first of the trio to regain conscientiousness. She wasn't sure if either of the men was alive, but praised the Lord for her deliverance from the jaws of death. The young rancher soon discovered that her left arm was broken when she tried to push the aging messenger of God's body to the side. China did accomplish this feat with great difficulty and pain, and in doing so, discovered that she had several cuts on her head and three gashes on her arms and legs. She wasn't sure if she could walk, so she pulled herself out of the coach using her right arm. Outside the death trap that had doubled as a means of transportation, the young woman pulled herself up to a standing position while leaning on the coach.

Suddenly, China heard a moan from within the wreckage indicating that at least one of the men was alive. But which one? The Colonel's daughter slowly bent down enough so that she could see inside the coach. And she let out a deep sigh when she realized that it was the old circuit rider who was moving some and groaning. China crawled back inside the ruins of the coach in an effort to aid her fellow traveler. As she did so, she noticed that the outlaw's gun was lying beside him. The young lady grabbed the pistol and stuck it inside the waistband of her skirt. Then she continued on to the old preacher.

"Brother Jeremiah!" she said softly so as not to startle the Bible-man. "Can you hear me? Can you move your legs? We've got to get out of this tinder box before it collapses. Brother Jeremiah!"

The old itinerate preacher could feel blood running down the sides of his face, and the situation reminded him of the Ashtabula Horror. Brother Jeremiah quickly took inventory of his aches and pains. . . like the pains in his side, obviously from broken ribs. . . and the pain in his left wrist which indicated that, too, was broken. But his legs felt like he could move them if he needed to do so.

"I can hear you, Miss China," answered Brother Jeremiah in a shaky voice. "I think I can get out OK on my own. How's Westerfield?"

Miss Jones looked behind her at the body that lay dormant in the corner of the rubble. He was breathing, but he was covered in blood.

"I don't think he's in very good shape, Preacher," answered China. "But he's not goin' anywhere. . . at least not on his own."

The young cattlewoman helped Brother Jeremiah turn his body as best she could amid gasps of pain from both of them. Then they crawled outside the crumbling coach, the wood making terrible noises all the while. Finally outside, the two leaned against the coach. China looked around for her trunk. She had some petticoats and dresses in there that could be used for bandages. Neither of the two survivors could do much alone, but with God's help, and a reliance on each other, they could at least ease the pains they were experiencing.

Then it happened. . . the creaking hulk of the crumbling public conveyance broke just about where the cabin met the roof, and leaned awkwardly against a fallen log on the opposite side from where the two passengers were standing. This opened up the rescue area for the young cattlewoman and the old preacher. They could see the wounded outlaw more clearly. . . especially the blood flowing from his side.

"We need to stop that bleeding on Westerfield, Miss China," said the old Scripture-reader solemnly, "then we need to bandage each other."

"If I could get to my trunk," answered the half-Oriental cowgirl, "we can use most of my stuff for bandages. But my trunk's in that tree yonder."

Miss Jones indicated a rather large-trunked mesquite tree to her right about 20 yards up the embankment. Brother Jeremiah assessed the situation and decided on a temporary, alternative plan.

"Do you think you can reach my satchel, Miss Jones?" asked the bleeding Bible-expositor.

The young woman nodded her head that she could. She remembered seeing a bunch of money in the preacher's bag, so she wasn't sure what he had in mind.

"Good," replied the old churchman, "Get the bag. . . underneath the money, I have a couple of shirts and another pair of pants we can use for bandages for the time being. Just not sure how us two cripples can bandage up each other. You've only got one arm. . . and I can't lift mine very high."

"Wellllll," drawled a voice behind the old sermonizer, "I can use both of my arms. . . just can't seem to move my legs or sit up. . . got a hole in my side. Reckon I shot myself when we was tumblin' down here."

Miss China and Brother Jeremiah turned their gaze towards the wounded bad man who lay helpless on his back. He was trying to put pressure on the whole left by his own bullet.

"You might want to hurry things up a bit, Jonesy," grunted Zac, "don't know how long it's gonna be before I pass out again."

Miss China walked quickly but carefully over the debris to retrieve the old Psalm-singer's little black bag. She noticed it was kinda heavy, and she noticed that it had gold writing that said "Dr. J. Black, M.D." The young lady undid the latch as she approached Brother Jeremiah, opening the top of the bag, revealing a worn-out Bible wedged in one end and a Colt .45 in the other. . . both on top of packages of wrapped bills.

Brother Jeremiah squatted on the ground and removed the revolver and the Bible while rummaging to the bottom for a pair of clean long-johns, two plain white shirts, and a pair of black woolen britches. The old sin-killer tried to tear one of the shirts, but his own wounds kept him from that task.

"Might work better if'n you use the knife stuck in my right boot, Preacher," mentioned the bleeding bandit with a slight smile.

Miss Jones pulled the knife from its scabbard and used it to cut strips in the preacher's shirts.

"I think we need to set and splint your arm, Miss Jones," suggested Brother Jeremiah. "There are a couple of pieces of the stage over there that look the right length. We might have to cut one of them."

The youthful landowner brought the pieces of wood to the aging Satan-beater who trimmed the pieces to be about equal in length. Then, he motioned the girl to lean against the exposed coach-seat. He sat down close and placed his left foot against her shoulder. There was a certain degree of fear in the eyes of the little lady from Coleman County. . . mostly from the pain that she knew was coming. The old circuit rider grasped her wrist in his hands, grinned reassuringly. . . and yanked hard.

Miss China groaned, but didn't scream out as both men expected. Westerfield winced at the same time and turned his head so that the others couldn't see the tears in his eyes. The young cattle-breeder was much tougher than she looked. She was in a great deal of pain, but refused to show it openly.

Brother Jeremiah placed the boards on the top and bottom of her arm, and wrapped it with the homemade bandage the two had created. The splint allowed some movement in her hand, but immobilized the arm.

"Now," breathed the saddlebag-parson, "let's see if we can stop Mr. Westerfield's bleeding."

Brother Jeremiah crawled on his knees to the bleeding thief as Miss Jones followed. She had forgotten that she still had his gun in her waistband. Westerfield eyed the weapon as the young lady approached. The old Gospel-wrangler gently rolled the wounded man over slightly to determine if they had a bigger problem.

"Thank, God," he said, "seems the bullet went clean through. . . and from the angle, I don't think it hit any internal organs. We just need to pack the wound to help stop the bleeding. Here, use my. . . uh. . . personal garments."

Brother Jeremiah looked at Westerfield who had a funny look on his face. The old Bible-jockey grinned big, assuming he was interpreting the criminal's expression correctly.

"They're clean, Zac," muttered the old Bible-teacher, "much cleaner I suspect than anything you're wearing." Both men chuckled some, and the young lady blushed.

"While you're occupied with that, Preacher," said Miss China, "I'm gonna climb that tree yonder and push my trunk out of the branches. Oh, don't worry, Gentlemen, I've been climbin' trees for most of my life. . . and I'll be careful."

Before either man could issue a protest, the lady cattle-raiser was off to the trees. Brother Jeremiah and Westerfield watched as the lass skillfully climbed the tree with only one hand. The hardest part was dislodging the trunk from the branches where it had been entangled. Finally after much grunting and shoving, the trunk plummeted to the ground some ten feet below. The impact broke the chest open. The young lady shook her matted hair, smiled broadly like a circus acrobat, and descended the tree with ease without getting scratched.

While the girl rancher was struggling with her luggage, Westerfield confronted Brother Jeremiah with more bad news.

"You know, Preacher," said Westerfield softly, "my boys'll be comin' down this here riverbottom 'bout sundown or so. . . they'll be after the strongbox. . . and the girl. . . and they'll find your money. . . and kill us both. Worst one of the bunch is named Rio. Now he's a mean 'un. . . hates everybody 'cause their alive. . . looks at a feller like he's takin' him apart one bone at a time."

"The money ain't mine, Zac," replied the old black-coat. "Belongs to the church folks in Van Horn. . . a gift from the folks in the Piney Woods. . . to help 'em rebuild their meetin' place after it burned down. So I reckon this Rio fella will just have to try and kill me. That just might make me exceedingly happy."

"Don't you understand, Preacher!" said the wounded highwayman, "In about two hours you're gonna be exceedingly dead!"

"Well, Son," responded the old minister, "this year it'll take a heap of doin' to kill me. And you can bet your bottom dollar that I ain't gonna just sit down and give up what those folks back in the

East Texas woods sacrificed to scrape together for a love offering to their fellow brothers and sisters in Christ. . . not without a fight I ain't." The old Bible-thumper grinned his 'I-know-something-you-don't' grin at the pale former lawman just as Miss China came back with some petticoats to be used as bandages.

****

Mark McClure had avoided talking about the tragedy that had befallen his favorite cousin since the day that Susannah had died. Mark had hoped that Tom would have opened up more during their trip westward. But Tom McKelroy had a way of changing the subject to something about the Lord whenever he didn't want to talk or answer questions.

"The woods can sure be peaceful at times," said Mark while he heated up the coffee at dusk.

The young cowboy was determined that this would be the night that he would try and get Tom to open up. Mark had a first-hand knowledge of how tragedy could build up an all-controlling inner hatred. He could see slight changes in the former card-sharp's demeanor. . . like his sullen attitude for one and the way he looked past people and things as if they weren't even there. And that just wasn't the Tom McKelroy that Mark knew.

"Don't reckon we ever recognize real peace," commented Tom, "until it's taken away from us."

Mark put a pan of beans on the fire and poured a cup of coffee for his traveling companion. Then the red-headed future cowhand took off his hat, rolled up his sleeves, and sat down cross-legged close to Tom.

"Why are you out here, Tom?" asked Mark, determined he would not let his cousin change the subject this time. "I mean, what are you searching for? Are you gonna go back to gambling? Are you gonna become a preacher like Susannah wanted? Or are you just gonna become a drifter. . . riding aimlessly from one place to the next. . . no rhyme or reason. . . 'til you wind up killin' someone or they wind up killin' you?

Tom took a swig of his coffee as he pondered his younger cousin's questions. The former poker-player/farmer had considered these same questions and a dozen others ever since the two had left the family farm in Georgia. He kept trying to figure out just how God was gonna work-out something good from Susannah's illness and death. Perhaps it would be best if he talked it out.

"I'm not real sure of the answer, Mark," stated Tom rather matter-of-factly. "I told you how I had convinced myself that the Lord wanted me to take up preachin' when He led me away from the gamblin' halls last August. Brother Jeremiah was the one who started me thinkin' hard about takin' some time to study the Book and pray, seekin' out what God wanted me to do." The tall Georgian took another swig of coffee to help clear his thinking.

"Then I met up with Susannah at that party Pa throwed," continued the lanky plowman. "And I felt sure that the Lord wanted me to take care of her. . . settle down. . . start a family. And I figured I could do just that and still maybe preach some, too. And I was happy takin' care of Susannah. . . she hardly ever complained of the pain, but I could tell when she was hurtin'. She'd cuddle up as close as she could to me. . . and hum 'Amazing Grace'. She did that the night before she died, only that time, she sang that song ever so softly."

Mark moved the beans off the fire so that they wouldn't burn, poured himself some coffee, resumed listening to Tom.

"I just couldn't believe that God would actually take that sweet girl from me," added Tom in a heart-broken voice. "I started thinkin' that maybe I'd read the cards wrong when I left the *Delta Queen* last year. . . or maybe the Lord was just punishin' me for somethin'." The former card-shuffler played with the dirt under his boots for a few seconds then continued. "Then I remembered somethin' that old preacher told me aboard that boat before I left it. . . he said that whatever I decided, that I just needed to give up all control and let the Lord lead me one day at a time 'cause He wanted the best for me, and He wouldn't steer me wrong."

Tom looked over at his younger cousin with a perplexed look on his face like he was ready to surrender, but didn't know exactly how.

"Reckon that surrenderin' thing is mighty hard for anybody, Tom," stated Mark who was just as confused. "Wish I could make that decision for you, but then I'm not completely sure why I have this hankerin' to go back out to Fort Harrison."

"Reckon it's just gonna take a heap of prayin' before I get it all figured out, Mark," added Tom, "but I'm glad you're concerned. Thanks. I reckon I'll just go on to Shreveport. . . there's a good-sized church there that Brother Jeremiah told me about. Maybe they can tell me how to find that old preacher. . . maybe I can follow him around for awhile. . . learn how to preach."

"You got any idea as to where Brother Jeremiah might be, Tom?" asked Mark as he served up a helping of beans for his older cousin.

"Nope," replied Tom, "but wherever he is, he's probably tellin' someone about Jesus and doin' it in such a way as it's just a normal part of the conversation."

Both men chuckled a bit as they each formed mental pictures of the old circuit rider's activities. Night was comin' on, the food was hot, and the sounds of the Mississippi woods seemed to reinforce the calmness of the evening.

****

By the time the sun was setting out in west Texas, China Jones had used most of her petticoats for bandages for the three survivors of the stagecoach wreck. None of the three knew exactly where they were, other than at the bottom of a mostly dried up creek bed that had formed a ravine some hundred feet below the normal landscape and somewhat off the beaten path of the main road between Ft. Stockton and Van Horn. The doctored passengers looked like refugees from the Battle of Shiloh.

All three had some sort of binding around their heads and each had several facial lacerations that had been cleaned as much as possible by the lady rancher after she found the stage-driver's canteen amidst the rubble of the wreckage. Miss Jones had a splint on her left arm, and dressings over large wounds on her legs. Zac Westerfield, the man who had planned the hold-up, had a large compress around his stomach where he had accidently shot himself and a splint on his broken right leg. And Brother Jeremiah had his left wrist bandaged tightly as well as his broken ribs. Individually, they all would have been helpless, but together, working as a team of sorts, they were well on their way to overcoming the hazards of the accident.

Miss Jones had gone down stream about 50 feet to re-fill the canteen from a shallow watering hole in the creek bed. Brother Jeremiah had made a small fire close to the wreckage for warmth during the night. Westerfield had been propped up against the side of the crumbled mess of the coach.

"My boys will be along any minute now, Preacher," commented the wounded outlaw in a caring tone. "You got any ideas about how to save yourself. . . and Jonesy?"

"Funny you should say that, Zac," grinned the old traveling-minister. "I've been wonderin' if you got a plan to get saved."

Westerfield sighed deeply. "Are you talkin' 'bout bein' saved from my boys?" asked the unarmed thief shrewdly. "Or bein' saved from a life of sin and debauchery? 'Cause if'n it's the last. . . you're flat wastin' your time. . . there ain't no way I can be 'saved'!"

"Really?" asked Brother Jeremiah in a rather mocking tone. "Why not?"

"You remember me tellin' about trackin' down my wife and the feller she ran off with?. . . and killin' 'em?" asked the injured bandit. "Well the part I didn't tell you was that the man she ran off with, that I killed. . . was a preacher. . . or so he claimed to be. He had long stringy blond hair and a big burly mustache. He wore buckskins and carried a .50 caliber Hawken. Said he'd been preachin' up in the Rockies for a dozen years or so. Anyways, he held some meetin's out in a little clearin' along Brushy Creek. . . about a mile or so from town. Collected money from folks for healin' he claimed he could do. . . took $100 from my wife. . . she had been so tore up after the death of our son, she couldn't see straight."

Westerfield paused in his story for a moment as his mind relived every detail. He was trying to decide just how much to tell the old circuit rider. Brother Jeremiah noticed the outlaw's breathing had become deep and heavy, like he was stirring up a big anger.

"I chased 'em for nearly 50 mile," continued the lawman-gone-bad. "When I caught up with 'em, I tied my wife to a tree. . . then I hung that preacher-man upside down from that same tree. . . and I cut him to pieces with an old bullwhip I used to carry in my saddlebags. I sliced him and sliced him. . . 'til he stopped screamin'. Just left him hangin' there. . . figured even the night critters needed somethin' to eat. Then I drug my wife to a deserted old cabin I knew about close by. . . and I watched her starve to death. . . while I sat in front of her eatin' and drinkin'. . . and laughin' at her pleas for mercy. Been robbin' and killin' ever since. That's why I cain't get saved, Mister! Now what have you got to say to that?"

Brother Jeremiah walked slowly to the campfire and threw another piece of the broken stage on the fire. The old man-of-God straightened up as much as he could, clicked his teeth a couple of times, and responded, "I think you're wrong, Zac. I think you could be saved because the blood of Jesus can cover any evil we could ever do. But I don't have time to talk to you about it right now. I hear some horses comin'."

Westerfield perked up some and listened closely. Miss Jones returned to the make-shift campsite just as Brother Jeremiah made the comment about the horses.

"You reckon the stage company's sent folks to rescue us, Preacher?" asked China innocently.

"They're not from the stage company, Jonesy," stated Westerfield matter-of-factly. "That's my boys come to kill us for the money. You got a plan old man?"

"Well, Sir," answered the old backwoods Bible-thumper calmly as he checked the cartridges in his .45, "I gave God the reins to my burro a long time ago. . . and He's gotten me outta worse scrapes than this. Reckon He's got the right to call me home tonight if'n He wants to. . . but I don't think He wants to just yet. So, I'm gonna try and purswayed them varmints that if would be in their best interest to leave us alone."

The big preacher walked close to the dilapidated coach, grinned at his fellow travelers, scratched his beard and nose, and said softly, "Miss Jones, you might want to put a little more pressure on Mr. Westerfield's wound, as I see the bandage turning crimson and wet. Now, Zac, which one of them yahoos is the meanest?"

"That would be Rio, Preacher," stated Zac, trying not to wince from the touch of Miss Jones against his bullet wound. "You could bathe him for a full week and still smell him!"

Brother Jeremiah caught the shadow of one of the boys still sittin' on his horse, holding the reins of the other two cayuses. He cocked his pistol and took careful aim. . . and prayed.

"Sure wish these jaspers had come about a half-hour earlier," whispered the old soul-wrangler.

The sound of the gunshot echoed through the trees along the ravine as the bullet whizzed through the air cutting the reins of the horseman. The sound of the bullet and the rider's exclamation frightened his mount, and the stallion reared and bucked his astonished rider off. All three horses galloped away.

"Help me, Nate!" screamed the would-be-thief. "Somebody's down scared the horses, and I think I done broke my collarbone. . . can't even raise my gun-hand none! Help me, Nate! Help me!"

"Stop your catterwallin', you old bag of wolf meat!" hollered Nate from behind a tree off to the left of where Odie was fightin' the dust. "Yew gonna let 'em know we's a comin'!"

"They already know, you stubborn old sidewinder!" hollered back Odie who thought he was about to die. "Get yore midget-hide over here and help me!"

"Raf ain't gonna like this, Odie," screamed Nate. "You know how he told us to be as quiet as a churchmouse!"

Nate holstered his gun, and ran over towards his fallen comrade. The little man had a difficult time trying to get his overweight friend to his feet so that the two of them could find a place to hide. Suddenly, another bullet exploded from the direction of the pile of wood that had been a stagecoach, and it cut the scabbard from the belt of the diminutive bandit. Another shot was heard, and that bullet cut the belt-buckle off Odie's gunbelt, dropping both weapons to the ground. The two criminals looked at each other and took off for the hills as fast as their little feet could move them.

Zac and Jonesy had been watching the activity through the broken pieces of the coach. Both were astonished at the circuit rider's marksmanship, but both also wanted to laugh. Then Westerfield caught the movement of someone in the shadows behind the old preacher.

"Nice try, Mister," said the meanest of the foursome as he cocked his six-shooter and raised his arm to look down his site at the back of Brother Jeremiah's head.

"Look out, Preacher!" yelled Westerfield while pulling his own pistol from the ranchin' lady's waistband and firing just before his former partner in crime could pull the trigger. Westerfield's shot struck true. . . right between the eyes of the Irish-Mexican thief.

Jonesy had forgotten that she still had the pistol and looked at the former lawman the way she had looked at him just before the wreck. Brother Jeremiah turned and grinned at his adversary. Westerfield looked at the pistol in his hand and pitched it over by the body of his former business associate. All three laughed out loud.

"Jonesy," said Westerfield, "reckon you can catch one of those horses? Somebody's got to ride for help. The Preacher can't sit a horse with those ribs of his. . . and I'd probably bleed to death before I got more than five miles. So that leaves you."

"I can track them and catch them, Mr. Westerfield," smiled the lovely rancher. "And I'll be back with help before you know it. We've survived a plunge off a cliff and an attack from outlaws. . . God must be with us. . . nothin's gonna hold me up now, Gentlemen. See you in the morning!"

China hurried off into the early darkness on a mission. Brother Jeremiah walked slowly over to the campfire while re-loading his three spent shells. He picked up the fallen gunman's pistol and tossed it into the bushes. Then he looked back at the scrubby outlaw that had saved his life.

"I swear, Preacher," said the former bad-man, "one little thing that don't suit your Sunday manners, and you get you feathers all ruffled." The outlaw smiled for the first time in a very long time. He knew his fate, but was not afraid to face the consequences.

"You want to continue our discussion about redemption, Zac?" asked the old puddle-jumpin' parson.

"Might as well, Preacher," answered the former desperado, "I got a feelin' you're gonna win that argument, too." Both men grinned from ear to ear.

****

Chapter Nine

The Entrance

B rother Jeremiah had been traveling for at least 34 years now, riding from one town to the other in the heart of the Texas farmland region preaching the Gospel, baptizing in a nearby creek, and performing weddings and funerals whenever the need arose. He had held church services among brawling and blaspheming cowboys wherever he could. The experienced sky-pilot had carried the Gospel to far-flung outposts throughout the tall pines of east Texas. Preaching the Word of God to anyone who would listen was truly a labor of love, despite his mission being filled with hardship and danger.

This itinerant preacher carried his entire fortune in his saddle bags. For bedding, he packed a quilt and a buffalo hide, gifts from an appreciative convert from Arkansas. For food he depended on "parishioners" for enough bacon, dried apples, biscuits, and coffee to see him through to his next stop. In addition, he carried his Bible, a hymnal, and a pistol for protection against four-footed or crawling varmints.

Whenever Brother Jeremiah entered a town, the aging sin-hound would preach at every opportunity to whatever group of settlers, miners, or plain riffraff he could draw together. Faithful to his chosen mission, he announced the threat of hellfire to sinners with none-too-receptive ears. But still he preached.

With only his faith and determination to sustain him, and the knowledge that he was doing a good work in a territory that seemed entirely lacking in refinement, Brother Jeremiah sought out even the most incorrigible souls and traveled into new areas whenever he heard that the need for someone to proclaim the Gospel was great. That's how the seasoned Psalm-singer came on this quest to Miller's Bluff.

"You'd do better to stay in the East Texas piney woods," warned Johnson Malone, a fellow circuit rider who served the area around the city of Marshall just a day's ride west of the Louisiana border. "That town is too close to the capital. . . and the woods around there are full of bears and cougars. Besides, I heard that the Indians just to the west of that territory ain't even been tamed yet!"

But Brother Jeremiah ignored the warnings of his friends and even the folks he served in and around Nacogdoches, and so he had set out bright and early one August morning on horseback, as usual, to traverse the trails and streams in the wilderness of east and central Texas. He was still on the trail when daylight deserted him. Trudging forward through the dense night, the big preacher strayed from the trail that Malone had mapped out for him, and not being sure which forest creatures might be watching him, the aging Bible-expositor decided to start singing as loudly as he could while searching for suitable shelter for the night. He prayed, too, that Homer might accidentally stumble on a stream, for his canteen had long been drained of the last of his water.

Finally, after singing a hundred verses or so of "Amazing Grace", the old black-coat heard the distinct sound of hounds chasing a raccoon through the woods. He followed the baying and crossed the trail of two hunters who hurriedly pointed the preacher in the direction of their cabin just over a mile or so further west. Brother Jeremiah thanked the two men for their kindness and wished them well on their hunt. Then he reined Homer towards the faint glow of lights coming from the direction of the homestead to which the hunters had alluded. The weary evangelist knew that God had once again provided for his needs, and he went merrily on his way.

****

The sun was just creeping its way over the horizon when the circuit rider, half asleep in the saddle, peacefully topped a small hill outside the little village of Miller's Bluff, Texas. Brother Jeremiah sat up straight in his saddle as he gazed at the town some 100 yards away, just sittin' there like a Christmas apple. Most of the farmers and ranchers in the area had been up a good while and were busily and methodically going through their early morning chores. It was still too early for the town's merchants to be up and about, and there was not yet movement at the one room schoolhouse being as there was no need for a fire in the middle of August in central Texas. No one noticed the entrance of the long, black-coated figure on the big Appaloosa stallion that morning, but everyone in town would mark his departure.

The elderly Gospel-wrangler had never before ventured as far south as Miller's Bluff, but had been compelled by the Spirit to make the journey. He still wasn't quite sure of the reason the Lord had sent him to the small, south-central Texas community, but he was glad to have arrived. As usual, the first thing he did was kneel just outside of the little town and pray. The old Psalm-singer was known to fall on his knees, any place, at any time. Weather conditions never seemed to bother him, nor did the taunts from children who sometimes jeered at him or threw handfuls of dirt on him while he knelt in prayer.

On one occasion, the aging Gospel-pusher had knelt in prayer just outside the main entrance of a ranch he had stumbled upon. The rowdy cowboys watched him for a couple of minutes and then riddled the ground around him with bullets, instructing the gray-haired preacher to "get up or get shot". Lead spattered the earth all around him, but Brother Jeremiah stayed on his knees, engrossed in prayer, believing in the Lord's deliverance while his assailants holstered their hoglegs and slunk away like whipped pups.

Prayer was very important to Brother Jeremiah for he believed he was totally powerless without it. Traveling like he did provided him with ample time to pray, and yet he was accustomed to spending the first two hours of each day on his knees seeking direction from the One who knows the future. Jesus was not only Lord of Brother Jeremiah's life, but his closest friend, also. Perhaps that is why Brother Jeremiah's sermons contained such power.

With the sunrise the sleepy little town of some 300 residents called Miller's Bluff began to stretch out her arms to meet the new day. At the time, no one was aware of their meeting a new preacher also.

Miss Gayle Murphy, the young substitute schoolmarm, was one of the first to meet Brother Jeremiah. She was on her way to the schoolhouse near the edge of town when she saw the unfamiliar Appaloosa stallion standing rider-less by the roadside. It wasn't until she had drawn up alongside the big animal that she saw a man, apparently clutching his heart, leaning against an old oak tree. Being a very sensitive young woman of eighteen, she supposed the man with the long, black coat to be hurt. As she hurriedly jumped out of her navy-blue carriage, she thought she heard the faintest mumbling sound coming from the man whose concentration she mistook for a face of pain.

"Good heavens! Are you alright?" Miss Gayle gently touched the man's left shoulder as she spoke.

Startled by the sudden appearance of the young teacher, Brother Jeremiah banged his head against a low hanging branch as he leaped to his feet.

"Yes, Ma'am," he answered, "except for this little bump here." Embarrassment covered both faces as each suddenly realized what had happened.

"I'm so sorry, Sir," she offered, "but I thought you were hurt. You really shouldn't bend over that way so early in the morning, clutching your fists to your chest and mumbling. . . you weren't. . . praying were you?"

Brother Jeremiah looked at the beautiful, auburned-haired young woman some forty years his younger, and saw both human concern and spiritual unbelief.

"I'm sorry I frightened you, Ma'am. Indeed. . . I was praying. I just didn't think anyone was nearby. Folks call me Brother Jeremiah," he said as he took off his straight-brimmed, black Stetson.

"Oh no, I'm sorry for interrupting you," Miss Gayle said with an embarrassing tone. "We haven't had a preacher-man in Miller's Bluff for at least eight or ten years. Are you planning on staying or just passin' through?"

"Well, the Lord led me here for a special reason that He hasn't quite explained to me yet. So, I reckon I'll be around for a spell. . . least ways till He tells me what I'm here for," Brother Jeremiah answered with a smile.

Miss Gayle's green eyes sparkled with delight as she grinned, "God knows we need some preachin' alright. How much do you know about Miller's Bluff, Preacher?"

"Nuthin' yet. Why?" responded the gray-haired man of the cloth.

"I think you'll find out more than you want to know when you walk down the main street. Anyway, I'd best be getting on to the schoolhouse before the children get there. If I were you, I'd do some strong prayin' to see if you ain't made a mistake," suggested the young schoolmarm with a soft smile.

"Oh, me and Jesus always talk things out real good each morning, Miss. . . uh. . ."

"Murphy. Gayle Murphy. I'm not the real teacher. Just fillin' in for a spell, 'til we can find us a new one."

Miss Gayle had come to the little central Texas farm community from the hamlet of Dunnyhoo, another small town in nearby Bell County, when she was just ten years old. She was the oldest of five children and had always been more mature than her youthful looks displayed. The auburn-haired beauty had been forced to grow up fast after her dad had been killed at the Second Battle of Bull Run defending his native land during the War of Northern Aggression.

Miss Gayle's grandmother, Molly Ford, had become somewhat of a legend about the same time as her dad had been killed. Granny Molly had been walking along Dunnyhoo Creek on her way to a friend's sickbed when she slipped into some quicksand. Neighbors had heard her screams, but the old lady often screamed and shouted out praises to God as she traveled, so no one paid attention. Two days later, her body floated back up to the top of the quicksand, and the two farmers who discovered her buried her close to the creek bank as a warning to others. Granny Molly, though in her mid-60's, had made a living making quilts and selling them in the Dunnyhoo General Store. And even though her contribution to the family was meager, the absence of the handful of extra dollars each month put a great strain on the family's livelihood.

The accident involving Miss Gayle's grandmother, coupled with the death of her father, caused her widowed mother to fret something fierce about how she would put food on the table. At least their small farm was paid for, and friends and neighbors had been extremely helpful for a while. The widow Murphy took in wash and prepared pies and cakes for special occasions, but those activities brought in little income. So Hannah Murphy had welcomed the opportunity to send one of her flock to Miller's Bluff to help take care of her husband's aunt.

Miss Gayle had definitely been blessed physically over the next eight years, and all the young, single men had at one time or another, vied for her attention. But her heart had been reserved for a young cowboy she had fallen in love with the first time he had chased her around the playground at school some seven years earlier.

Brother Jeremiah helped Miss Gayle back into her two-seater carriage. "Do you know my Jesus, Miss Murphy?"

"As a matter of fact, I do, Brother Jeremiah. Only we aren't on good speakin' terms right now. Maybe someday, when I'm older, I can get reacquainted, but right now, I'm late for school. Giddyup!" she said as she slapped the big, reddish-brown mare hitched to her buggy. "See ya around, Preacher."

Brother Jeremiah watched the petite, olive-skinned young lady drive her buggy down the steep path that led to the little red school house on the northern edge of town. Being a veteran of many revivals in small towns, the gray-haired, but now balding, preacher's mind flashed back to tearful scenes of triumphant joy when folks who had somehow forgotten the love of Jesus got "reacquainted" with His presence. Miss Gayle was embarrassed and caught off guard by Brother Jeremiah's question, but since he knew their meeting was not by chance, he could hardly wait to see what the Holy Spirit had in store for the young educator.

Brother Jeremiah walked over to his old tired horse, Homer. The big Indian pony had been the old preacher's traveling companion ever since a rancher-friend from Dallas had given the oversized mount to the young evangelist. Appaloosa's were specially bred by the Nez Perce tribe and were mostly native to the northwestern portion of the United States. Homer's ma had been mixed with a quarter horse from Texas as an experiment to herd cattle. Unfortunately, the horse grew to be three hands higher than normal, and though beautifully marked, was a bit ornery. He was headed for a soap factory when Brother Jeremiah heard about his plight at a revival in the Oklahoma Territory.

"Ned," said the Gospel-wrangler during a pleasant supper with his stockman friend, "I'm gonna need a strong horse to carry me across the miles on my circuit in East Texas. I ain't got much money, but I'd be willin' to give you $20 for that Appaloosa of yours."

"Soap factory offered me $25," answered Ned as he lit up his after-dinner cigar. "That there ain't no run-of-the-mill horse, Preacher. That horse is just pure mean. He don't take to humans much. . . or cattle. Maybe he needs some religion," said the cattleman. "If you can get down to Ft. Worth by next Tuesday, I'll wire the station master to let you have that hay burner. And good luck to ya." That was some fifteen years earlier, and the two had become fast friends.

"What do you reckon she meant by 'mistake', Homer?" questioned the veteran Scripture teacher as if his horse could answer. "Let's go talk this out with the Lord over yonder in the woods so we won't be disturbed."

****

Two hours later, Brother Jeremiah stepped down from his weather beaten saddle and tied Homer to the rail in front of Taylor's General Store. Sometimes traveling from town to town causes one to not view the structure of a town as very prominent. Brother Jeremiah had been riding the circuit for Jesus for some time now, but had never seen a town designed the way Miller's Bluff had been. Every store, shop, cotton gin and saloon on the east side of Main Street was owned by men named Taylor while the stores, shops, saloons, and cotton gin on the opposite side were owned by men named Bell. Directly across the street from Taylor's General Store was Bell's General Merchandise. And so it went. . . store for store, shop for shop, saloon for saloon, gin for gin. . . either Taylor or Bell.

Isaiah Taylor, owner of Taylor's General Store, was busy rearranging shelves of canned good items that had apparently been hit by a tornado. Isaiah was a short, plump, grey-templed, balding man in his fifties, wearing bright red suspenders that had long since been too short, making his trousers leg come to the top of his boots. He had a bushy grayish-red moustache that covered his mouth. His thick eyebrows wiggled up and down as he spoke, as did the unlit, half-smoked cigar that protruded from his round face. He seemed to be more preoccupied with the appearance of his store than himself. Brother Jeremiah had never heard anyone use so many curse words before. Obviously Mr. Taylor thought he was alone.

"Ahem. . . ahem." Brother Jeremiah cleared his throat rather loudly in order to get Isaiah Taylor's attention.

"Now, look, Bell, if you've come to gloat," shouted the fat little shopkeeper as he turned around. "Oh, excuse me. I thought you were that lame-brained idiot from across the street come to laugh at the job his boys did last night. Look at this mess!"

A mess it surely was. Cans were ripped open and turned upside down or sideways, labels ripped off some, pickles in the honey jar, coffee and sugar mixed in little piles, egg yellow dripping off the walls, and licorice whips strung from shelf to shelf like Christmas decorations.

"You think Mr. Bell's sons did this?" the old preacher asked.

"Think nuthin'! I know they did it!" shouted the plump shopkeeper. "And just wait'll I get a chance to get even tonight!"

"But Jesus said to 'Turn the other cheek. Love your enemies. Do good to them that hate you'," commented Brother Jeremiah.

"Jesus Rodriguez, the stable boy?" shouted the portly merchant incredulously.

"No. . . Jesus Christ, the Son of God," answered Brother Jeremiah in his I-can't-believe-you-don't-know-who-I'm-talking-about voice.

"Oh. You're a Bible-thumper. Listen, Preacher, we don't need your screemin' and stompin' around here. We can settle our differences peaceably," sneered Mr. Taylor.

"Yes, I can see the pieces," commented the circuit rider with a grin.

"Small splinters'll be all you see of Bell's place after I'm done. That'll teach 'im good!" screamed Taylor, "Why I'll pulverize that no good, low-down, skunk of a human being. I'm gonna take his scrawny little neck and . . ."

"Excuse me, Mr. Taylor," interrupted Brother Jeremiah, "but why not let the sheriff handle the affair? If Mr. Bell is guilty?"

"If he's guilty? Bell was born guilty, Mister!" exclaimed Taylor rather loudly.

"Funny you should say that, Mr. Taylor, 'cause that's jest what this here book says in Romans, Chapter 3. But you know, it says that you and I have the same problem as Mr. Bell. We're all born guilty of sin. And we all deserve the same punishment. . . a burning hell."

"Then it won't make no difference if I add an extra piece of coal to the flames tonight by gettin' back at old man Bell now will it? Good day to you, Preacher!"

"Mr. Taylor, Jesus wants you to. . ."

"Good day, Preacher!" growled Taylor as he interrupted his frocked-coat visitor.

Brother Jeremiah had been preaching long enough to recognize a man embittered by hatred whose receptiveness to the Gospel was non-existent at the moment. The look on Mr. Taylor's face coupled with the devilish arch of his bushy eyebrows proclaimed loudly that it was time to back off.

"Good day, Mr. Taylor," countered the circuit rider while tipping his hat.

There were several people milling around in the streets and stores of Miller's Bluff on that lazy morning in late August. Brother Jeremiah stood on the boardwalk outside Taylor's General Store silently talking to his friend, Jesus, asking for strength and wisdom. He couldn't forget the look of hatred in Isaiah Taylor's eyes and the warning of the young school teacher.

As he stood there gazing across the street at Bell's General Merchandize, a tall, rather skinny man in his late fifties stepped through the open doors sweeping the early morning dust from the boardwalk. Walter Bell was dressed as neatly as a politician at a church social. He wore small glasses that continually slid down his prominent Roman nose. His neck was long and seemed to stretch clownishly high above his wide, red bowtie which hung tightly around a collar that left ample room for his protruding Adam's apple.

Brother Jeremiah knew that he had to speak to the tall shop-keeper who was the target of Isaiah Taylor's wrath. Mr. Bell deserved to be warned of the impending danger of Mr. Taylor's retaliation. . . as well as the impending danger of not knowing Jesus.

As the old circuit rider crossed the dry, dusty main street of Miller's Bluff, another tall, large framed man rode up to Walter Bell's store on an animal that only vaguely resembled a horse. This man's wardrobe was one which appeared to have been thrown together in a dark room by a blind man. His black trousers were two inches too long while his blue coat was two sizes too small. His faded green vest was missing three buttons at the bottom, and his gun-belt hung low on his hip. The man's brown hat sat nervously on the back of his head, and his rumpled grey-plaid shirt hung half un-tucked beneath his vest.

The aging circuit rider would find out that the big, husky, smiling man named Owen North had a childlike lust for life and an inherit curiosity of just about everything. Born to share-croppers in 1854 in the land of magnolias, Owen stood just over six-feet-two and was well muscled, his physical strength was obvious. As a boy, he was the runt of the family and was constantly cuffed around by his elder brothers. Before he turned 10, Owen saw his father hacked to death by abolitionists in northeast Mississippi. The boy gunned for chicken thieves, coyotes, and roving Indians by the time he turned 13 since all four of his older brothers had been killed in the War Between the States. What little schooling Owen received came at the knee of his mother, who herself was only five foot tall. The big man learned about broncs and cattle on the range, having worked as a trail-hand when he was only 17. But the simple-minded fella decided that herding cattle just wasn't his idea of spending his time and so took on the job of Deputy Sheriff in nearby Taylor, Texas, in 1875, and two years later became the Sheriff of Miller's Bluff.

Owen constantly brushed his jet-black hair out of his eyes with hands large enough to hold three apples each. His face was puckered like wet sheepskin before a hot fire. The most prominent item of his wardrobe was the extra-large, five-pointed tin star that shone with the brilliance of the sun, pinned to his left jacket lapel. Brother Jeremiah followed the two men into Bell's store unnoticed.

Sheriff Owen, as the townsfolk called him, rarely fought, partly because of his size and potential strength if angered, and partly because very few of Miller's Bluff's citizens took him seriously. Few thought he had brains enough to fill a walnut shell. Many a Saturday–night-bar-room fight started over a discussion between local cowboys as to whether the town's lawman could even read and write. And because of his extra-slow Texas drawl, many argued over his ability to speak English. The larger-than-life peace officer was a rugged-looking man, but was actually quite kindhearted, usually apologizing when he had to place someone in jail.

"I'm awful sorry to bother you, Mr. Bell, but Mr. Taylor claims your boys broke into his store last night and messed the place up bad," stated the sheriff.

"I don't give a hoot what Isaiah Taylor says! He's a liar! My boys got better learnin' than to set foot in that rat-infested, flea trap he calls a store!" exclaimed Bell in a rather loud voice that sounded like a burro with a bad cold. The slender shopkeeper was mad enough to swallow a horn-toed backwards.

"Well, Sir. . . Mr. Taylor says. . ." began the lawman.

"Only a fool would listen to that old fool, Owen," interrupted Bell. "And Taylor ain't the bull goose around here just yet, Sonny Boy. Did he see my boys mess up his store?"

"No, Sir, it happened sometime last night while Mr. Taylor was over to Miss Hattie's'," explained the sheriff.

"Then you got no case! 'Sides, Taylor was probably so drunk he did it himself tryin' to get to bed," commented Bell. "You know he couldn't track an elephant in the snow when he's been drinkin'," continued Bell as he returned to his regular duties.

"But he's convinced you're responsible, Mr. Bell," added Brother Jeremiah.

"Who the devil are you?" asked the startled shop-keeper. "Owen, put your gun away."

"Folks call me Brother Jeremiah," answered the tall sin-buster as he gently moved the barrel of Sheriff Owen's gun away from his midsection. "I'm here to preach the Gospel of Jesus Christ. I was just over to Mr. Taylor's store. It certainly is in a mess. And he does blame you."

"Well, the old buzzard's wrong!" shouted Bell.

"He plans to do you hurt to get back at you," added Brother Jeremiah.

"Yeh, well, let him try! He'll get a load of double ought buckshot in his fat backside for his trouble!" promised Bell.

"Now wait right there, Mr. Bell. We can't have no violence in my town," said the sheriff in his bass-toned authoritative voice. Sheriff Owen thought this might be a good time to try and impress the new preacher by demonstrating his ability to control his constituents.

"Owen, go polish your badge. . . and hobble your lip while you're at it," teased Bell.

The big soft-spoken giant-of-the-law dropped his head, obviously embarrassed in front of the new visitor to Miller's Bluff, and shuffled through the doors of Bell's place into the warm sunshine. All the while he mumbled to himself in a way not unlike the muffled growl of a grizzly bear.

"He's a good old boy, Owen is. . . he's just a might weak North of his ears," stated the willowy merchant.

"Mr. Bell, did you know that Jesus said that if anybody had a grudge against us that we ought to go to him and ask his forgiveness and settle things according to the Scriptures?" asked the veteran preacher-man.

"No offense, Preacher, but we've got our own ways of settlin' things 'round here," Mr. Bell said calmly with that same glint of hatred in his eyes that the old revivalist had seen in Taylor's eyes just moments before. The lanky retailer proudly nodded toward the gun case in the corner of his store.

"But the Bible says, 'He that lives by the sword shall die by the sword'," continued the experienced, itinerate preacher.

"Well, I'll just have to take my chances, Preacher," answered the skinny merchant with a sneer.

"Then what? What do you accomplish by striking back at one another? Each time you plan a bigger and more violent retaliation. When will it end?" asked the preacher.

"When ever last one of them good-fer-nuthin' Taylors is pushin' up daisies. That's when it ends," growled the angry merchandiser.

"And what does that do to the town? The Bible says, 'A house divided cannot stand.' Have you no concern for those caught in the middle?" asked Brother Jeremiah.

"Why don't you save your preachin' for Sunday and church. . . if you can get anybody to come. I'm too busy to listen right now," countered Bell while smoothing a few wrinkles from a bolt of cloth.

"Oh I intend to do just that, Sir. You do have a building for worship here, don't you?" asked the old preacher.

"You'll find a building down the street at the end of town. Course it's a long time till Sunday. Maybe you won't be stayin' that long," glared the lanky businessman.

"Oh, I'll be stayin'. And I might get to preach before Sunday. . . I just pray it's not at a funeral. Good day, Mr. Bell." The old circuit rider tipped his hat and walked away.

The itinerant preacher had carried the Word of God into more small towns and new towns than any other man he knew. But he had never seen a town quite like Miller's Bluff. Brother Jeremiah strode into the bright morning sunshine, leading his horse down the main street of Miller's Bluff, looking straight ahead and yet seeing peripherally the signs of a town torn apart with hatred. The Taylors on one side, the Bells on the other. Both men seemed hell-bent on making things happen in Miller's Bluff regardless of who was hurt. Could it be a coincidence that the church stood in the middle?

As the Bible-teacher rounded the curve in the street, he came face to face with the structure that Walter Bell had mentioned and in which he was convinced that Jesus had led him to serve. His heart sank as he gazed intently at an unfinished, framed, one-walled structure, worn and weather-beaten, overgrown with weeds and thorn bushes and sunflowers growing through the cracks in the wooden floors. It looked like a trash dump. Most imposing of all were the buzzards that perched atop the one wall at the rear of the structure. The great feeders-on-death looked at the preacher standing alone in the doorway and stretched their wings and circled the building time and time again slowly winding their way upward as if to say, "We'll be back."

Brother Jeremiah clutched his worn Bible to his heart and, bowing his head, slowly sank to his knees. His mind flashed back to his earlier meeting with the pretty, young schoolmarm. Had she said Miller's Bluff had been without a preacher for ten years? Or was it twenty? The old preacher's thoughts went back to a small town in north Louisiana. In that town the old circuit rider built a church almost on his own, the first church that town had ever had. Before completion, however, civil authorities decided to take back some of the land and began moving fence posts. But when Brother Jeremiah picked one of the posts up and threatened them with it, they backed down.

The work facing the veteran man of the cloth momentarily looked awesome and more dangerous than anything he had ever faced. But even now Brother Jeremiah could feel his being flooded with hope. . . for he knew Jesus never makes mistakes.

****

Chapter Ten

The Helper

Brother Jeremiah pushed back the curtains of his second story room in the only independent boarding house in Miller's Bluff. He breathed deeply the fresh summer air in the early morning hours before sunrise. The old circuit rider was the servant of Jesus, always willing to go wherever the Lord instructed, preaching, singing, praising, baptizing. Never before in his almost thirty-five years of riding the circuits of small towns had Brother Jeremiah been faced with such a huge "giant" challenging this man of God to hand to hand combat. But like the Biblical hero, David, Brother Jeremiah had a simple, all encompassing faith in Christ for deliverance. Armed with the Gospel of Grace and the patient love of a true shepherd, he stood convinced of final victory over the enemy of hatred that jeered so defiantly, as did Goliath against the people of God.

Such confidence comes easily with a man of prayer as was Brother Jeremiah. He had spent the night in prayer, searching the Scriptures he so treasured, for just the right ammunition, the right "stone" for the sling of ministry to allow him to conquer through Christ all enemies. Being where God wanted him to be made him determined to carry out the Great Commission no matter what the price. He had seen in the night a vision of victory, of a town united, of a beautiful high-steepled, white building bursting with praise from the inside, from the mouths of young men and women trained to spread the Good News of the Savior. There would be many, hard, long battles he knew, but that would make the victory so much the sweeter.

The first task would be to make the building ready for services. As Brother Jeremiah walked down the stairs to the breakfast table, he began organizing the day's work in his mind. He had prayed for help and was confident that God would send someone willing to build a structure for worship. He was somewhat surprised, but not startled, to see the young substitute school teacher sitting at the table, for he was more prepared to see Miss Ida, the owner of the boarding house, scurrying around the feasting place. The aging Devil-shaker could hear noise coming from the kitchen and concluded that his host was busying herself preparing another delicacy for the breakfast table which was already covered with everything from scrambled eggs to pancakes. Brother Jeremiah's mind recalled the story of Martha's stress over setting a good table for Jesus once when He came to visit her family.

"Mornin' Preacher," said Miss Gayle with a big smile on her face. "You're sleepin' kinda late aren't you? It's near 6 o'clock already."

"Good morning, Miss Murphy," answered the gray-haired Psalm-singer as he seated himself at the table. "I've been awake awhile, Ma'am. . . just been talkin' to my best friend for a spell. I always do that first thing in the morning."

"Yes, Sir. . . I seem to recall you doin' that very thing yesterday mornin' outside of town. So how did your first day in Miller's Bluff go? Did you notice anything unusual?" inquired the auburned-hair educator with a sly smile.

"Nothing the love of Jesus can't handle. Are you planning on coming to the services Sunday?" he asked as she passed the gravy for the biscuits.

"Sure. You seem to have a lot of faith in Jesus. My mother is like that. She constantly sings hymns all day while doing her chores," commented Miss Murphy.

"Then you do have a Bible background?" Brother Jeremiah inquired.

"Oh, yes, I know Jesus personally. In fact, Momma taught me to read the Bible when I was five. It's just that. . . well. . . I came to stay with my Aunt Ida several years ago when she was ill. And since there was no church, I've just lost contact with religion," she offered. "I'm really glad you're here. And if there's any way that I can help out. . . just let me know." Gayle looked a little embarrassed as she noticed the entrance of a young man named Jesse Lane.

Jesse was an average looking fellow with dark brown hair and eyes, strongly built and mentally older than the twenty years of age that his features showed. His olive complexion was framed by a well groomed, dark-brown beard he had grown to make himself look older. The young cowboy appeared to be a quiet fellow whose shyness belied the heavy Colt dangling at his hip, and he had a glint in his eyes that set him apart from others as a man not to be taken lightly.

The young wrangler had been born into a ranching family, but had been orphaned at an early age. Still, he learned to ride before he began to wear long pants. The handgun that Jesse wore seemed to almost be a part of him. The way he carried himself showed his confidence in his ability to use the weapon at his side if need be. While he had never shot anybody, all the folks around were quick to refer to countless blue ribbons Jesse had won at the county fair for marksmanship and fast draw. He bore no resemblance to the fictional western gunman. He had never shot up a saloon or forced a tenderfoot to dance for his own enjoyment. Jesse was, in fact, rather mild-mannered and courteous to most folks. Still, he was a deadly shot. Brother Jeremiah noticed the special way that Jesse and Miss Gayle looked at one another over the breakfast table. It was the same look that he had shared with a young woman named Jenny Jones, some thirty years his younger a couple of years ago, or so he recalled.

The aging circuit rider had been on his way to a meeting in a small town in northwestern Louisiana. It was dark and a storm was raging, and Brother Jeremiah was soaked to the bone. He stopped at a small cabin in the woods. A young woman answered his knock at the door of the rough-out. She carried a double-barreled shotgun. The pretty young farm girl allowed the preacher to enter her house and warm himself by the fire, but she held the gun on him the entire time. Jenny told her visitor that her folks were down at the church meeting at the crossroads where a circuit riding preacher named Brother Jeremiah was to conduct the services.

"On a night like this?" queried the graying sin-buster before introducing himself.

"Apparently you don't know Brother Jeremiah," stated the young, black-haired lady with the most beautiful smile that the country parson had ever seen. "Ain't nuthin' keeps him from preachin' at a meetin'!"

The still soaked Gospel-pusher was ashamed that he had sought shelter and so excused himself and hurried on to the meeting at the forks. Later, he returned to the farm house with the girl's parents where both discovered that despite the large difference in their ages, they had fallen in love at first sight. However, Jenny's parents wanted her to be educated to the duties of a pastor's wife. While away at school, she died of the consumption, and the old evangelist's dream of a home died with her.

"Jesse," said Miss Gayle, "this is Brother Jeremiah. He's the preacher I told you about last night. . . come to build a church."

"Howdy," Jesse said. He seemed to be a little uncomfortable in the presence of the circuit rider. By the way Jesse looked at Miss Gayle, the old Bible-wrangler detected a mutual admiration shared by the two young people with whom he was having breakfast.

"Here, Jesse. . . have some of these biscuits and eggs," offered Brother Jeremiah. "Miss Gayle, do you know anyone who might play an organ or piano for us on Sunday?"

"Well, I used to play some, but it's been a long time. 'Sides, there's only one organ in town," she said. Both Jesse and Gayle turned a little red-faced.

"Where might that be?" asked the old preacher while buttering a hot biscuit.

The silence was deafening. Finally, Jesse broke the silence by clearing his throat.

"Over to Miss Hattie's," he said while playing with his food.

"Where is Miss Hattie's?" asked Brother Jeremiah in a purely inquisitive tone.

Again there was an embarrassing silence while Jesse and Miss Gayle looked sheepishly at each other. Gayle chose to occupy her hands and mouth with the disposing of breakfast. Brother Jeremiah somehow sensed that Miss Hattie's might not be the best topic to discuss at the table. . . especially in mixed company.

"It's the big, red, two-story mansion on the hill at the west end of town," Jesse answered while nervously applying a large amount of pepper to a pile of eggs on his plate.

"Oh," was all the old preacher said. Again there was a silence for awhile. After several minutes, Brother Jeremiah started the conversation again.

"Well, I'd best be gettin' to the church. Got lots of weeds to pull and boards to replace by Sunday," he said.

"Jesse does lots of odd jobs around town. Maybe he could help you some, Preacher," added Miss Gayle rather quickly.

Jesse had grown up learning how to do first one thing and then the other in order to make a living. He was a good carpenter but a better ranch-hand. He enjoyed the "loner jobs" like mending fences and breaking horses or repairing roofs. The tough, outdoor life hardened the young man into an anvil of strength. He was even a fair hand at making simple furniture.

Jesse was a young man who had a tremendous amount of confidence in himself and his abilities. While he was always willing to lend a helping hand to anyone who asked, he seldom offered his help freely. "Don't want to push myself onto nobody," he'd once told Miss Gayle.

The wisdom of age told Brother Jeremiah that the look on Jesse's face meant he was not overly excited by the prospect of spending the day pulling weeds in the hot August sun. But he also sensed the urgency in Miss Gayle's voice.

"I'd be glad to have some help, Son, if you've got some time. 'Course I realize a payin' job would take first priority," he said, offering a way out for the young man.

"We'll see," Jesse said casting a correcting eye in Miss Gayle's direction.

The veteran preacher changed the subject to the weather as the three of them finished their breakfast just as Miss Ida, Gayle's aunt, came into the room with a large bowl of oatmeal and to see if anyone needed anything else. The aging Psalm-singer excused himself, as did Jesse, and the two men walked through the door of the boarding house and headed in opposite directions.

****

Brother Jeremiah never knew there were so many different kinds of weeds. The church building, started some ten years prior, appeared to have every variety known to man. He thanked the Lord over and over again that whoever had started building the church had left some three feet of space between the floor and the ground. It had taken all morning to clear just the front side of the church of the tall grass and weeds with just his hands and a shovel Miss Ida had loaned him. What he needed was a weed-scythe. To make matters worse, apparently several folks had come to consider the church yard as a place to deposit unwanted or broken articles like furniture and dishes.

By lunchtime, the blistering central Texas sun was beginning to take its toll on the aging preacher. Brother Jeremiah decided to take another short rest and enjoy the cool well water provided by Miss Gayle's aunt. He was hot, tired, and wringing wet. The aging Gospel-pusher licked his parched lips with his tongue and tasted the mixture of sweet water and salty sweat. Using his shirt sleeve as a handkerchief, Brother Jeremiah wiped the perspiration from his brow and face to the tip of his chin where the drops had accumulated.

Bits of grass and weeds and sunflowers clung to his clothes, his hair, his eyebrows, and his beard as if they had been planted in the dirt that covered his wardrobe and exposed body parts. Brother Jeremiah poured a liberal dipper full of water over his head allowing the coolness to flow over himself. As he did so, he burst into song and leaned against the half-rotten steps. With his eyes still closed, he began reciting aloud favorite Scriptures dealing with labor, rest, and rewards.

Suddenly, Brother Jeremiah felt he was being watched. He slowly opened his right eye and looked around. There, standing about 30 feet away against a half-broken fence, was Jesse Lane, with arms crossed and hat pushed back on his head.

"Been there long, Jesse?" inquired the old preacher with a slight grin on his face.

"Long enough to know that you're either crazy or. . . somethin'," he answered.

"What's the verdict?" questioned Brother Jeremiah, sitting up straight with both eyes opened wide and a grin on his face that exposed his dimples while the sweat made mud out of the dirt on his brow.

"Ain't sure yet," was the young man's reply. The young cowboy examined the old Gospel-pusher from his dusty boots to his dirt filled hair like an experienced rancher might examine an animal that Ben Schroeder, the livery owner, might be trying to sell as a horse.

Suddenly, Jesse stiffened and slowly moved his right hand towards the butt of the pistol on his hip. The old Psalm-slinger took notice.

"I overheard some folks in town yesterday talkin' 'bout your marksmanship, Jesse. The Lord could use some straight shooters in His work," offered the grey-haired preacher rather nervously.

He had seen the look of death in men's eyes before, and he knew that the slow deliberate movement of the young gunman and the cold stare meant that Jesse was ready to demonstrate his fast draw ability. Brother Jeremiah whispered a quick prayer concerning Jesse's favorable acceptance of preachers.

"Don't move, Preacher," said Jesse coolly.

Brother Jeremiah only blinked momentarily, but that was almost enough for him to miss the smooth swiftness with which Jesse's hand removed his shinny, black, pearl-handled revolver from its resting place at his side to become a flashing instrument of death emitting the tiny explosion that propelled an ounce of destruction toward the old, but still well-muscled, man of God. There wasn't time to move, even though the circuit rider heard the blast that split the stillness of the mid-day air. Brother Jeremiah waited for the kick-of-the-mule he had felt before so many years ago. . . but there was no pain. Then, as his sweat-filled eyes focused more closely on the young gunman, he realized that the barrel was pointed towards the ground to his left.

"Rattl'r," said Jesse as he nodded at the headless diamond-backed serpent lying in the weeds by the steps.

Then just as smoothly as he had pulled his six-shooter, he re-holstered it. Jesse walked over to where the preacher was still sitting and plopped down on the steps. The young cowboy leaned back, resting both elbows comfortably on the decaying steps of the unfinished church. Then the young pistolero unconsciously stretched his long legs over the bottom step, resting his rough-out boots on the dirt.

Brother Jeremiah could tell that something was bothering Jesse, but the old preacher didn't want to push the young cowboy into a decision. He had a feeling about Jesse that he could not explain. He thought he'd just wait and see what would happen.

"Folks sure were right about you bein' a pretty good shot with that hogleg, Jesse," ventured Brother Jeremiah.

"Yep," Jesse answered, absentmindedly placing his hand on the holstered pistol.

Most everyone in Miller's Bluff knew of Jesse's desire to have a reputation as a slick gun hand. He was a hard worker and ambitious, but not one to look for trouble. All the local boys were well aware of Jesse's ability with the .45, and so he went unchallenged. So far, his fame rested in his county fair excursions.

"Miss Gayle's a right pretty young lady, doncha think?" asked the veteran Psalm-singer, trying to start up a conversation with the young boy-man that he hoped would turn naturally to Jesus.

"Yep," was all Jesse replied. He then reached down and pulled up a lone weed between his feet and tossed it to the side.

Brother Jeremiah could see conversing was not going to be easy. But he was determined.

"Guess I missed that one," the old preacher said smiling, "but there's plenty more where that came from." The aging man of the cloth gestured with his right hand at the menagerie of plant growth that had worked its way up between the boards in the formerly-forgotten structure.

The young cowboy surveyed the scene, clicked his teeth, and answered, "Yep". Then Jesse cleared his throat and crossed his arms.

"Sure got a mess of weeds to pull before Sunday. Probably take one man the better part of the week to get all the work done." Brother Jeremiah glanced out of the corner of his eye to see if Jesse was responding. He wasn't.

"Of course, two fellas could get the job done in no time," continued the old Scripture-pusher. Still no response. Then a long silent pause.

"Listen, I could go on talking with you for hours, Jesse, but I jest gotta get back to work," Brother Jeremiah said as he rose from off the front steps.

Still Jesse said nothing. He just leaned against the floor of the unfinished building again and played with the hole left by the weed he had pulled. Brother Jeremiah knew from experience that something was bothering Jesse. There was much work to be done on the building before Sunday, but the preacher felt the work which needed to be done on an eternal soul took precedence.

"Jesse, has anyone ever told you the story of Jesus?" asked the circuit rider rather bluntly.

"Jesus who?" Jesse still played with the weed hole.

"Jesus, the Son of God. He was sent to earth to die on a cross so that folks like you and me might live forever," replied the aging Bible-thumper.

"Nobody can live forever, Preacher. There'll always be someone faster somewhere. Besides, the older yuh git, the slower yuh git," countered the young cowpoke.

"I'm not talking about physical life, Jesse. I'm talking about the spiritual man deep inside of you. . . that's the real you. And that's what can live forever, if you have faith in Jesus."

"Right now, Preacher, I have all the faith I need in this," answered the young man pointing to the Colt slung low on his hip.

"That kind of faith will fail you someday, Jesse. You've already admitted that," said the preacher. "What will you do then?"

"By then it won't matter much. Everybody'll know who Jesse Lane is. My name'll be in all the history books."

"Better that your name be in the Lamb's Book, Jesse," replied the Bible-teacher.

"Look, Preacher, I came out here to help you only 'cause Gayle asked me to. Save your Bible stories for the kids. Don't waste 'em on me. Just let me help yuh build a church in peace and quiet," retorted Jesse.

"OK, Jesse. Let's build a church," grinned Brother Jeremiah.

Thoughts flashed through the circuit rider's mind of the previous night spent in prayer as the young rebel-without-a-cause joined the old warrior-of-the-faith in the laborious task of getting a worn-out structure ready for Sunday services. Brother Jeremiah had prayed for help and here was a young man willing to help, even if for the wrong reasons.

But a structure is not a church. While the veteran minister of God knew that Jesse was probably unaware of the significance or meaning of his words, the old preacher held a deep-seeded faith in the absolute control of Jesus over every situation. . . the kind of control that left no room for mistakes. . . or coincidence. There would be more chances for the aged evangelist to present the Gospel to his young helper, and Brother Jeremiah began to have mental visions of him and the young cowboy working side by side to reach this small, central Texas farm community for Jesus.

Religion was actually a strong and influential force on the frontier, once preachers settled permanently. While Brother Jeremiah and Jesse Lane worked to get the partially erected building into shape for Sunday, the old Bible-thumper envisioned a room full of folks held spellbound by the passionate preaching of himself and his young, future-partner.

Miller's Bluff would not be a temporary home for the veteran of many a camp meeting'. Brother Jeremiah had always enjoyed those special days of revival usually held just before harvest when families would gather at the campground and pitch their tents or build makeshift dwellings. It was, in fact, at a camp meeting the previous year that the old preacher had heard about the churchless little town in central Texas just a day's ride north of the state capital in Austin. Brother Jeremiah had talked to one of the farmers who had brought their produce to the meeting about the absence of a

Spiritual influence in the farmer's former hometown. After a week of impassioned sermonizing from several of his colleagues, the old circuit rider had decided to travel to Miller's Bluff to see if God might use him to start a church there.

Now, Brother Jeremiah had found a home and a possible friend in the young, clean-living cowpoke that neither smoked, drank, or used profane language. It seemed to the old frontier minister that God was putting every piece of the puzzle together to form a picture of a town where the folks would one day take their religion very seriously.

****

Chapter Eleven

The Feeling

T here is an extra special good feeling that comes over a person when they have done something good for another person. Jesse Lane could not explain his inner self at the moment, nor did he understand just why he had decided to help Brother Jeremiah fix up the old rundown framework that at one time might have been the most beautiful building in town. Brother Jeremiah was a strange sort of fellow to Jesse, and yet, he seemed to be drawn to the smile and easy going contentment of the old circuit rider. They had both put in a hard day's work pulling weeds and clearing the front of the building of the debris, and yet neither man seemed to be feeling the physical exhaustion that should have accompanied their labor.

Brother Jeremiah had stayed at the old church building to "catch up on his prayin'," although Jesse had caught him praying several times during the day. Jesse liked the old preacher despite his constant singing, and Bible quoting, and hinting that "the Lord had something for him to do." Jesse didn't like to think about religious things much, especially when he considered his plans for making a name for himself as the fastest gun in Texas. Another year and he planned to join the Texas Rangers. Being a Ranger would give him plenty of opportunity to face down desperadoes and get his name in the paper. He figured it would only take a couple of years for him to clean up Texas so that he could have a name that Miss Gayle would be proud to share. Of course, being the wife of a Texas Ranger was not the kind of life a real lady like Miss Gayle might want, so Jesse figured on being on "courtin'" terms with her till he made his reputation. Then they would settle down to an easy life where his reputation would do him the most good. . . politics. Maybe then Jesse would have time to squeeze in some of that Bible stuff the old preacher kept talking about all day.

There was much about the future on Jesse's mind as he walked up the steps of Miss Ida's boarding house, and all of it centered on Miss Gayle Murphy.

"Hold it right there, Mister," said a guttural voice behind Jesse as his hand touched the doorknob. "I hear yore pretty fast with that there six-gun yore a totin'. I come to see how fast. I come all the way from Waco jest to see how fast yew really be. And when I count ta three. . . I'm gonna send yew to Angel land. One. . . two. . . thr. . ."

Before the last part of the word sounded, Jesse had spun around, ducked, and pulled his gun, ready to shoot for his life.

"Jimmy!?! Are you crazy?" Jesse shouted. "You coulda been killed!" Jesse looked down at the young boy shaking on the porch with the toy gun hanging halfway out of its holster.

"Wow, Jesse. . . you are fast. Don't shoot though. I was only playin'." Little Jimmy, more frightened than he let on, was Miss Gayle's star pupil in school and one of Jesse's most loyal fans. Ten-year-old Jimmy was an orphan himself like Jesse, who lived at the boarding house. He paid for his keep by looking after the chickens and cows in the barnyard behind the old mansion run by Miss Ida, Gayle Murphy's old maid, fifty-something aunt. Little Jimmy was also a "matchmaker" who had been trying to get Jesse and Miss Gayle together for quite awhile.

"You better be more careful how you play, kid. Don't sneak up on a man when he's got other things on his mind. It's dangerous," scolded Jesse. The young cowboy knew that Little Jimmy thought him to be some sort of special "god" or something for the lad pretty-much shadowed every move the young gun-hand made.

"I'm sorry, Jesse," Little Jimmy said. "Can I put my hands down?"

"Sure." Jesse uncocked his .45 and twirled it in a fancy manner before holstering the weapon again.

"Man, you're filthy, Jesse," suggested Jimmy. "Miss Ida ain't never gonna let you set to the supper table like that."

"I reckon I do need a bath," Jesse said as he dusted off his clothes with his hat.

An impish grin crossed Little Jimmy's freckled cheeks, and his blue eyes sparkled through his straight red hair that hung down in his face.

"There's a preacher man in town, Jesse. . . kind that marries up folks," hinted the tyke.

Both Jesse and Gayle knew of Little Jimmy's desire to get them hitched. They also knew that he had dreams of the three of them becoming a family, a thought that entered both of their minds from time to time.

"I know," Jesse replied. And with a sly grin of his own he added, "Been talkin' to him most of the day."

The little boy's eyes shone with excitement, and he grinned like a weasel in a hen house. "'Bout gettin' married?" he almost shouted.

"No, Jimmy. . . 'bout a fella named Jesus," answered Jesse.

"Jesus? Who's he?" asked Jimmy. He had never been to church before or heard the Gospel. Except for the yellow-paged, dusty Bible in the parlor, Jimmy had never even heard of religion.

"Preacher says He's the Son of God that loved us so much that He died on a cross to save us," parroted Jesse. He had heard the story so many times during the day that he almost knew it by heart.

"Save us from what?" asked Jimmy.

"From hell, I think. Or sin. Or was it death?" mused Jesse.

"Do you believe it, Jesse?" inquired the young boy.

"I don't know, Kid. I don't have time for that stuff right now," concluded Jesse. "Besides there's lots more important things to think about." Jesse grinned and patted his holstered Colt.

"Yeah, but you better think first about gettin' a bath. You sure can't go a callin' like that," said Little Jimmy pointing to Jesse's clothes.

"You're right, Kid. Can't let that old cowhand beat my time, can I?" answered Jesse while sniffing at his musty-smelling clothes.

Little Jimmy knew the "old cowhand" was the foreman of the Double Bar TB Ranch, Jeff Rutledge. Rutledge was fifteen years older than Jesse, a little taller with curly red hair and cold, steel-blue eyes. The thirty-something cowhand always dressed in black, and he carried a yellow-pearl handled .45 in his fancy holster, slung low on his hip, and always well oiled. He kept a back-up derringer in his hat just in case and a cuttin' knife inside a special slot in his right boot. And woe to any man who crossed his path. . . or crossed him.

Rutledge was mean and distrustful of most folks. He seldom traveled the same trail twice whether the red-headed cowpuncher was coming to town, going back out to the Double Bar TB, or checking on the dozen or so cowboys who worked under him. Rutledge didn't make friends easily mostly because of his rough manners. He left the impression with most that he simply didn't like people. . . men, women, children, older folks. . . anyone. Even the windows on the little cabin he called home were painted dark green and heavy shades hung over those windows at night so that no one could see the shadows of the man inside. And what few times he and the boys spent the night on the range tending to his boss' cattle, Rutledge always sat back beyond the campfire light just in the edge of the shadows.

"That old cowhand", as Jeff called him, ran the Double Bar TB with a fist of iron and intimidated the cowhands into doing his bidding. Those who refused or grumbled about unwanted chores were found roughed up some. . . always after falling off their horse somewhere. Those clumsy cowboys more often than not pulled out late at night without giving anyone a clue as to where they might be headed.

On Sundays, the red-headed terror would drink as much oh-be-joyful as he could hold, and then mount his old roan horse and ride around town looking to start a fight with someone. Occasionally, Rutledge would ride his horse into one of the four saloons in the small central Texas hamlet and drink at the bar while still mounted, daring anyone to say anything. He was just as fast with his fists as he was with his gun.

Most of the folks around Miller's Bluff thought Rutledge was just a tad bit crazy. . . crazy enough to eat the devil, horns and all. Perhaps it was the way he squinted his eyes and glared at people. . . or the way he sort of growled when he made even the slightest mistake. Or perhaps it was Rutledge's fondness for getting into fights that made everyone in town believe he was mean enough to take the coins off a dead man's eyes. And when he fought, he fought like a burnt bear in a cave full of hornets. The mean-spirited cowboy wanted everyone in the area to believe that he was harder to handle than a mule on ice. He was quite successful with his bullying ways in his attempts to influence people to think that very thought.

Rutledge saved as much of his money as he could, and he had a good nest egg set aside to buy a small ranch near the San Gabriel River a few miles east of town. The ranch had been for sale since last winter when Old Ike Kelly, the owner, drowned after falling through the ice on the creek running down the middle of his property, which emptied into the San Gabriel.

Nobody seemed to know much about Jeff Rutledge's past other than that he had come from New Mexico Territory a few years back. There had been rumors, unproven of course, that the young cow-hand had originally been raised in Kentucky or Tennessee and had run to New Mexico to escape murder charges. The rumors insisted that Rutledge had skinned an old farmer who accidentally spit tobacco juice on his mother's shoe. Charges were not filed because the young cow-puncher's mother insisted that her boy was at home the night that the farmer was killed.

Another rumor that kept folks wondering about the character of the black-vested ranch hand was that he had stomped a man to death in a saloon. Seems that another cowboy had made a comment about the brutality to the livestock caused by the Mexican-style spurs Rutledge wore. Rutledge knocked him to the floor and brought the heel of his boot down hard again and again into the face of the younger wrangler, scarring the boy's cheeks with his spurs each time the angry line-rider brought up his foot. The boy's face was so mutilated, his own mother wouldn't have recognized him. Those who witnessed the cruel act believed the threats Rutledge made and so refused to testify against him. A few days later, the red-haired cowpoke arrived in Miller's Bluff.

Rutledge usually only came into Miller's Bluff once a week, but he was always dressed in the fancy black courtin' duds with the black-leather vest sporting the Mexican Conchos that Mr. Theo Bell, the owner of the Double Bar TB, had brought back from New York. Jeff had bragged to everyone in the county about the plans he had for making Miss Gayle his wife. Trouble was, Miss Gayle couldn't stand him. Each time he approached her, she gave him the mitten.

"Jeff's just. . . pure-dee mean," the young school-marm had once told her aunt. "He's so mean, he'd probably steal a fly from a blind spider."

Rutledge knew how the young lady felt about him, but that didn't stop his planning and bragging. He figured that she could grow to love him if Jesse Lane wasn't around. He just had not figured how to get rid of Jesse without getting himself killed by Jesse's fast draw and amazing marksmanship. . . at least in a way that wouldn't force him to spend most of his life behind bars. . . or wear a California-necktie.

"Jesse," said Jimmy with a serious tone in his voice, "when you gonna quit beatin' the devil 'round the stump and ask Miss Gayle to marry up with ya?"

Jesse looked down at the little man who kind of worshiped every move the young cowboy made, grinned, and tousled the boy's hair.

"Well not right now," answered the Ranger hopeful, "Least ways not until I get me a bath and splash on some of that stuff to make me smell more like a cactus rose." Both fellas laughed as Jesse opened the door to Miss Ida's place.

Jesse and Little Jimmy sneaked into the entrance hall and bolted quickly up the stairs before anyone could see them. Jesse hurried inside the small room with the one bathtub while Little Jimmy stood guard outside.

****

Jesse was still all smiles as he combed his hair in front of the mirror. Absentmindedly he began to whistle. . . one of Brother Jeremiah's hymns.

"Where'd yew learn that tune, Jesse?" asked Little Jimmy. "I ain't never heard it afore."

"What tune, Kid?" Jesse continued making sure each hair was in just the right spot.

"The tune yew been awhistlin' for the last five minutes," insisted Little Jimmy.

"I don't know. I think I heard it from that preacher I worked with today," answered Jesse.

"That parson rubbin' off on yew, Jesse?" queried the youngster with a big grin.

Jesse put down his comb. "Don't worry, Little Jimmy, I ain't gettin' religion. There ain't no way I'd ever be like him. I got too many plans at stake. It's just a catchy tune that's all. Come on. Let's go get us some supper."

"Miss Gayle made supper tonight, Cowboy," said Jimmy in a teasing way, "reckon mebbe she's practicing for later?"

"Mebbe," answered the young cowhand, "she said this mornin' that she'd rustle up somethin' special for supper if'n I helped that old preacher pull weeds. And from the smells comin' out of that kitchen, I 'spect I'll have to work twice as hard tomorrow to keep from gainin' a hunnert pounds!" Little Jimmy giggled his approval.

"And Miss Ida's makin' some of her biscuits," added the boy who shadowed Jesse's every move. "And you know they're so big, nine of 'em makes a dozen!"

Both Jesse and the small fry beside him breathed deeply to take in all the culinary odors coming from the kitchen. Little Jimmy grabbed his hero's hand and almost pulled the young reputation-seeker's arm out of socket as he led Jesse down the hall to the stairs that led to the dining room of the old boarding house. The two clomped down the stairs in their usual manner ready to sink their teeth into Miss Gayle's famous fried chicken.

Jesse noticed the empty chair where the circuit rider should have been, but didn't think much about it as the two young men joined Miss Gayle and her aunt at the table. Miss Ida gave Jesse a stern look and sighed deeply because of the noisy entrance of her two favorite guests. Then the older woman glanced at her niece, who herself was trying to suppress laughter. And Miss Ida just grinned slightly and shook her head, then pushed back her chair to place the food on the table.

"Jesse, do you know where the Reverend is? I told him last night that we always eat at six o'clock sharp," said Miss Ida as she set the beans and hot biscuits on the already filled table. Despite the fact that Miss Ida's Boarding House had only four residents beside herself, she always set a full table. On this night she was trying to impress the town's new preacher with a small feast that she had helped Gayle prepare.

"I left him at the old church. Said he had somethin' important to talk to Jesus about. He'll be along d'recly," answered Jesse as he tucked the checkered napkin into his white shirt collar.

****

Brother Jeremiah was just getting up off his knees when he felt the surge of joy that comes from answered prayer. He had spent the last hour thanking God for sending a helper and asking for wisdom to say the right words that might cause Jesse to accept Jesus as his Savior and be a great testimony. The old preacher understood the power of prayer and the reality of faith that allows one to sometimes get a glimpse of the future. More and more he was understanding God's leading him to the divided community of Miller's Bluff. He could hardly wait for Sunday to come. He just knew there would be victory in Jesse's life.

The old preacher sported mental pictures of victory all along the dusty main street of the black-land farming town as he ambled on down his way towards his "home". He tipped his hat to all the passersby, smiled and bid them a good evening, all the while visualizing the spiritual transformations of each. Once in awhile he would stop to make polite conversation to those citizens who returned his greetings. The aging Scripture-beater even stopped Sheriff Owen and shook his hand like the unkept lawman was an old friend that the soul-healer hadn't seen in years. Isaiah Taylor and Walter Bell came out of their respective places of establishment at the same time, and the grey-haired Gospel-sharp waved vigorously to the both of them. Of course both men simply grunted a response and hurried down their boardwalks in opposite directions. But not even deliberate snubs by the town's leading citizens could take the spring out of the veteran sermonizer's step.

The old Psalm-singer was all smiles as his hand touched the doorknob of Miss Ida's Boarding House. Brother Jeremiah knew that extra special good feeling that comes over a person when they have done something good for another person.

****

Chapter Twelve

The Trick Shot

The sun was just beginning to set in Miller's Bluff as the tired, middle-aged preacher stepped back to admire the work of restoring the half completed structure-of-praise which had laid dormant the past ten years. As he rolled down his sleeves, Brother Jeremiah recalled the past week's seemingly never ending task that he had shared with his young friend, Jesse Lane. Brother Jeremiah had taken great pains to constantly whistle or sing tunes that clearly presented the Gospel and had managed to recall a different verse of Scripture for each situation that had perplexed the mismatched duo.

Jesse's only outward sign of response to the Circuit Rider's witnessing was his failure to wear his Colt .45 that Saturday morning as he and Brother Jeremiah had put the finishing touches on the one-walled building. Much of the old preacher's prayer life the last week centered around the young man who dreamed of a reputation as a fast gun on the side of law and order. Jesse had just left in an effort to find some type of seating for tomorrow's meeting. The young cowboy had decided to check out the old warehouse where a dozen or so chairs were stored. Both saloons in town kept a regular order of chairs and tables to replace those broken during the occasional bar-room brawls on Saturday nights. But Jesse figured neither the Bells nor the Taylors would begrudge the temporary use of the chairs for this one day. He also figured the old Bible-thumper would leave town within two, maybe three weeks, just like the other two frock-coated evangelists before him.

The old weather-beaten, half-finished room no longer looked as foreboding as it had when Brother Jeremiah had been directed to the location by Walter Bell. Gone were the weeds and sunflowers. The front steps had been replaced with some boards Jesse had found in Miss Ida's storage shed. Several other holes in the floor had been fixed, and the back wall had received a fresh coat of whitewash which could hardly be seen. Jesse had surprised Brother Jeremiah with a homemade pulpit he had fashioned out of an old fence post and two apple crates that Isaiah Taylor had discarded. Two side walls were only partially framed, and there was no roof, but it was a start from which Brother Jeremiah believed would grow a fine House of Prayer for Jesus.

There were only three details left to handle before Miller's Bluff could experience its first worship service in over ten years, and the old Bible-thumper figured the three together would take the rest of the night. The first detail was to make sure everyone was informed about the meeting.

Just about everyone in town knew about the existence of the Circuit Rider. Little Jimmy had spread the word to anyone who would stop and talk with him; Miss Gayle had the school children practice writing sentences at home that contained the announcement which had to be signed by parents; and Miss Ida had aptly informed all the ladies in her sewing circle of the tall, handsome, mysterious parson who rented the smallest room in her boarding house.

Jesse had told Brother Jeremiah of the bets being placed by several of the men-folk as to how long the new preacher would stay. In fact, there was even a bet as to how long the old rickety building would stand if the Taylors and the Bells attended and started to fight during services. Most folks had planned on staying away for fear of getting caught up in the feud. In addition, Brother Jeremiah knew that ten years of late Saturday night salooning and late Sunday morning sleeping would be a tough habit to break. He figured it was time to draw on the special talents with which God had supplied him.

Down in the town's saloons, most of the area cattle ranchers and cowboys were bent over their whiskies and cards discussing the usual events of the day. And against the din of clinking glasses, billiard games, and fancy banjo picking, there was talk, too, of the new preacher that had come to town.

Taylor's Four Aces, like all the other businesses, was directly across the street from Bell's Cattlemen's Club. Brother Jeremiah stood in the middle of the street trying to decide what method to use to draw a crowd. The old preacher stood with his hands on his hips, his long black coat pushed back, with one eyebrow raised in concentrated thought looking first at the Four Aces and then to the Cattlemen's Club.

The experienced sermonizer considered an easy trick called Bottom the Bottle to impress the men with his marksmanship. This was done by placing a bottle on its side with the neck of the bottle facing the shooter who would then put a bullet through the neck without touching the sides. The bullet would take out only the bottom. If the bullet touched the neck, the bottle would be smashed to pieces. He had done that trick hundreds of times, but decided that this town might need a little something more eye-opening.

"If you're thirsty, Reverend, you'll have to find someplace else to go," said Sheriff Owen who had come up behind the statue-like figure. "'Gainst the law for Bible fellas to go inta either one of them places. On account of the feud."

"Oh, I wasn't plannin' on goin' into either establishment, Sheriff. But, I would appreciate you asking the gentlemen inside each place of business to step outside for just five minutes," answered Brother Jeremiah.

"Yew ain't figurin' on preachin' in the middle of the street are yew?" asked the sloppily-clothed gentleman behind the twinkling tin star.

"No, no. I just thought I'd make a sportin' proposition to the men concerning tomorrow." Brother Jeremiah grinned slyly.

Jeff Rutledge had just come out of the Cattleman's Club when Brother Jeremiah had answered the Sheriff's question. Rutledge was a tall, square-jawed, broad-shouldered man with a devilish grin who made sure everyone knew he was around. His black hat was pushed far back on his head allowing a straight lock of reddish-brown hair to fall on his forehead. Jesse had mentioned his "feud" with the foreman of the Double TB, and that Rutledge was not at all opposed to using violence if it would help him get his way. The Double TB's top hand was the kind of man that lived to hurt people who appeared weaker than himself. Rutledge's thick, black moustache glistened with beer suds in the evening light coming from the Cattleman's Club. He staggered on the porch propping himself against one of the painted ladies from Bell's saloon.

"Whadcha got in mind, Parson?" interrupted Rutledge, "a Bible drill contest?" The two other men with the young cowhand laughed heartily.

"No, Sir. A shootin' contest," replied Brother Jeremiah.

"Aw, everybody knows Bible-thumpers cain't shoot nuthin' but their mouths off," hollered Jeff amongst drunken guffawing and shouts. The drunken cowboy took a long swallow from his mug, wiped his sleeve across his mouth, and glared at the old Psalm-singer standing in the middle of the street.

"Would you care to make an honest wager on that?" inquired the old preacher in total control of himself. "Like whether I stay or leave?"

"Sure, Mister Bible-man!" shouted Jeff. "Owen. . . get them boys in the Four Aces to step out chere whilst Sandy gets the men from the Cattlemen's. We gonna run us a Jesus feller out of town on a rail."

Brother Jeremiah stood squarely in the main street of Miller's Bluff eyeing the loud-mouthed cowhand dressed in black that now leaned drunkenly against the porch support of the Cattleman's Club saloon on a hot August night. Again, the experienced preacher of thousands of sermons saw the cold stare of indifference in the grey-blue eyes of a human being that had the added danger of carrying a weapon famous for snuffing out the lives of mortal enemies. As the men emptied both saloons that night, Brother Jeremiah knew that Jeff Rutledge would prove a formidable foe of the Gospel. And just for a moment, the old Gospel-wrangler thought he saw a faint familiarity in the face of the drunken cowhand standing on the porch.

"What's this all about, Mister?" shouted Jacob Taylor, owner of the Four Aces. "We ain't got no time for no sermon tonight."

"This will only take a moment, Sir," promised Brother Jeremiah. Turning first to one side and then the other so that all could hear, he continued speaking. "My name is Brother Jeremiah. God sent me here to preach the Gospel to you kind folks. Jesse Lane and I have spent the week cleaning up the old church building for services tomorrow. I know some of you don't plan on coming to hear the stories of my Lord Jesus. Let me make you an offer concerning your attendance in church tomorrow. Sheriff, may I borrow one of your guns, please?"

Sheriff Owen, whose brothers had ridden with a Quantrill-like militia group during the War of Northern Aggression, reluctantly handed over his gun to the preacher after a nod of approval from Jacob Taylor.

"Now," continued the Jesus-seller, "if someone will place a bottle with a cigar stuck in the neck and an upturned whiskey glass balanced on the cigar on the far table in the Cattlemen's Club, please. Now, Mr. Taylor, if you'll be so kind as to open the doors of your establishment so I can see the big mirror on your back wall I shall attempt to drop the whiskey glass intact onto the neck of the bottle by shooting the cigar in two."

Jeff Rutledge and his friends led the laughter.

"That's impossible, Mister. Be a heap easier buildin' your Gospel mill outta toothpicks than makin' that shot. No one could do that," stated Mr. Taylor.

"But the Bible says, 'I can do all things through Christ,' Mr. Taylor. If I miss or break the neck of the bottle or break the shot glass, I'll ride out of here tonight. If I accomplish the task, I'll expect to see each and every one of you in church tomorrow. Deal?" commented the old preacher with a grin.

There was silence from the crowd of men standing in front of both whiskey houses as each tried to reckon in his own mind the impossibility of the stunt. Finally Jeff Rutledge broke the silence, just as Jesse Lane walked up beside the Sheriff.

"You're on, Preacher-man," said Rutledge gruffly. "Boys hold them doors open! But I'd hide behind 'em if'n I was you."

134

The men on both sides talked with each other as they backed away from the doors of the saloons. Brother Jeremiah stood sideways facing the huge mirror in the Four Aces. As he cocked and raised the Sheriff's gun, he silently prayed, "Lord, let this be for Your glory. . . that folks will come to know Jesus."

Jesse could feel the tenseness of the crowd as the veteran preacher raised the pistol to shoulder level still keeping his head turned so that he could see the reflection of his target in the mirror. Suddenly, the night air was filled with the explosive crack of gunfire as all the men strained to see the whiskey bottle or hear the sound of breaking glass.

"Well Golly Bill. . . I don't believe it!" shouted the bartender in the Cattlemen's Club. "He did it! He shot that thar ceegar clean through!"

The men from the Four Aces poured across the street to stare at the whiskey glass sitting neatly over the bottle with the half cigar in the neck. Jesse gazed at the preacher with a puzzled look. He never figured that the old preacher even knew how to hold a gun. . . much less use one. As he studied the face of the circuit rider, Jesse began to wonder if there was more to this frocked-coated fella than met the eye. Everybody was somethin' else before he became what he was at the moment, or so Jesse reasoned in his own mind. But just what had this Jesus-man been before he became a pulpiteer? The others in the audience shared similar questions with each other as they glanced first at the elderly man-of-the-cloth and then at his target.

"Services start at ten tomorrow morning, Boys. See ya there," shouted Brother Jeremiah with a huge grin on his face. The Circuit Rider tossed the six gun back to the open-mouthed sheriff and turned, whistling "Shall We Gather at the River" as he walked down the street towards the boarding house while the men clamored and retold the tale. One more detail had been taken care of.

All the while Jeff Rutledge glared at the preacher with an intense hate-filled stare. "Keep your saddle cinched, Churchman," said the mean-spirited cowhand so that no one else could hear him.

****

Miss Ida Murphy, in her mid-to-late 50's, had been anxiously watching for her most honored guest to arrive for supper. Though she had only gone to school for four years when she was a child, she possessed a rare sense of hospitality. She was a tidy housekeeper and careful in her personal appearance with a fondness for decided colors. Widowed after only two years of marriage, Miss Ida was proud of her Christian heritage and the decision she had made to follow her Lord when in her late teens. She prayed daily, offering her prayers with earnestness and eloquence, but she seldom read her Bible.

Miss Ida would have made a good mother. She had given her full time to her great niece, Gayle. . . ensuring her comfort and position within the community as co-hostess at her boarding house. The gray-haired widow made sure that there was always an abundance of wholesome food on her table. And despite all of her outward gentleness and apparent frailty, she carried a derringer in the pocket on her apron and knew how to squeeze a trigger almost as well as her gentleman friends.

Brother Jeremiah had already missed supper, again, but Miss Ida had kept his food warm for him. He hadn't really planned on eating any food, but decided he'd use the opportunity to question the portly widow about the Sheriff's remark concerning the feud between the Taylors and the Bells. The old sky-pilot had visited enough towns to realize that, like all other places, Miller's Bluff had its curious and heartrending stories. And the story behind the anger between Walter Bell and Isaiah Taylor might give him an idea for a strong message on Sunday.

"Well, it started nigh on to thirteen. . . no it was closer to fourteen years ago, Brother Jeremiah," began Miss Ida as she passed the preacher dish after dish of mouth-watering delicacies that she had kept warm just for the old Bible-wrangler. "A preacher came to town just after the War. He stayed in the same room that you're occupyin', Reverend. Oh it truly pleasured us so to keep his vittles warm whilst he visited the folks around town. He was so very handsome in his long black coat and knee-high boots."

Miss Ida started starring at the small couch in the sitting room as if in a cloud of memories. Then she came back to the present with the rattling of the stew bowl by her favored guest.

"Anyway," continued the elderly matron, "he started holdin' services in Abe Taylor's saloon, bein' as it was the only buildin' in town that could hold a group of folks. So, Abe Taylor began to act righteous as a deacon. . . on Sundays anyways. . . because of the church services bein' held at his place. Well, Jake Bell decided that the town needed a real church buildin' to worship in on Sundays, and since he owned the town lumber company and general store, Jake got his boys to start a buildin'."

"Well," she continued after freshening the circuit rider's coffee. "It sorta made old Abe Taylor kinda mad, but then the worst came about when Abe offered to help pay for the materials, and old Jake Bell refused to take his money. Said it was tainted with sin. Before anybody could do anything, them two got in the awfulest fight you ever did see! Finally old Abe Taylor pulled a gun and shot Jake Bell plumb dead right there on the steps of the church building! Old Jake's brother, Walter, whacked Abe upside the head with a hammer, and Abe died two days later. Walter Bell was arrested, but the jury couldn't reach a verdict. Everybody was arguing as to whose fault the whole thing was. The poor preacher thought that what had happened was his fault, and after a nice, dignified buryin' of Mr. Taylor and Mr. Bell, he just up and left town without saying good-bye to me or anybody. Walter Bell decided not to finish the church since there wasn't no more preacher. Several fellas tried to start a church since then, but each time the old arguments and feelins' come up and folks just run 'em off!"

Miss Ida waddled over to the oven to retrieve two warm biscuits so that Brother Jeremiah could continue sopping up the gravy from the beef stew.

"That's why there's two of everything in town, Preacher," she sighed as she sat down next to the greying travelin'-preacher. "That's why everybody figures you'll leave, too," she said sadly.

Miss Ida cocked her head a bit, lowered her chin and looked up at the old revivalist in her best "it'd break my heart if you left" look. She blinked her eyes a couple of times, trying to get the old preacher's attention and possibly a pledge that he'd stick things out longer than his predecessors.

Brother Jeremiah listened carefully to the whole story, merely chewing and swallowing his meal, and not actually enjoying the flavor.

"Excuse me, Miss Ida," interrupted the aging Bible-expositor, "but I really do need to take care of a couple of details before morning."

****

Brother Jeremiah closed the door to his room without lighting the lamp by the bedside. If the church had started the feud, then the church must put an end to the feud. Brother Jeremiah knew that the task in front of him now was much harder than shooting a cigar in two. The stubborn pride of the Taylors and the Bells made each family loathe each other for the very same reason. And the petty rivalry became a contest of wills, and sooner or later the little central Texas town just wouldn't be big enough for the both of them. Still, the hatred spurred on by so many years of bitterness would take much prayer to conquer.

As the seasoned soldier-of-the-cross poured out his heart in prayer to Jesus, he knew the answer would be found in the love of the One who died for the sins of the world; the One who said that love would be the sign of salvation; the One who said that we should love our enemies.

And then the old circuit rider felt his spirit moving within him to shape the third detail. . . a message to the people from the Lord. The preacher would stay because of the strength of Christ. The church through Christ would mend broken relationships. The church, through Christ, would be the answer to the warfare that threatened to tear a town apart. The old minister walked purposefully to a small table in the corner of his room near the window that let in the wondrous beams of moonlight. He reached for a small can of red paint that his host had found in her basement. And by the light from the moon shining through the window, the frontier parson hurriedly began painting on a large signboard Jesse had found:

WELCOME TO
PHILADELPHIA CHURCH
The Church of Brotherly Love

****

Chapter Thirteen

The Fire

W hat a difference the past week had made! Brother Jeremiah had spoken boldly his first Sunday morning in Miller's Bluff about "loving one's neighbor" to the thirty or so people who had made the effort to attend the opening service of Philadelphia Church, most of whom came to see if the old preacher could holler out the Scriptures as well as he could shoot. Two of the towns-people had asked Jesus to come into their hearts. Little Jimmy had been the first to the altar followed by the barkeeper from the Cattlemen's Club. None of the Taylors or the Bells had ventured out that morning, but all present knew that Brother Jeremiah had been speaking about the feud.

"The only way to end this devil-inspired split is through the love of Christ shown through the lives of those who claim His name," the circuit rider insisted, "and you and I must bring an end to this thing. Do as Jesus would do for one week!"

The veteran revivalist explained skillfully how the love of Christ had made the difference in holding together his two disciples, Matthew and Simon the Zealot, bitter enemies of different political persuasions, to the point that they spread the news of that same love throughout the world.

While no one had actually made any public commitment to his challenge, Brother Jeremiah felt that several would attempt to meet every situation with genuine Christian love. The past week had seen a significant change in the attitudes of the folks staying at Miss Ida's Boarding House, and Brother Jeremiah believed that this change would eventually spread throughout the small Texas farm community.

Very little work had been done during the week on the unfinished structure that had started the civil unrest of two of Miller's Bluff's most prominent families. Brother Jeremiah had managed to finish only half of one side of one wall without the aid of Jesse Lane. Jesse had not been around much since last week's message, and the aging preacher suspected that the Holy Spirit was working hard on the young reputation-seeker.

Miss Gayle had explained to the Gospel-wrangler that Jesse often rode out into the surrounding countryside alone to "sort things out". Sometimes he would stay for weeks at a time. He was a man of deep feeling as well as quick, accurate observation, and he often felt self-conscious and reflective. The outdoors spoke to him in a way that the hustle and bustle of city life never could. He truly enjoyed the streams and the hills covered with bluebonnets and Indian paint brushes in the spring.

"I deeply enjoy ridin' a steep ledge," Jesse once told Miss Gayle, "and viewin' the hills at sunrise or smellin' the dew on the cedar trees and listenin' to the mocking birds and marvelin' at the magnificent cloud displays at sunset."

Jesse really enjoyed being alone and would often seek out the line duty jobs at area ranches. He had memorized the trees, shrubs, and flowers in their season, and the signs and legends belonging to each. He had fed wild turkeys and quail with the bread and beans from his saddlebags. The hoot of the owl and howl of the coyote were music to his ears. No one in Miller's Bluff knew where to find Jesse on these occasions, and even Miss Gayle had stopped worrying about him. He always came back when he was through thinking.

****

The early morning hours of Brother Jeremiah's second Sunday in Miller's Bluff seemed to be full of hope for a mutual cease-fire between the participants of the emotional rivalry of the Taylor and Bell feud. Both Isaiah Taylor and Walter Bell had agreed to come to the services that morning. Of course neither man was aware of the other's intention of lending his support to the work of the old Scripture-hound. Brother Jeremiah had talked to each one privately after the paint and window incident of the previous Thursday.

Sometime Wednesday evening someone had broken every window out of Walter Bell's General Merchandize and had poured red paint over every item on the display. Of course Mr. Bell accused Isaiah Taylor of being responsible and promptly marched across the street, with red shotgun in hand, ready to add to the violence which mounted weekly. Sheriff Owen had tried to stop Mr. Bell, but was unable to do so. Walter Bell stomped into Taylor's General Store in a rage.

"This is the last straw, Taylor!" Bell shouted at the top of his lungs. "I'm gonna blow your insides all over the wall!"

Walter Bell raised his shotgun, cocked both barrels, aimed squarely at the plump, unkept shopkeeper who was taken totally by surprise, and pulled both triggers at the same time. Luckily, for both men, this shotgun was brand new and, therefore, contained no shells. Taylor fainted. Bell was so angry that he plunged the shotgun, barrel first into the pickle keg by the front counter. As the lanky merchandiser stomped out of his rival's store, Bell tripped on the front porch and landed head first in the horse water trough outside.

Predictably, all those witnessing the event laughed hysterically. Both mercantile stores were closed for the day as Bell and sons tried cleaning the mess made by the vandals, and Taylor tried to regain his composure. Brother Jeremiah took advantage of the situation and boldly talked to both men.

The town's new preacher lambasted both men individually with the same Scriptures and lecture. Neither appeared to be listening too well, but both promised to come to the Sunday service in exchange for the departure of the country prophet from their respective establishments. Each secretly planned vengeance on the other. But both had decided to wait a couple of days. . . until their enemy least expected reprisal.

Brother Jeremiah had overheard the many discussions, some heated, among the townsfolk concerning which of the men was almost responsible for murder. The wise old minister had let slip while at the supper table that he intended on settling the feud through preaching about Jesus' love or challenge Walter Bell and Isaiah Taylor to a duel. Little Jimmy quickly spread the word around town "the preacher was gonna face down Mr. Taylor and Mr. Bell this Sunday after church." Word of Brother Jeremiah's cigar shooting trick had already circulated all over the community, and most everyone thought the worst would happen. Of course, all wanted to see the gunfight. That's why Brother Jeremiah had arisen so early before sunrise on that third Sunday in August to enter into concentrated prayer that God would use him in a mighty way that morning to preach the plain and simple message of the Gospel. The veteran of many a camp meeting knew that this Sunday morning message had to be packed with an extra anointing of the Holy Spirit.

"Lord, use me as an instrument of Your love and peace," the old circuit rider began as he approached the steps of the unfinished frame-of-a-building. Brother Jeremiah took time to pray a special word or two at each level of the steps. Then, he slowly walked the aisles of the church praying all the while for the sin-killing, convicting Spirit to be present with whomever sat in that particular chair. The experienced Bible-expositor did not know very many names of the citizens of Miller's Bluff, and so he simply described people whenever he thought of someone. Finally, he reached Jesse's homemade pulpit, and there he poured his heart out to God to send a Savior-exalting, saint-edifying revival. So intense was the prayer, that he didn't hear the masked, black-clothed cowboys walk down the aisle. Neither did he notice the strong smell of coal oil coming from the buckets the men were carrying.

When the aging country minister finally looked up, he only caught a quick glimpse of the man in front of him before his head exploded with pain from the blow of the rifle butt. Brother Jeremiah slumped to his knees, stunned but conscious.

"We don't like Bible-thumpers in Miller's Bluff," said a muffled voice the dazed preacher thought vaguely familiar. He even thought he saw splotches of red paint on the lower pant leg and right boot belonging to the voice, through eyes that had already blurred. Four hands grabbed the man-of-God under the arms and jerked him to his feet.

"And we don't want no Bible-thumping in Miller's Bluff," proclaimed the faceless voice. This time the admonition was accompanied by a forceful blow from an iron fist to the midsection followed by a destructive uppercut to the face. Blood was pouring from the mouth and nose of the old churchman, who though conscious, did not comprehend anything the voices said. Again there were words which by now held no meaning whatever, followed by blows from imaginative cannonballs to the ribs, stomach, and face. As the circuit rider crumpled to the floor, he felt the hard leather of boots plunge into his chest and back.

Just before Brother Jeremiah lost all consciousness, he saw three black-clothed figures splashing the contents of wooden buckets all over the one room, planned building. As his eyes closed on reality, the battered warrior-for-Jesus caught the flicker of a small light that illumined the face of one of the attackers. Brother Jeremiah knew he had seen that face before, for it contained the grey-blue eyes of a young man filled with hatred.

"Burn the Doxology works, Boys," growled the cowboy, "and everythin' in it!"

****

There was ever so faint a glow coming from the western end of town that Sunday in the darkest minutes before dawn. Sheriff Owen had just stepped from his office to make his last rounds before going to Mary Bell's Restaurant for breakfast. Several seconds elapsed before the Sheriff focused his attention toward the golden hue coming from the direction of the church building.

"Fire!" he shouted as he finally realized what his eyes beheld. "Fire! Fire! Help! Everybody. . . help! Fire!" Sheriff Owen was not too bright when it came to matters of law or dress, but Nature had endowed him with a powerful set of lungs and a deep bellowing voice. As a result, heads bobbed out of windows all along Main Street as the gangly sheriff clomped down the boardwalk screaming, "Fire!"

Most of Miller's Bluff's residents responded to the scene of the blaze, but the flames had already reduced the one and a half wall and flooring into a big bonfire. All the folks could do was watch and stand ready to keep the fire from spreading to nearby buildings. Few noticed the two figures over in front of the newly erected location sign. Jesse Lane had ridden into town the same moment a black-leather vested figure tossed a match onto the steps of the unfinished building. It was Jess that saw the familiar, old, worn-out Bible on the crude pulpit in the light of the flames and knew its owner could not be far away from his most prized possession. It was Jesse that ran through the flames to pull the bleeding, unconscious body of the preacher to safety just before the entire structure was engulfed in fire. Jesse had propped the circuit rider against the signboard proclaiming the "church of brotherly love" and gently placed the old Bible in his lap.

Brother Jeremiah was alive, badly beaten, but alive. As Jesse stepped back with the crowd and stared at the bloody face of what he felt was most assuredly a defeated man, he wondered which of the feuding parties had committed such a crime. Jesse looked down at the preacher's Bible and secretly vowed to begin his reputation by seeking vengeance on the men responsible for the brutal attack against the peaceful old parson.

At that moment, Brother Jeremiah opened his swollen eyes as best he could. His gaze met that of the young gunman, and he seemed to read Jesse's mind like he read the Bible.

"Vengeance is mine sayeth the Lord; I will repay," quoted the preacher. "Let God take care of them, Jesse."

Jesse looked at the old, worn Bible once again. He squatted next to the old Psalm-wrangler, picked up the Treasure but didn't open it. He stared at the words on the cover. . . Holy Bible. . . then laid it gently down onto Brother Jeremiah's lap once again. As the young man stood up, he looked the old preacher in the eyes. Without a word, Jesse turned and walked away.

****

A bed in an enclosed room is not the kind of place an outdoorsy type of fellow wants to spend much time. For many years now, Brother Jeremiah had spent most of his time in the outdoors riding from town to town with the Gospel. He had spent many a night lying on the cold ground gazing into the heavens, praying and recalling that the Master of his life had experienced the same discomforts of riding the circuit. Part of the preacher's uneasiness came from the fact that he had missed another service.

The aging man-of-God set up on the side of his bed, wincing some from the pain in his side that indicated his ribs had not healed just yet. Brother Jeremiah gazed out the window in his room at the trees and pastureland that he could see, and his mind returned to the week he had spent in bed, burning up with fever.

Just a couple of months after surrendering to carry the Gospel message wherever his Lord led, Brother Jeremiah had gotten himself lost and without a horse while traipsing the woods of east Texas. In those years, this fearless man of God didn't have enough sense to seek shelter when the clouds and the wind indicated the approach of a Texas norther. The temperature took a sudden drop, and the Scripture-peddler found himself freezing. He happened upon a muleskinner who had made a sort of shelter out of an old tarp and the wagon he was driving. The campfire and the smell of hot coffee was a great temptation to the young traveling preacher.

"Hullo the camp!" shouted Brother Jeremiah as he recalled the surprised look on the face of the teamster.

"Hullo yer own self, Mister!" replied the wagoner. "What in tarnation are yew adoin' out in this weather. . . afoot!?"

"My name's Jeremiah. . . I'm a preacher. . . on my way to Gainesville for a meetin'," answered the Soul-wrangler. "Reckon I got lost a might."

"Yep, I reckon so," commented the muleskinner while pouring a cup of coffee for his guest. "Yur a mite nearer Crockett City then yew aire Gainesville, Mister. Have a cup of java. . . it'll help warm up yur insides."

Brother Jeremiah took the cup in his shaking hands and sipped generously of the liquid heat. The look on the face of the Bible-thumper must have been priceless.

"How's it taste?" asked the wagoneer.

"Fine," answered Brother Jeremiah. "Probably the best I've ever had."

"Hmmmpph! Sounds to me like yur a bit tetched!" said the mule-skinner. "It tastes like riverbottom to me and everbudy else. Never could make descent coffee. . . but I keep tryin'."

The freight-man offered to share his fire and shelter and an old buffalo hide with the saddlebag minister for the night, and Brother Jeremiah graciously accepted.

The next morning, the muleskinner pointed the young sin-buster in the direction of the nearest town, a small settlement called Wearysville. Brother Jeremiah thanked the teamster for his hospitality, shouldered his pack and headed off in the direction indicted by the freight-hauler. By the time he reached the little village, the Scripture-slinger was burning up with fever, and he was barely able to stand. A group of dirty-faced cowboys allowed he could take shelter in an old, abandoned cabin on the outskirts of town.

"This here's the best we kin do, Preacher," said one of the fellers who wore a ten gallon Stetson and a week's worth of whiskers. "We ain't gut no fancy hotels here or much of anythin' else in the way of civilized comforts."

For days, the young Bible-teacher lay sick in the abandoned hut, with no one to care for him. Then an elderly Irish couple learned the plight of Brother Jeremiah, and so they moved him to their modest farmhouse where the wife nursed the sick man back to tolerable health. That was the first time Brother Jeremiah had missed a Sunday preaching opportunity, and he had vowed that it would never happen again. And with the exceptions of those five times over the past two years, it hadn't. . . until now.

****

It had been a week since the senseless attack in the church and the fire, and Brother Jeremiah decided that his bruises had healed

146

sufficiently. Besides, it was Sunday, and the old warrior-of-the good-news couldn't bare the thought of missing another worship service, no matter how he still ached. The beating he had sustained was not his first since riding the circuit for Jesus, and he figured it wouldn't be his last. And he had faced the fear of death before.

Once, he remembered, about four or five years after making his decision to take the Good News of Jesus Christ to wilderness areas, the Gospel-herald was almost hung as an outlaw. Brother Jeremiah had packed his broadcloth in his saddle bags and was outfitted in the regular garb of a range-rider. By accident, he rode into an area where he fit the description of a horse thief. He was caught and taken to the hanging tree on the outskirts of Muleskin, Texas.

"You're making a big mistake!" protested the young Bible-jockey. "My name is Brother Jeremiah! I am a preacher! Look in my saddle bags and you'll find my credentials!"

"Tell thet to yore Maker," quipped a self-appointed vigilante as the other men laughed.

"Hold on here jest a minute!" replied a member of the would-be promoters of justice. "I heard tell that Brother Jeremiah was a mighty fine shot with a pistol. If'n yore him, then yew oughta be able to prove it with just one shot!"

"Pete," yelled the leader of the group, "give him yore pistol. . . and one bullet. . . and let's see whut he can do. Don't want nobudy ever accusin' me of not lettin' a feller prove his innocence."

Another of the group untied the accused and removed the California collar from the young parson's neck. The cowhand named Pete handed him his pistol with the one bullet, and Brother Jeremiah prayed that the Lord would steady his hand and his aim.

"What should I shoot?" asked the misidentified horse thief.

The leader of the pack took a silver dollar from his pocket. "Pete, put this here dollar in the fork of thet tree over yonder. Let's see if this supposed Bible-thumper can knock it out of the tree."

Pete took the coin and ran to the small pine tree some fifty feet away. Only a true marksman could possibly hit the coin. . . only a handful of people could even see it. Brother Jeremiah cocked the gun in his hand and took careful aim. The shot echoed through the little valley, and birds nesting nearby flew into the air.

For several minutes Pete searched the area behind the tree for the coin, finally bringing the now ruined dollar to the party's leader. There was a hole in the very center. The leader apologized to the young preacher, and Brother Jeremiah quickly changed his clothing into his black frockcoat, never donning the comfort of cowboy clothes when traveling again. Brother Jeremiah thought how silly the whole thing would look in a dime novel.

Only Little Jimmy noticed the battered Jesus-man slowly tip-toeing past the parlor opening in Miss Ida's Boarding House on his way outside. Little Jimmy grinned with excitement as he watched Brother Jeremiah open the squeaky front door with such noiseless patience. Even though the whole town, including Miss Gayle and Jesse, believed that the old preacher would be riding on soon, Little Jimmy had stuck by the man with the big Bible.

"He'll stay with us," Little Jimmy would say. "I just know he will. And he'll rebuild that old church, too. And I'm a gonna hep him! He'll stay and keep on a preachin'. 'Sides he ain't balpatized me yet!"

Little Jimmy's child-like faith had begun to open a few other eyes in the community. Walter Bell and Isaiah Taylor had both offered a $100 reward for the arrest of the persons responsible for the fire and the beating of the circuit rider, partly out of rage that such a thing could happen in Miller's Bluff, but mostly to dispel the rumors that one of them had hired someone to scare the Bible-thumper out of town.

****

There was nothing left of the little framed church building, but ashes and the sign Brother Jeremiah had painted two weeks before. Of course, there was no congregation either since everyone anticipated the soon departure of the old preacher.

Brother Jeremiah sat down on a stump looking half defeated at the ground. Then he noticed the shadows of the large-winged birds circling above the site of the building.

"Y'all ain't gonna win that easy, you pallbearers-of-the-sky," the old Gospel-soldier said to the circling bone-pickers. "I ain't dead, yet! This here church ain't dead yet neither! And God sure 'nough ain't dead!" shouted the pulpit-pounder as he stood to his feet shaking his old, worn Bible at the buzzards that had greeted him here once before.

"Preacher. . . you OK?" asked Little Jimmy shyly. He had followed Brother Jeremiah out of the house and had stood behind the corner of one of the buildings spying on the old parson. Brother Jeremiah, startled, turned to face the voice.

"Yes, Sir, Jimmy! I'm fine as cream gravy! And you know why? 'Cause Jesus is alive and well! You go tell the folks I'm here to stay! No devil's gonna run me and the Lord off! You go tell 'em! And you tell 'em they might as well come out here to hear the Gospel 'cause I got a special message from the Lord about who did this," the preacher said boldly pointing to the pile of ashes that had been a building.

"Yes, Sir!" grinned Little Jimmy as he turned, running down Main Street. "The preacher's gonna stay! The preacher's gonna stay!" He ran and screamed with all of his might.

Brother Jeremiah looked at the sign a moment and fell to his knees clutching his Bible. The old sermonizer raised his eyes to the skies and talked to a "face" only he could see.

"Thank you for the fire, Lord. Now we can start fresh and new. The old memories of the building that caused the feud won't stand in the way anymore. Now give me wisdom and strength to preach Your message boldly."

Brother Jeremiah knew that the beating and the fire had been sent by Satan in an effort to destroy the work. He also knew God had allowed Satan to think the Old Destroyer had won, but God had actually taken Satan's plans and worked them against him just like He had done so many times in the Bible stories the old preacher loved and told so well. The old church building had been destroyed, but with the fire had come the destruction of the symbol of the feud and the hatred between the Taylors and the Bells. In addition, these two families were working together for the first time in over ten years, even if it was to salvage their own reputations.

The old circuit rider knew that a miracle was about to take place in a town that had so desperately needed a miracle. He knew, too, that the miracle would cause the Enemy to fight harder than ever, but Brother Jeremiah was confident of his mission now, and he knew that God would eventually win. He would stay, and the Gospel would be preached to a town hungry for spiritual food. Revival would come, and lives would be changed forever. He knew, too, that Old Slewfoot would not give up his interfering ways. . . more battles would come. . . but the victory was the Lord's.

****

As the news of the "preacher's stayin'" echoed through the streets of Miller's Bluff, a black-gloved hand clenched tightly around the empty glass of beer on a table in the Cattlemen's Club. Those sitting with the young cowboy dressed all in black noticed the tenseness in his jaw and his mesmerizing, grey-blue eyes full of hatred that stared out the window towards the frocked-coated figure kneeling in the dust beside the charred ruins of the former House of Worship. Those eyes exposed a pent-up antagonism that would soon be unleashed against those unlucky persons who had foiled his plans. If facial expressions alone could kill, then the graveyard would soon have some new residents. Rutledge's friends knew that look meant that the ranch-boss would be mighty disagreeable until he removed the one who troubled his mind. . . so disagreeable that Jeff would have trouble getting along with his own shadow.

"Next time," he said so softly that only those close by could hear, "I'll make sure that old man stays permanently."

His hand moved instinctively to the gun at his side as the black-leather-vested cowpoke stood to his feet, still gazing at the praying sermonizer. Rutledge's right index finger tapped the small cannon in his holster.

"Next time," he breathed slowly, "and Jess Lane'll get the same thing if he interferes again."

Rutledge kept searching the bottom of his tankard of beer as if he were reviewing a way to wreak havoc on the old sin-hound. The suds-covered-bottom of the glass became like a crystal ball for the mean-spirited cowboy. And life for the black-clothed hombre would not be relaxed or casual until the old Bible-thumper was gone.

****

Chapter Fourteen

The Celebration

Miller's Bluff, Texas, had not witnessed the kind of community celebration that Isaiah Taylor and Walter Bell were planning since the nation's centennial birthday two years earlier. Several factors had evolved to produce the citywide spirit of sharing and joy, not the least of which was the revival of hope and worship experienced by those who had attended the previous Sunday's services at Philadelphia Church.

More than a hundred folks had come to see if the circuit rider was indeed staying as Little Jimmy had so enthusiastically announced. With the crowd, that was forced to stand around the ash covered spot of the location of Miller's Bluff's only church, came a bold and powerful message from a bruised and battered preacher about the results of sin in a person's life, and the only release of Satanic bondage through the blood of Jesus Christ. Brother Jeremiah whirled around and stomped and screamed and rattled off Scripture after Scripture dealing with salvation and forgiveness and the removal of sin barriers with such zeal, that almost everyone present that morning made some kind of commitment to Jesus.

What really broke the ice of indifference was Brother Jeremiah displaying his bruises and cuts and then tying his beating into what happened to Jesus at Calvary.

"An ordinary man would've called it quits like I thought about doing for awhile," preached the Bible-orator, "but Jesus tweren't ordinary! He looked down from the cross at His tormentors and persecutors, the ones responsible for the bruises and the blood and the torn flesh and the pain, and with a heart breaking with love for folks who didn't care, Jesus raised His eyes t'wards Heaven and said, 'Father, forgive these folks; for they ain't got nary an idea as to what they're doin'.'"

At that point, with his own eyes looking toward Heaven, Brother Jeremiah raised his arms, open Bible in hand, and pointed directly at Isaiah Taylor and Walter Bell standing on opposite sides of the crowd. After a long pause that seemed like an eternity to the two embarrassed men, the old preacher lowered his head and spoke, arms still raised and pointing, "If Jesus could forgive you, don't you think you should forgive each other?"

The veteran revivalist stared first at one and then the other, but neither man wanted to match his gaze for more than a second. Then, as if cued individually by an unseen director, both men stepped out of the crowd and walked slowly across the ashes of the burnt structure until they stood just a fist's distance away from one another in front of the old circuit rider. Isaiah Taylor's unlit cigar spun in large circles as the short man nervously chewed the green-leafed pacifier. Walter Bell's Adam's apple bobbed up and down like a cork on a fishing line as he tried to utter words without sound. Finally Mr. Taylor offered his hand, and Mr. Bell responded with a firm grip. Brother Jeremiah placed his hand on top of theirs as all three men sank to their knees, heads bowed in prayer, tears streaming down their faces.

That was all it took for a genuine spirit of revival to break out amongst the crowd. Neighbor turned to neighbor, husbands turned to wives, and Taylors turned to Bells and asked forgiveness for wrongs done or said. Before the day was over, fifteen people had asked Jesus to be their Savior. Jesse Lane was not one of them. Jesse had only grinned slightly at the sight of grown men and women washing their conscience clean with tears of happiness and repentance. Then he walked away.

Almost immediately Isaiah Taylor and Walter Bell began making plans with the other citizens of Miller's Bluff for a church raisin' and community picnic for the following Saturday. Miss Ida and Miss Gayle began making arrangements for different ladies to bring food, and the Cattlemen's Club helped encourage even disinterested cowboys to donate some time and labor. Taylor's Four Aces donated chairs for the new building, and Sheriff Owen began construction of an oak pulpit.

As the week wore on, Brother Jeremiah spent more time in his room at the boarding house praying. Jesse had not been heard from since Sunday, and the old preacher still had a hankerin' for good organ accompanied music. God had proved He was still in the miracle working business, and Brother Jeremiah knew that some miracles just took lots of prayer and fasting. Beside, the Taylors and the Bells had everything under control as far as planning the celebration was concerned, so the only thing the old Bible-teacher had to do was pray. Prayer had always been important to the circuit rider, but there seemed to be an extra urgency in making sure that Jesse Lane would be reached soon. Almost as if the whole situation was on some fleeting time schedule. Brother Jeremiah had never felt such an urgency. He even thought of riding into the hills to search for his young friend, but Gayle discouraged the idea.

"Jesse will come back to town when he feels like whatever it is that is bothering him, isn't bothering him anymore," Gayle had told the saddlebag-clergyman.

****

By the time Saturday had arrived, the spirit of cooperation had touched most of the residents of the small Texas farm-town. The sun had risen on folks busily hurrying along the dirt streets of Miller's Bluff towards the newly cleaned and cleared plot of ground that would serve as the site for the town's new church. Walter Bell's sons had worked most of the week getting the property ready for the church raisin' using tools donated by Isaiah Taylor. Several other members of the Taylor and Bell family worked side by side setting the 24 large, eighteen-inch-tall stumps that would serve as the foundation for the one-room House of God.

Miss Ida and Miss Gayle were up early checking their list of supplies needed to help feed the men expected to turn out for the town's special celebration. Both women were busy with the sunrise setting up tables to hold the abundant foods and pastries.

" 'Sbeen a long time since any of us wanted to do somethin' for God, Preacher. You been brandin' for the Lord for a long time now, so let us do the hammerin' and such," insisted Walter Bell. Still, Brother Jeremiah felt he needed to help raise the building.

The townsfolk worked enthusiastically sawing lumber and wrestling the heavy beams and planks into place. Brother Jeremiah rolled up his sleeves and helped lift the timbers whenever he could. Philadelphia Church would be a simple building of rough lumber that would be whitewashed later. Thad Bell, one of the town's bankers, placed a new silver dollar bearing the date 1878 in a corner post.

By midday, the Philadelphia Church was beginning to look more like a meeting place than it ever had. All four walls were up, and the men were almost ready to raise the roof. The food was holding out adequately, and the older teens were keeping the younger children busy playing games. Everything seemed to be in apple pie order. Not one of the folks at the celebration could have imagined that this festive occasion would end in a tragedy.

"Preacher," Little Jimmy said excitedly, "I found a great spot for the balpatizin' tomorrow. Come and see! Come on, Preacher!" he said as he tugged at Brother Jeremiah's shirt sleeve.

"OK, Jimmy, OK," answered the old circuit rider, "the boys don't seem to be needin' me here. Let's go look at the balpatizin' hole."

Little Jimmy took the old warrior-for-Jesus by the hand and led him through the woods behind the place where the men of the community were busily constructing the building that would house Philadelphia Church. Neither party saw the lone figure dressed in a black-leather vest lurking in the shadows.

"There it is, Preacher! See!" announced Little Jimmy. "And it's not too deep neither! See how the sun shines on the water!"

The sun reflecting on the surface of the clear little creek appeared to be spreading fingers of silver from bank to bank.

"Yes, Jimmy, it's a great spot for baptizin'," answered Brother Jeremiah matching the small boy's excitement. "And folks can sit on the slope here next to the river. And this rock next to the bank here will make an excellent pulpit. Tomorrow's gonna be a great day for the Lord, Jimmy."

Brother Jeremiah sat down on the rock, pulled off his boots and placed his tired feet in the cool waters of the creek. Little Jimmy was still talking expectantly about the "balpatizin'" while skipping flat rocks across the water.

The old glory-roader was excited that his mission was progressing so well. He took an envelope from his coat pocket that contained a letter written by a young man whom Brother Jeremiah had helped three years or so before. Tom McKelroy had written of his surrender to preach, his first churches in northern Louisiana, and his desire to see the old rebel-rousing-black-coat to ask a special favor. Brother Jeremiah read again of Tom's plans to come to Texas possibly in a couple of months. In the preacher's mind, he saw the former card-sharp standing behind his new pulpit in Miller's Bluff's new church, expounding the Scriptures to an awed crowd.

Gentile, happy music could be heard in the background as the final touches were being put on the roof of the new church. Walter Bell and his sons had planned on building a steeple complete with a bell during the first part of the next week. Brother Jeremiah closed his eyes in thought as the warm afternoon August sun seemed to make light of all the problems of the previous weeks.

For just one quick moment, time seemed frozen as Little Jimmy, turning to pick up a rock, caught the shimmer of the sun's rays on the barrel of the rifle that pierced the shadows of the woods.

"Preacher! Look out!" screamed the little orphan boy.

Brother Jeremiah turned just as the assassin's bullet exploded from the high powered weapon. His eye caught the flash of light at the same time his body felt the weight of the young boy who had thrown himself through the air to knock the old preacher off balance and into the creek.

Momentary silence filled the August air as the sound of gunfire drowned out the laughter and the music. Several men who were working on the ground instinctively ran towards the creek just a few yards behind the structure of praise. Horror filled the minds of those who had fought a fire set to destroy the work of God and the old evangelist who had come to town. Hammers stopped pounding and heads turned towards the heart-stopping thud that meant something. . . or someone. . . had been shot.

****

Chapter Fifteen

The Commitment

T he dark-grey, mist-filled skies of Miller's Bluff seemed to match the attitude of most of the town's residents as every bench and chair was filled at the first service of Philadelphia Church in the newly erected community-built sanctuary. Quiet sobs of grief and confusion were heard from many of the townsfolk, both men and women, as the tall, somber-faced circuit rider rose to deliver the funeral message of Miller's Bluff's youngest hero. Little Jimmy had succeeded in warning the preacher of the danger from the shadows and had in fact knocked an off balanced preacher into the shallow waters of the clear little creek that ran behind the church. Unfortunately the belligerent missile projected from the barrel of the Winchester hurdled through the air on target.

"Little Jimmy sacrificed his life yesterday so that a friend might live," began the old preacher, his voice cracking with emotion, "and you know. . . Jesus did much the same thing for all of us."

The veteran sermonizer compared each detail of Little Jimmy's deed with something in the life of Jesus with such skill that all in attendance that dreary Sunday morning eagerly listened to each word. Then, to tie everything together, Brother Jeremiah expertly weaved in the message of the Resurrection.

"Only those who have trusted Jesus to save them from the wages of sin will live forever in Heaven with the Father. Even now, Little Jimmy stands with Christ receiving partial rewards for his short ministry on this earth," Brother Jeremiah said.

No one in Miller's Bluff had ever heard of a preacher inviting folks to get saved at a funeral before, but then no one in Miller's Bluff had ever heard of Brother Jeremiah before. Ten people came to the Mourner's Bench to repent of sins done and to ask Jesus to be their Savior.

Halfway through the message, Jesse Lane walked quietly into the sanctuary and seated himself in a chair near the back. The unshaven Jesse had not heard of the brutal attempt on the preacher's life that placed Little Jimmy's body in a plain, pine box at the front of the room. For the first time in many years, the rough and un- emotional young cowboy's eyes filled with tears as he thought of the little orphan boy that used to follow him everywhere. He remembered, too, the change that took place in Little Jimmy just a couple of weeks before as a result of the boy's profession of faith in Jesus and how excited the youngster was at the thought of being "balpatized". It was Little Jimmy's excitement that had started Jesse thinking seriously about the message that the old Jesus-warrior kept telling him each time the two were together. But the sight of Little Jimmy's body made Jesse decide abruptly that he wanted nothing to do with a cruel God that would allow an innocent young boy, to be murdered. He vowed to find the killer and put an end to him. He then concluded that Little Jimmy's death was caused by the old preacher's presence in Miller's Bluff. Jesse knew he could do something about that, too.

****

Long after the last spade full of black dirt had covered Little Jimmy's grave in the area marked off by Brother Jeremiah close to the church building, the old preacher still knelt in prayer beside the little wooden marker, pouring out his heart to God in the driz-zling rain. Brother Jeremiah had nearly convinced himself that he had indeed made a mistake in coming to Miller's Bluff and that his actions were being punished. Guilt can cause even the strongest man to weaken and question his choices or even his very existence. Brother Jeremiah knew that the passing of Little Jimmy was a critical point in his ministry. Just as the aging saddlebag-preacher had finished another tearful plea for a "sign" as to what to do, Jesse Lane angrily interrupted his prayer.

"I wish I'd aleft yew in that fire, Preacher!" Jesse shouted.

Startled, Brother Jeremiah turned to gaze into frustrated eyes reddened by mourning over the loss of a friend. The veteran Psalm-singer hung his head and clutched his worn Bible even more tightly and answered, "Me, too, Jesse. Me, too."

"I b'lieve it's time for you to move along, Mr. Preachin' Man. You've caused enough trouble here," Jesse proclaimed.

"But, God hasn't given me the word to go, yet, Jesse. So, I reckon I'll be stayin' awhile," answered the country-parson.

"This is all the word you need, Fella," countered Jesse, pulling his big Colt from its holster. "Git movin'. . . now!"

Somehow, Brother Jeremiah knew this was the sign he'd been praying for. He finally had Jesse's complete attention. The old preacher rose slowly from his kneeling position and walked even more slowly to the young reputation-seeker. Jesse's eyes began to fill with tears again as Brother Jeremiah stepped closer and closer. Finally, the experienced Bible-teacher reached for Jesse's gun.

"Give me the pistol, Son," said Brother Jeremiah, "and let's talk."

"No!" cried Jesse as he slapped the preacher's face.

The old-time peacemaker reacted quickly by slapping Jesse's face. Frustrated and angry, Jesse planted a left hook to the old Bible-reader's chin, which sent him stumbling backwards.

"You know, Jesse, there's a story in the Bible about a young man that tried to fight with God. His name was Jacob," grinned the old soul-wrangler as blood trickled down the right corner of his mouth. "He ended up bein' a preacher."

"I don't wanna hear it!" Jesse screamed.

With that statement, Jesse once more opened his knuckles on the old Bible-thumper's teeth, knocking the preacher to the muddy ground. The two rolled and wrestled and kicked and grunted, with Brother Jeremiah, as best he could between breaths, telling Jesse about Jacob's wrestling with the angel all the while. The more Brother Jeremiah preached, the more Jesse fought. . . which made the learned devil-chaser talk even more. Brother Jeremiah held onto a confused and emotionally drained Jesse as tightly as he could during the struggle, which matched young untested strength with seasoned will of iron. The old Gospel-orator was going to convert Jesse to the Lord's side even if it killed them both.

Finally after several minutes of kicking and gouging, Jesse began to do more crying and less fighting. When he stopped altogether, the battered Scripture-slinger breathed a prayer of thanksgiving. Jesse had taken his frustration out on God by striking out at God's representative, and by doing so, had been conquered by the One he sought to destroy. By instinct, the old preacher knew the young cowboy was primed.

Brother Jeremiah began to speak again between gulps for air, "You ready to talk about Jesus now, Son?"

"What would Jesus want with me?" asked the exhausted, young rebel.

"He wants to use you as an instrument of His salvation," insisted the aging Bible-expositor. "He'll use whatever we give Him, Jesse. But first He wants to save us from death and Hell."

"Can He save me, Preacher?" inquired an eager Jesse.

"He can save anybody that lets Him. He saved me, Jesse. I used to be quite a cutter in my younger days over in Lou'z'ana. Good with the guns and the gals. . . and a cardsharp to boot. Folks called me Kid Jeremy. I've done a heap of things I ain't proud of. Most of 'em started when I was about your age. I wanted lots of folks to know my name, just like you, Jesse. Then I met Jesus."

Brother Jeremiah began relating his life story to the defeated young cowboy, a story very similar to Jesse's own. The two were almost carbon copies of each other except that Brother Jeremiah had actually lived out the fantasy of the big reputation.

"By the time I was sixteen," began the mud-soaked preacher. "I had decided that I was gonna make more money and have more material things than any person I knew. So I left my folks' farm and worked wherever I could find a job. T'weren't long afore I met a naturally mean character that went by the name of Tug. In my book, Tug had all the answers."

The old preacher paused momentarily trying to decide just how much he should tell the young man sitting in the mud at his side. Then he continued his story.

"One day, when we were havin' trouble gettin' money together for a poker game, Tug suggested an easy way of gettin' lots of money. 'We'll jest git us some girls to go to work fer us' Tug says."

Jesse was not playing with the mud the way he had that day he had offered to help build the church. He listened carefully to every word that the old preacher said. The young cowboy searched the eyes of the aging Bible-teacher for the truths hidden within the words being spoken.

"At first, I didn't realize what he was talkin' about," said the circuit rider with a downward embarrassed glance. "When the truth dawned on me, I didn't even jump back at the thought. 'Sides by now I had slipped to the bottom of the pits of sin without realizin' it. So, I responded with, 'Do you think we can git away with it?' My question and his answer had become the new standard for my conduct."

Tears began to form in the reddened eyes of the Bible-banger as he recalled his sin-filled past. "I had everything. Lots of money. Lots of women to make money for me. A reputation as a gunslinger. I often made it a point to practice my pistol shootin' in public. I knew all along I was doin' wrong. My momma used to read the Bible to me when I was a youngster. But because of my life style, I was jest too embarrassed to think about God, let alone talk to Him about my deepest feelings."

The drizzle turned to light rain now, but neither of the two men made an attempt to move indoors.

"I'd heard about God savin' others," continued the old churchman, "but I figgered I'd gotten too deep inta sin. My thoughts focused on the mindless violence that had become a way of life for me. I thought of a man Tug and I had once cut up in Baton Rouge jest for the fun of it. I remembered the young cowboy my friends and I had almost beaten to death. Then, there was the girls I had introduced to a life of prostitution. I just didn't think God could ever forgive such ugly things like I had done. By this time, many of my friends were either in prison or on their way there. Tug was hung for killin' a customer whose hat he didn't like. What hope was there for me?"

As the rain continued to drench Jesse and Brother Jeremiah, the old preacher could sense that the time had come to tell the best part of the story.

"One day," he said, "I happened to walk into this little church in town, and I noticed the big Bible on the Mourner's Bench. God spoke to me through the Scripture verse in front of me. It said, 'He that cometh to me, I will in no wise cast out.' I flipped some pages and another verse jest jumped out at me. It said, 'And ye shall seek me, and find me, when ye shall search for me with all your heart.'"

Brother Jeremiah's voice got shaky again as he continued, "I dropped to my knees and prayed, 'Lord, if you'll let me know right now that Jesus Christ is your Son, and if you'll let me know that He can do what my momma always told me, I will accept Him.' I turned some more pages, and another verse caught my eye. 'For whosoever shall call upon the name of the Lord shall be saved,' it said. At that moment, all the guilt and the burdens of my life were lifted off my shoulders. They were gone. And I had total peace. It was true. Even a person like me could be forgiven!"

The seasoned Bible-instructor took a few moments to let his story sink into Jesse's brain, expecting some questions. When they didn't come, the old preacher continued, "When I finally understood the love of Jesus, I couldn't do nuthin' but tell other folks 'bout what He'd done for me. Now, I only use a gun to help draw a crowd so's I can preach to folks and let the Holy Spirit do the savin'. And the way things have worked out over the years, I've learned that I've gained more recognition than I ever thought possible. . . stored up in a Place that gives eternal rewards."

****

Drops of rain glistened on the flowers and grass in the little cemetery of Philadelphia Church as the soft early morning rays of the sun peeked through the clouds above the horizon. Miss Gayle Murphy had spent a restless night, mourning over the death of Little Jimmy, wondering how God could make anything good come out of that tragic event like Brother Jeremiah said would happen, fretting and praying over the preacher and Jesse. She had studied the faces of both men and had seen the signs of decision. She could only hope God had heard her prayers in the night.

As she stepped to her bedroom window and pushed back the curtains, breathing deeply the fresh, morning air, she turned her head towards the memorial of death where only yesterday, the town had laid to rest a young orphan-boy. Tears of joy slowly filled her eyes as she recognized the form of two men silhouetted against the red sky. . . kneeling with heads bowed beside the small wooden marker of a little hero for God. And for the first time in many years, the young school-marm felt the joy that comes when one knows that He, indeed, hears prayers.

"Thank you, Lord," whispered Gayle, "for doing the things that only You can do."

****

Chapter Sixteen

The Challenge

The fall breeze of November brought chills to the people of Miller's Bluff and reminded them all that another winter would soon be arriving. Many folks harbored early thoughts of the Thanksgiving services, realizing that all truly had many things for which to be thankful. Fifty men and women had found Christ as their Savior since the arrival of the old circuit rider, and the town had a beautiful one-room sanctuary, complete with chimney and steeple, in which to worship. Other changes were even more miraculous.

The Cattlemen's Club stopped being a saloon and began serving the finest steaks west of the Brazos. Isaiah Taylor and Walter Bell began raising money together to build an orphanage on land outside of town that both had previously declared was their own. Sheriff Owen even become more particular about the clothes he wore, though his color combinations still caused quite a few giggles from some folks. Miss Ida and Miss Gayle sponsored weekly sewing circles and prayer meetings at the boarding house, and Jesse Lane accompanied Brother Jeremiah on his visits to folks whenever he could. . . without that big iron on his hip.

The ladies of Miller's Bluff were most thankful for the closing of Miss Hattie's at the edge of town. Business had slacked off to next to nothing as a result of Brother Jeremiah's hard Bible preaching and the prayerful efforts of the Thursday afternoon sewing circle. Even more surprising was Miss Hattie's reaction to losing some of her best girls to Jesus. Those girls either decided to go back home to their folks. . . or accept the marriage proposals of some of the men in the little farm community.

"I'm leavin', Preacher Man, 'cause my daddy always taught us to admit defeat and then start over. Wouldn't be no point in tryin' to start over here. You'd probably jest come after my new girls, too. Got my eye on a place in La Grange. I hear you been askin' around fer a piano or somethin' fer that church of yours," stated Miss Hattie.

"Yes, Ma'am," replied the old Psalm-singer, his hat in his hand. "Piano music or organ music would certainly add to the services."

"Be willin' to buy my organ for. . . $100?" asked Miss Hattie.

"No, Ma'am," came the quick reply. "Too many other things the Lord's money needs to go for. Besides, I hear several keys don't play, and I understand it'll cost you $200 or more to have it shipped most anywhere. 'Course it would be a shame to just let a beautiful instrument like that ruin 'til you figure out what to do with it. Just out of curiosity I was askin' Luke Taylor how much he would charge to store that organ for you in the freight office, and I gotta tell you, Miss Hattie, I was plumb exhausted tryin' to figure up costs he talked about just for one year. I never realized it would be so expensive! 'Course you might find somebody who'd be willin' to charge you less or maybe even nothin' at all, if you could leave that big music machine in the house there 'til Mr. Bell finds a buyer. But then you might have a problem if'n somebody wanted to move into the house real quick like. How much time you got before the stage leaves?" Brother Jeremiah was baiting his hook with a skillfulness matched only by the smoothness of the painted-lady adorned in red velvet standing before him.

Miss Hattie grinned as she recognized what the preacher was hinting at. "Preacher, do you reckon the church folks might let me keep my 'music machine' in the church building for a while?. . . for a nominal fee?"

"Now that's a great idea, Miss Hattie. Why didn't I think of that. I'm sure I can persuade the folks to do that as a favor to you," grinned the crafty old sky pilot.

"And I suppose you'd make sure that the rest of the keys wouldn't ruin due to lack of use?" queried the lady of leisure.

"Naturally," grinned the expert Bible-teacher.

"Naturally," Miss Hattie repeated shaking her head. "OK, Preacher, I know when I'm licked. And I ain't a sore loser. . .just a little wiser. You can have the organ. 'Sides, I got nobody can play it since Carey took religion and moved home back east. Do me a favor will you? Don't ever come down to La Grange?"

"Cain't make no promises, Ma'am. I jest go wherever the Lord leads," Brother Jeremiah replied still grinning. "Yew ever think of givin' your life to Jesus, Miss Hattie?"

The painted lady laughed so hard her hat almost fell off. "Preacher, it's way too late for that to happen."

"Not 'til you're six feet under, Ma'am," commented Brother Jeremiah soberly.

Miss Hattie's voice got serious as she felt the sincerity of the preacher's statement, and her highly rouged cheeks paled. "Not now, Preacher. . .maybe someday. . . I better get on down to the stage depot before those boys leave me here. Goodbye, Preacher."

"Goodbye, Miss Hattie," said the preacher as he offered her his hand. "I'll pray for you. Every time I see or hear that fancy organ of yours. . . I'll send up a little prayer just for you."

A tear came to Miss Hattie's brown eyes as she fumbled with her purse and straightened her hat. The lady from the big red mansion blinked her eyes and daubed them with her silk handkerchief.

"Thanks, Preacher," she said softly as she clasped his big right hand. Then she quickly turned and walked as swiftly as she could in her red-velvet outfit to the waiting stage.

****

Folks would have thought that Brother Jeremiah was putting Jesse and the seven other men through some type of religious torture judging from their grunts and groans as they carried the beautiful oak-wood pump organ down the steps of the "Tay-Bel Spread", Miller's Bluff's newest hotel and restaurant, formerly owned by Miss Hattie, now a joint business venture of Isaiah Taylor and Walter

166

Bell. The men were certainly relieved when the big music machine was lifted onto the wagon waiting to deliver the prize to Philadelphia Church for the Wednesday night prayer service.

"Drive her slow, Jesse," said an out-of-breath Isaiah Taylor as he wiped his bald forehead with the red-checked handkerchief loaned to him by Walter Bell. "I mean for safety's sake," the portly storekeeper added as he caught the preacher's eye.

"Don't worry, Fellas, I'll take it slow. For all our sakes," Jesse said as he climbed into the driver's seat of the overloaded wagon.

As he did, he noticed a man of light build, medium height, and dark complexion with a big moustache and wide brimmed hat ride slowly down the town's dusty main street up to the tired organ-movers. His pace was slow and certain, his face stern, and his eyes were large, restless, quick and sharp. His hair was long and jet-black and hung in shiny ringlets from beneath his black hat. An ivory-handled six-gun sat in the silver studded holster on his hip. By instinct, Jesse and Brother Jeremiah both knew that he was a hired gunslinger.

"Anybody of yew gents know where I might find a fella calls himself Kid Jeremy?" asked the stranger as he spit tobacco juice at the feet of Sheriff Owen. Jesse looked at the circuit rider as he moved his hand to an empty hip.

"I used to go by that name. . . thirty some odd years ago, Mister," answered Brother Jeremiah, "before I met Jesus Christ." None of the others seemed to know what was going on.

"Yeh, the man said yew wuz a Bible-thumper," drawled the gunman as he spit at the Sheriff's feet again. "Don't reckon yew got no gun, huh, Parson?"

"He don't need a gun, Mister. What the Lord don't take care of, I handle," offered Jesse who had not yet realized that he was unarmed.

"Who might yew be, Sonny?" asked the steely-eyed man with the fancy holster and saddle.

"Name's Jesse Lane."

"Yeh. . . the man said yew might cause some trouble," countered the gunman, "but nuthin' ah cain't handle. 'Sides. . . yew ain't even heeled."

"Now hold on there, Mister. I don't allow no gun fightin' in my town," ordered Sheriff Owen.

The gunfighter looked down at the multi-colored sheriff in an expressionless manner and spit again, this time hitting Owen's boots.

"Heh!" the sheriff cried as he jumped back. By the time he looked back up, he gazed into the dark bore of the gunman's .44.

"Got no quarrel with yew, Sheriff, but for $2,000. . . one more ain't gonna make no never mind," said the gunman coldly.

"$2,000?" said Walter Bell.

"That's what I get fer killin' Kid Jeremy there. . . in a fair fight, of course. And I'll kill yew, too, Sonny, if'n yew git in the way," answered the stranger looking squarely at Jesse in the wagon.

"Well, I'll git in the way, Mister. You can count on it. Fact is you better stop me first," replied Jesse standing up tall.

"Now wait a minute, Jesse," said the foxy old preacher. "I don't want you goin' ta jail for murderin' no lousy bit of scum like him."

"What'd yew say?" asked the man gruffly.

The crafty old sermonizer hoped that the stranger would take the bait. "Son," he had once told Jesse when they were making a visit to an ornery old lady, "Sometimes ya got to let the Lord take control of your tongue and let Him talk ya out of touchy situations."

"Well, Mister, I just seen you draw. And I've seen Jesse draw. And if that's as fast as you can get that hogleg out of that fancy holster. . . as sure as stink on a skunk. . . that boy will put a bullet between your eyes before you clear leather," answered the preacher. When the old Gospel-teacher finished, he grinned big, raising his eyebrows and showing his dimples.

The gunman looked first at Jesse's expressionless face to the glimmer in the eye of the pulpit-pounder. After a full minute of silence the gunman said, "Ah bet yore blluffin', Parson. Jest tryin' to shake me."

"You willin' to bet five silver dollars?" asked Brother Jeremiah, knowing from experience the hired killer was hooked.

"How?" asked the stranger.

"Well, you hand over five silver dollars. I'll throw 'em all into the air at once. Jesse here'll draw and fire, hittin' each one smack dab in the center. . . before they start comin' down," offered the preacher with a grin. "Reckon that'll prove what I said. Your life is worth five dollars ain't it?"

Again the man paused as he chewed and thought and looked back and forth at Jesse and then the old Devil-beater. Then, he put his left hand into his vest pocket and fished out five silver coins and said, "They ain't all dollars. Don't matter none though. Cain't be did. Yore bluffin', Parson, and I'm acallin' yore bluff." The gunman pitched the coins to Brother Jeremiah.

The old Gospel-warrior inspected the coins, and then said, matter of factly, "Owen, I wonder if you'd be so kind as to let Jesse borrow your gun and holster for a short demonstration of marksmanship?"

"Sure, Preacher," answered a bewildered Sheriff Owen as he fumbled with the buckle of his holster. The other men just stood by the organ in the wagon, trying to figure out what the old minister was up to. . . and hoping some of the townsfolk might see what was going on and come to their rescue.

Jesse climbed down from the wagon and walked over to Brother Jeremiah after taking the gun belt from Sheriff Owen.

"Preacher, I ain't never done nuthin' like this afore," whispered Jesse. The preacher put his arm on Jesse's shoulder and walked to the middle of the street.

"Remember young David and Goliath, my boy," whispered Brother Jeremiah. Then he turned his head towards the heavens and said softly, "Lord, take over now." Then the veteran revivalist backed off a few steps and asked, "Ready?"

"Ready," answered Jesse confident that the Lord would steady his shaky hand. Brother Jeremiah whispered another short prayer and tossed the five coins into the air. While the coins fought against gravity, and just as they split apart, Jesse pulled the sheriff's Colt .45 from the holster and fanned the hammer to score five quick hits dead center. Then as if a part of the same motion, he spun around and pointed a cocked gun at the head of the surprised gunman who had relaxed his hand on his drawn pistol. The old circuit rider marked the spots where the coins fell and quickly rushed to pick up the disfigured shinning targets. After collecting them all, he hurried back to the gunman, who by now was quite concerned with the small cannon pointed his way.

"Care to inspect 'em, Mister?" asked Brother Jeremiah, holding the coins in his palm to the stunned gunman on horseback.

The man with the big moustache carefully and slowly picked up each coin, finding each had been struck exactly in the middle. As he picked up a small silver ring that had moments before been a dime, Brother Jeremiah broke the silence.

"Mister, if you were to die today, do you know if you'd go to Heaven?" The old preacher couldn't help but grin, even though the question was made in true sincerity.

The hired killer looked at Jesse poised to shoot, then at his fistful of mutilated coins, spit again at the sheriff's boots, dropped the coins in the dirt, and slowly, using just two fingers, placed his .44 back into his fancy holster. Sitting up straight in the saddle, the gunman reached his right hand inside his vest to his shirt pocket and took out a folded envelope, full of money. Handing it to the preacher he said, "Tell Mr. Rutledge that my momma didn't raise no fool." Then he reined his horse and slowly rode out of town, staring straight ahead and sitting tall. Jesse followed the exit of the hired killer. . . still ready to shoot should the man change his mind about leaving.

Jesse relaxed as Brother Jeremiah walked over to him. "Wasn't as hard as shootin' a whiskey glass off a cigar stuck in a bottle while looking in a mirror, but it got the job done," joked a smiling circuit rider as he slapped his protégé on the back.

"He called you Kid Jeremy, Preacher," said Jesse seriously as he unbuckled the Sheriff's gun belt and handed the whole thing back to him, "and he said he was hired to kill you. You reckon someone from the past is tryin' to get even with you now. . . after thirty years?"

Jesse had not heard the last remark the gunman had made, and neither Mr. Taylor nor Mr. Bell were paying close enough attention to catch the name of the assassin's client. The men were all talking to each other, retelling the phenomenal sight they had just witnessed. Sheriff Owen just stood by the wagon, gun belt in hand, and mouth opened wide in astonishment.

Brother Jeremiah remembered the look of hatred in the eyes of the black-clothed cowboy the night of the saloon shooting and the voice of revenge the night of the fire. Then, he recalled the words of the gunslinger.

"I don't know, Jesse," was the sad reply, "I just don't know."

****

Norm Taylor, co-owner of the Four Aces, refolded his bar towel. Then, while watching Jeff Rutledge from the corner of his eye, he pretended to wipe the already spotless bar.

Rutledge was bent over the bar in Taylor's Four Aces, nursing a glass of beer whose head had evaporated, when one of the local cowboys walked through the white swinging doors. The foreman of the Double Bar TB had ridden into town early and had been drinking at the Four Aces nearly all day.

At first, no one noticed the rage that filled the grey-blue eyes of the young black-leather-vested man who listened with the others of the unbelievable tale of the shooting exhibition put on by Jesse Lane earlier that day. Rutledge gulped his whiskey with a vengeance as he heard of the man with the ivory-handled six shooter backing down from the sure death confrontation with the preacher's side-kick.

"Shut up!" screamed Rutledge as he hurled his empty whiskey glass through the large mirror in front of him. The sound of breaking glass quickly silenced the men in the half-darkened saloon.

"But he did it, Mr. Jeff," said the frightened cow-hand, "Look here. . . this here's one of the silver dollars that Jesse shot clean through the middle!"

"Shut your mouth tight, Boy, or I'll shut it for you, you bladder-brained know-it-all! I'll put everyone of you jug-heads in that bone orchard outside of town!" shouted Rutledge in a voice that made the veins in his neck and eyes bulge out so much that the men in the Four Aces thought for sure that he was gonna bust.

Jeff was screaming louder than anyone had ever heard before. The effects of the drink and the hatred in his heart for the old circuit rider had transformed him into a wild fury turned loose, ready to kill at the slightest provocation.

171

No one moved a muscle as the enraged ranch-hand grabbed the bottle from the bar, drew his pistol and seemed to dare the occupants of the room to even blink an eye. Jeff Rutledge had been known to carry violence with him, but not one of his compadres had ever witnessed him brandishing his six-gun in such a merciless and impulsive manner that regarded the men in front of him as impediments in his path, to be gunned down for no apparent reason.

Rutledge, breathing heavily and through clinched teeth muttered something unintelligible to those around him with a devilish guttural noise. Then, he suddenly stood tall, re-holstered his gun, straightened his black-leather vest, and slowly walked through the crowd of frightened, speechless men into the darkness of the cool autumn evening.

The bartender of the Four Aces was the first to break the silence in the room, "Well, Boys, I reckon ol' Jeff's on the shoot tonight! Lawd have mercy on any fool who crosses his path."

The crowd of men in the saloon returned to their frivolous pursuits, shaking their heads in agreement with the barkeep and prophesying the headlines in the paper within a few days after Rutledge brought an end to someone. Of course, the disgruntled drover might calm down and not hurt anyone. . . but few believed that to be any kind of possibility.

Outside, the frustrated cowhand trembled.

"There's a darkness hangin' over me, Ma," moaned the tortured cowboy aloud as he gazed into the stars from the porch of Taylor's saloon, "and a cold wind's blowin' away my dreams."

Then he slowly mounted his horse and rode off into the night. . . alone.

****

Chapter Seventeen

The Shooting

Miss Hattie's imported pump organ never sounded as clear and beautiful as it did with Miss Gayle pressing the keyboard to form the musical notes of "Bringing In the Sheaves". The electrifying strains of Gospel music flooded the streets of Miller's Bluff on the cloudless, star-filled, Wednesday night before Thanksgiving. All those in attendance, members of Philadelphia Church and non-members alike, could feel the excitement of the evening rise with each chorus. There seemed to be something in the air that had folks convinced that this would be a Thanksgiving that would not be soon forgotten.

With the completion of the last song, Brother Jeremiah stepped up to the large, oak pulpit Sheriff Owen had built, but he remained silent for just a moment as he delicately ran his hand across the top of the speaker's table. Then he stepped backwards one step and slowly looked around the room at the work done by a one-time divided community. As he gazed at the organ in the corner, he shook his head, a broad grin on his face, and let out a loud, ear-splitting shout of ecstasy.

"God. . . has been good to us!. . . but you ain't seen nuthin' yet!" he said to a chorus of amens led by Sheriff Owen's bass voice.

Again, he shouted at the top of his lungs, and, looking towards Heaven with hands raised, continued, "This. . . is just the beginning."

Suddenly the back doors of the little church building burst open, and there stood a very drunken Jeff Rutledge. With pistol drawn and cocked and aimed directly at the old preacher, Rutledge announced loudly, "No, it ain't, Mister Preacher Kid Jeremy. . . this is the end. . . for you!"

Jesse Lane, who had taken to wearing his six-gun again since the incident with the gunslinger, jumped quickly to his feet, hand on the big iron at his side, ready to draw. His movement was met promptly by a shot which barely missed him and lodged in the organ. The ladies screamed and ducked, along with most of the men and the children. Sheriff Owen sat near the front, mouth gaping in disbelief, unarmed and feeling so useless. He looked towards Walter Bell, but got no indication from the shocked storekeeper as to what to do. The lawman quickly panned the congregation to see if anyone might offer some resistance. . . but they were all scared belly green.

"Don't try anything, Lane," commanded Rutledge. "Nobody's that fast. And I don't wanna kill you. . . yet!"

The full-as-a-tick cowhand staggered a couple of steps forward past terrified men and women on either side of him, and took a large mouthful of whiskey from the nearly empty bottle he carried.

Brother Jeremiah, stepping from behind the new pulpit, spoke calmly, "Put the gun down, Jeff. You don't want ta hurt anybody."

"I wanna hurt you, Preacher Man!" screamed Rutledge as he threw the bottle of whiskey against the pulpit sending bits of glass and whiskey spraying across the front of the room.

"Why?" pleaded Miss Gayle. "He's never hurt you!"

The emerald-green eyes of the beautiful schoolmarm brimmed with tears as she feared the worst from the inebriated ranch hand.

"He hurt my ma!" Rutledge screamed back to the young educator. "Thirty years ago. You remember Becky Williams, Mister Fast-Talkin'-Bible-Man? You told her you loved her, and then ran off and left her. For twenty years she pined for you. She died hoping to see you again. . . but you never came back!"

Rutledge staggered forward a little more while reaching into his shirt pocket. "She followed yore movements close fer awhile," he continued, holding what looked to be an old, worn-out diary. "Then she lost track of you. She called you 'my Preacher'. Wrote about yore fancy shootin' as Kid Jeremy, too. 'Twuz the trick shot at the saloon that made me know who yew wuz."

Rutledge tossed the diary into the lap of Miss Ida who sat in a chair to his left.

"I swore the day they buried my ma that I'd find you someday and kill you slow, like you did her," continued the hate-filled cowboy.

Tears, combined with the effects of the 'who-hit-John', began to blur the angry wrangler's vision. And the hatred in his heart made his blood boil.

"I. . . I'm sorry, Boy. I. . . never knew," the old circuit rider said softly.

"Yew never knew," screamed Rutledge, " 'cuz she wuz afeared it'd destroy yew if folks knew that the Big Preachin' Man had a son by an unmarried saloon girl!"

The crowd murmured together as heads began to peek up from their hiding places. Jesse stared at Brother Jeremiah in quiet disbelief. The old Bible-teacher moved close towards the broken human in front of him that hatred had ravaged for so many years. He tucked his Bible under his left arm and extended his right hand.

"Give me the gun, Jeff," Brother Jeremiah said calmly as he stared straight into those grey-blue eyes. "I understand how you must feel. I knew your ma before I met Jesus. She was one of my girls, all right, but I loved her as much as any man could love a woman. Give me the gun, Jeff."

Brother Jeremiah walked slowly towards the drunken young man set on vengeance. The veteran Bible-expositor was trying his best to keep the angry cowboy calm while not getting anyone in his congregation hurt as a result of doing something that might set Rutledge off.

"Your ma didn't want to be a preacher's wife," continued the old circuit rider, advancing slowly towards his adversary. "I had to leave her. But I did love her. I always have loved her. Give me the gun, Jeff."

The old preacher spoke more sternly the closer he got to the young cowboy. Jesse was as tense as a tightly wound watch spring, ready to defend the old Psalm-singer if need be. As soon as Brother Jeremiah's body blocked Rutledge's view of the one-time-wanna-be gunman, Jesse moved his hand atop his revolver.

"Yore a liar!" growled the teary-eyed, drunken Rutledge as he raised his pistol to shoulder length, slowly cocked the hammer, and took careful aim.

"I ain't gonna listen to yore lies no more! Nobody is! Prepare to finally feel the wrath of Jeff Rutledge!!!"

"No!!" shouted Jesse as time for all in the little church building began to move at a snail's pace.

Jesse, horrified by the sight in front of him, instinctively drew his gun and fired two rounds just as the puff of smoke left the barrel of Jeff Rutledge's Schofield. The almost simultaneous triple explosions coupled with the screams of terrified innocent bystanders formed a nightmarish discord totally foreign to a House of Prayer. All three lead projectiles hit true, causing the old circuit rider's and young Rutledge's bodies to hurdle through the air.

The bullet from Rutledge's blast had passed through the veteran sermonizer and lodged in the big oak pulpit which actually broke Brother Jeremiah's fall. The wounded preacher still clutched his Bible as he slid down the pulpit to a sitting position, a dazed, foreign look on his face.

The impact of Jesse's two shots sent Rutledge sprawling helplessly into the laps of Walter Bell and his wife, Martha, breaking the chairs in which they were sitting.

In the momentary confusion of screams and sobs, Jesse felt for the first time the agonizing, gut-tearing pain that comes with the knowledge that one has just taken another human life. As he searched for a place to deposit his churning insides, he looked at Brother Jeremiah, propped against the pulpit, bleeding profusely from the hole in his chest.

Sheriff Owen was among the first to Rutledge, and so turned his body over after disarming the enraged ranch-hand.

Rutledge grimaced in pain and whispered, "Took me three times, but I did it." Then a frightening look came into his cold, grey-blue eyes as he screamed and kicked, "The fire. . . somebody put out the fire!. . . don't let 'em take me!. . ." And with one final pitiful gasp, he slipped into eternity.

Miss Gayle had rushed to the old preacher's side as quickly as the gangly lawman had reacted to the mortally wounded disturber of the church service.

"Somebody get the preacher to the doc, quickly!" she cried.

Three men close by picked up the bleeding, still conscious Bible-expounder and quickly carried him down the aisle and out the doors to the doc's office which was only about fifty yards away.

Jesse, gun still in hand at his side, followed along behind the men with Miss Gayle and Miss Ida, as the previously worshiping crowd quickly exited the palace of death. Gayle stopped just long enough to pick up the diary that Rutledge had tossed away just before shooting the old preacher. The personal history book had fallen out of Miss Ida's lap when she had jumped up to offer aid and comfort to Martha Bell. Instinctively, the young teacher thought the diary might hold a clue as to the motive of Rutledge's actions.

Just outside, Jesse paused by a water trough as the troupe continued their journey down the street. As he turned to see still frightened people evacuating the church building, weeping and comforting one another, his eye caught the movement of something on the roof. Straining his eyes in the moonlight, he thought he could vaguely make out the form of a large bird of some kind, resting near the church steeple.

Still sick to his stomach over the night's event, he turned towards the chambers where his wounded friend had been taken. As he moved slowly toward the doc's office, he purposely dropped his Colt into the trough at his side while reaching down to pick up the old worn, yellow-paged, blood-stained Bible of the circuit rider.

****

Several of Miller's Bluff citizens followed the men carrying the old preacher's body to Doc Evans' office while most of the crowd went to their respective homes to pray and speculate on what they had just witnessed. As Jesse approached the rear of the small group of men discussing what could have caused Rutledge to do such a dastardly deed, the young cowboy paused for just a moment and then half stumbled into the dark alley between the physician's office and the Cattlemen's Club. Unseen in the shadows of the darkest night Jesse had ever experienced, the young reputation-seeker dropped to his knees to do the only thing he could think of that might help his wounded friend. . . pray.

By the time Jesse walked into the doc's office, about an hour had passed since the shooting in the church, and the old warrior for the Lord's wounds had been bandaged, and he was lying peacefully in the small room at the rear of the office that served as a hospital. Doc Evans came out of the room shaking his head.

"How is he, Doc?" inquired Jesse.

"Bullet nipped an artery and punctured his left lung. I don't know what's keepin' him alive," stated the white-haired physician, shaking his head and rubbing his chin whiskers.

"Can I see him?" asked Jesse.

"He's asleep now. But you can go in. He needs a lot of rest if he's going to make it. Rest and prayer," mumbled Doc Evans.

Jesse opened the door slightly and saw Miss Gayle sitting beside the old preacher, who rested calmly even though he seemed to be having difficulty breathing. She held his right hand in both of her own; despite her eyes being closed, tears streamed down her face as she mumbled a prayer for the recovery of the old Bible-thumper. The bandage had already turned a deep crimson from the wound, indicating that Doc Evans was not completely successful in patching up the old soul-wrangler.

The young school-marm's prayer was interrupted by the squeaking of the hinges on Doc Evans' door as Jesse opened the door widely and entered the room. Neither Jesse nor Miss Gayle said a word. Both simply gazed deeply into the eyes of the other, sensing the hurt and shock shared by them as well as the whole town. Jesse leaned over and placed the aging saddle-bag parson's Bible under his left hand.

****

Several hours had passed since the shooting had disturbed the Philadelphia Church's first Thanksgiving service. A large crowd of people had gathered on the porch of Doc Evans' office, awaiting news of the condition of Brother Jeremiah. Most had spent much of the night praying for God's healing of the veteran preacher.

Inside the small hospital room, Miss Gayle had dozed off while Jesse stood at the east window and just stared into space.

"Jesse," whispered Brother Jeremiah, "come here."

The young cowboy hurried over to the fallen soldier-of-the-cross without waking an exhausted Miss Gayle.

"Jesse," said the old preacher, gasping for air, "my time. . . is come. . . my Lord awaits. . . here. . . take good care of this. . . it's yours now."

Brother Jeremiah, quite pale from the loss of blood, picked up his old, worn-out Bible with both hands, pressed it to his lips, and handed it to Jesse.

"Take it, Jesse," repeated the dying circuit rider, "read it. . . let God speak to you. . . through His Word. . . believe it. . . live by it. . . take it."

Miss Gayle awoke just as Jesse reached out a shaky hand to take the oversized, well-read Bible from the old servant of God.

"The mantle is passed," grinned Brother Jeremiah.

With that grin still on his face, the old circuit rider closed his eyes and began a new walk in a land where there is no death or pain. Brother Jeremiah had served his Lord faithfully for many years. He held no wealth or possessions that would amount to anything in this world, but the old revivalist was headed to a place where gold is so plentiful, they use it to pave the streets. This underappreciated servant of the Lord left no great record of exploration, but he had logged thousands of miles riding the hills, valleys, swamps, and prairies of Texas and Louisiana searching for lost souls. His obituary would not grace the pages of the nation's largest newspapers nor would his life's story be highlighted in one of those dime novels so popular with folks back East, but his passing would be heralded by the angels in Heaven.

Jesse, tears in his eyes, clutched his inheritance, rose slowly, and walked through the door into the pre-dawn blackness. Jesse's stepping onto the porch of Doc Evans' office caused the admirers of the grey-haired preacher to crowd close to the young man who just a few hours before had used the only means at his disposal to try and stop the ruthless murder of a close friend and teacher. No words were exchanged as Jesse looked through tear-filled eyes of grief at Walter Bell and Isaiah Taylor and Sheriff Owen and the other residents of Miller's Bluff who had received healing of an emotional illness that had strained the life and limited the growth of the small central Texas community.

Jesse swallowed a large knot that welled up in his throat as those huddled in the early morning broke into soft sobs at the sight of the old preacher's blood-stained Bible. The former cowboy made his way through the crowd of mourners toward the church building that had been the scene of an unimaginable horror the night before. He had a head full of questions. . . all beginning with 'why'.

There was no time for Jesse to ride off into the gentle rolling hills to the west of the little, central Texas farm community. Besides, the young convert didn't feel much like going anywhere. What he wanted was to turn back the clock a few hours to a time before the awful shootings the night before. Thanksgiving Day had never looked so bleak for the former-reputation-seeker. Jesse had begun to change his mind a bit about his future and his well-thought-out plans. He had actually begun to listen more closely to the old glory roader, dreaming of imitating the mannerisms of his "daddy-in-the-Lord", as the young ranch-hand would eventually refer to Brother Jeremiah. Now, all of those dreams seemed to be vanishing as the reality of his actions brought him back to the real world.

****

Chapter Eighteen

The Decision

J esse Lane sat in the front row of chairs in Philadelphia Church, gazing red-eyed at the big oak pulpit with the cross carved on the front, as the sun sent its orange rays above the horizon surrounding Miller's Bluff, Texas. He had been sitting that way for hours, just staring at the blood-stained cross on the pulpit. Brother Jeremiah's Bible lay closed on top of the handmade preacher's stand. The young cowboy had been trying to sort out the thousand and one questions racing through his mind and the haunting guilt of his actions the previous night. Jesse had never been the kind to let his emotions rule his life, but he could feel an inner war going on that he couldn't explain, nor did he know how to cope with his feelings about Brother Jeremiah and Jeff Rutledge and Little Jimmy. . . and Miss Gayle.

Finally, in desperation, Jesse spoke aloud as if Someone could hear his words.

"OK, Lord. . . so what'll I do now?" he began. "That old preacher sure has messed up my life good. All things totaled, I don't know much about much of anything compared to other folks. I know how to tote a gun and how to point it. Things sure wuz much simpler afore he showed up."

Jesse stood and paced back and forth in front of the pulpit, silently shaking his head. After several minutes he stopped and looked straight at the hardened reddish-brown streaks of life that seemed to be coming directly out of the carved cross.

"Brother Jeremiah gave me his Bible so's I'd be a preacher like him, didn't he? Did You put him up to that? Surely that's not right. I killed a man last night," Jesse said, tears returning to his already reddened eyes. "Who'd listen to a killer?"

Jesse began pacing again, but this time he walked around the pulpit and stood looking out over the empty room of dislodged and overturned chairs. His optical survey stopped as he focused upon two broken chairs beside a dried pool of similar reddish-brown type stain flowing from the cross on the pulpit. Saddened by the visions of last night and the echo of Jeff Rutledge's final screams, Jesse began randomly turning pages in the old Bible. He paid little attention to the notes the self-taught Bible-thumper had scribbled in the margins of the yellowed pages. Then by accident, he opened the well-used Scriptures to Second Kings, chapter two. There in the bottom margin were the hastily scribbled words, "The Mantle Is Passed". Jesse recognized those as the last words Brother Jeremiah had spoken. Intrigued, he read on: "1) Mantle of Life, 2) Mantle of Power, 3) Mantle of Service." Then to his utter amazement, he saw the words, "Elijah=me; Elisha=Jesse."

"What did that old preacher have in mind?" Jesse questioned himself aloud. Then he very carefully and slowly began to read the second chapter aloud.

The young cowboy was so engrossed with the story he did not notice Miss Gayle slip into the room and sit down on the back row. Miss Gayle listened to Jesse read, and she heard his comments, and immediately recognized the problem Jesse was having. For the first time in several hours, the young instructor of Miller's Bluff's children smiled.

"Sounds pretty much up to date to me," commented Miss Gayle.

Startled by the girl's voice, Jesse's reflex again moved his hand to his hip.

"How long you been there?" asked the embarrassed, young man.

"Just awhile," she answered. " 'Been lookin' all over for ya. Kinda figured you'd be in here. You reckon Brother Jeremiah had planned on trainin' you to take his place someday?"

"Maybe. Anyways. . . don't matter now. . . after last night," answered Jesse, hanging his head in disgust.

"What do you mean?" inquired the young, green-eyed school-teacher as she walked down the aisle towards the pulpit and her young cowboy.

"I mean, God wouldn't want to use no killer to be a preacher. . . if I wuz thinkin' about it," came the reply.

Jesse made the statement hoping that Gayle would have the answers to the questions he'd been asking himself most of the morning.

"Did Brother Jeremiah ever tell you the story about David and Goliath?" asked the young teacher as she sat in a chair close to the pulpit. "Or about Elijah and the prophets of Baal?. . .or about Abraham?. . . or the Apostle Paul?"

Gayle grinned at her chosen life-partner in much the same way that the old circuit rider used to grin when he was about to make a big point.

"No. . . at least I don't remember. . . he did mention David and Goliath a few days ago," replied Jesse with his brow deeply furrowed because he did not know exactly what Gayle was trying to say.

"Those fellas I mentioned killed God's enemies but were used by God to bring people to Him," mentioned the auburn-haired beauty. "How much do you know about Brother Jeremiah's life?" asked Gayle.

"Not much. I knew folks called him Kid Jeremy thirty-some-odd years ago. And I know he was good with a gun," answered Jesse.

"He ever tell you about the men he killed before he met Jesus? It's all here in this diary that Jeff Rutledge had. But there's a scripture beside the entry. Look up Mark 3:28 in that Bible, Jesse," suggested Miss Gayle.

"Mark. . . what?. . . where is it? The front or the back?" asked a confused Jesse rather shyly. Jesse was too frustrated to be embarrassed at his ignorance of God's Word.

"Oh, here. . . let me do it for you," offered Miss Gayle, approaching the platform. Turning the pages until she found the reference she read, "Verily I say unto you, all sins shall be forgiven unto the sons of men. . .'"

"Look!" cried Jesse, "he circled the words 'all sins' and put 'even killin' folks' out to the side here. But how did Jeff's ma know about that?"

"Well, the diary says that Brother Jeremiah came to her one day and explained what had happened to him, and the decision he had made to preach. Evidently he musta had the same questions you have now," answered Miss Gayle softly.

"Kinda makes you think that old preacher knew I'd need that verse, huh," said the puzzled, young cowboy.

"You know, Jeff made some entries in here, too," continued Gayle. "You need to read what he wrote! Why, it's enough to make a preacher cuss a blue streak," she said with a smile. "He tells all about how he kept the feud a goin' by destroyin' things of Mr. Taylor's and Mr. Bell's," continued the pretty school teacher. "Jeff was gettin' protection money from both of 'em. . . made 'em pay through the nose, too! Jeff stole mavericks from all the ranchers in the area. . . tore down their fences to make it look like the cattle had done it. . . then he'd drift a bunch of cattle out of one pasture into another and separate the calves and then put his brand on 'em. Says here in this little book that he hid almost 200 yearlings in a wooded area near the land he wanted to buy."

Philadelphia Church's pretty piano player paused for a moment to let that information settle in Jesse's head. Jesse didn't give any indication that he was listening much. . . for the young cowboy just stared at Brother Jeremiah's open Bible lying on the pulpit in front of him and braced himself against the wooden lectern with stiff arms.

Gayle stood behind her man and gently placed her left hand on his shoulder and continued the story.

"Jeff also wrote about the fire. . . and the ambush down to the creek that killed Little Jimmy. Rutledge was responsible for both of those events. Why he even murdered old Ike last winter just to get his land. Remember the rumors of him skinnin' a fella in Tennessee? Well it wasn't in Tennessee; it was in Louisiana. Jeff was just no good from start to finish. The years just soured him up like a persimmon."

Miss Gayle stopped to see if Jesse was listening. Jesse just continued staring at the Bible in front of him. There was silence for awhile.

"Sure is strange how things work out," insisted Miss Gayle with a deep sigh.

"Yeh," said Jesse slowly, "still, I don't know."

"Don't know what?" asked the young lady.

"Don't know nuthin' about the Bible. . . or preachin'. . . or even if God really wants me to do it!" said a frustrated Jesse. Again he started pacing nervously.

Miss Gayle began trying to console Jesse again. "Mr. Bell and all the other folks said you did what you had to do. Sheriff Owen told some of the folks that he was rulin' the shootin' self defense, because Jeff threatened to kill you, too. Everybody there heard him. Nobody blames you or thinks little of you, Jesse. Even Mr. Taylor said you sure saved the town a lot of fuss and bother of havin' a trial and a hangin' when you took Jeff last night. You did what you had to do. . . the only thing you could do. The strain of years of pent up bitterness just made something snap inside Jeff's head. He went crazy. No tellin' how many other folks he mighta hurt if you hadn't stopped him."

Miss Gayle placed her hand on Jesse's shoulder again and continued her discourse. "The Bible says God can forgive you, and none of us think you did anything that needs forgivin'. But the big question is can you forgive yourself?"

Jesse looked into the sparkling green eyes of the woman he loved and then began to walk slowly back and forth across the small platform again. Then the young seeker-of-truth stepped onto the floor to inspect the blood-stained cross on the front of the home-made preacher's stand. Jesse touched the stain ever so gently and ran his fingers to the bottom of the cross where the circuit rider's blood had pooled.

Miss Gayle spoke frankly again about God's forgiveness and His Will as she watched Jesse pace. Then Jesse walked behind the sacred desk once more and placed a hand on the Bible. He looked straight into Miss Gayle's big green eyes as if to say something worth listening to. Instead, he just sighed and began staring again at the opened book in front of him, trying to reason within his mind the seriousness of the decision he faced. The words on the page in front of him all ran together into one big blur as Jesse heard the last words of the dying preacher echo through his head. . . 'the mantle is passed'. . . 'the mantle is passed'.

"Brother Jeremiah said that God would speak to me through His Word," Jesse said more to himself than to the young school-marm standing at his side. Jesse took the Bible in both hands and raised his eyes toward the Heavens. "Lord, I don't wanna keep on wonderin'. So, please just tell me now what You want me to do," prayed the young cowboy.

Jesse then closed his eyes and opened the Book at random. With his eyes still closed, he placed his finger on a worn page. Opening his eyes, he read, "How then shall they call on Him in whom they have not believed? And how shall they believe in Him of whom they have not heard? And how shall they hear without. . . a preacher?" Jesse looked puzzled.

Miss Gayle grinned, "That answer your question?"

"Coulda just been a coincidence. I think I'll try it again," said Jesse. Again, the young cowhand closed his eyes, opened the Bible, and pointed to the page in front of him. "For after that in the wisdom of God, the world by wisdom knew not God, it pleased God by the foolishness of. . . preaching. . . to save them that believe," Jesse read slowly.

Miss Gayle giggled, but quickly restrained herself. "You gonna try again, Jesse?" she asked, smiling.

"No," breathed Jesse heavily, "probably just find a verse with my name in it that has to do with preachin'. Reckon I'll have to change my plans a lot. 'Specially all the plans I had for us."

Jesse grinned the way Brother Jeremiah did when he was 'settin' someone up for the kill.'

"For us?" echoed Miss Gayle, her eyes sparkling with interest. "What plans did you have for us? And why would they be changed?"

Jesse, grinning, closed the old, worn-out Bible and walked down the aisle towards the door, pretending to ignore the young educator.

"Jesse. . . Jesse!. . . Jesse Aaron Lane!. . . you come back here this minute and explain what you meant by what you just said! Jesse. . . do you hear me?" Miss Gayle didn't know whether she should be angry or happy, but she followed the future preacher out the door.

****

Tom McKelroy stepped down from his buckskin horse and walked slowly to the two-room house he shared with his young, pregnant bride, Sarah. The former hay-roller from Georgia had come to the hills of north Louisiana to preach the Gospel of Jesus Christ, just as Brother Jeremiah had expected him to do. On this first day of April in 1879, his mind was occupied with news he had received from his cousin, Mark McClure, who worked on a large ranch in the Texas Panhandle.

"Why so grim, Husband?" asked his smiling bride as her circuit rider entered their small house and hung his hat on the wooden peg near the door.

"It's Mark's letter, Darlin'," answered the tall man of the cloth.

Sarah placed her hand on her slightly swollen belly. The young, transplanted-Bostonian lost her usual smile as she placed parts of their usual daily lunch on the table. The blonde lady from Beantown recalled how disturbed her husband had become when the letter had first arrived.

Sarah had never met Mark, but Tom had mentioned that the serious-minded young man had become a loner long before his twenty-second birthday. The McClure side of the McKelroy family had served their country in the army since the first McClure, Horatio Justice McClure, had sailed from Scotland to the colonies just before the Revolution. Tom had described the last living member of that branch of the family as being tall, muscular, smart, and a dead shot. Mark had lived with the McKelroy's for awhile in Georgia and had asked Christ to be his savior after hearing Tom practice one of his first sermons out in a half-cleared forest near the family cabin. Except for Tom and Mark, the McKelroys were just plain farmers who raised bees and did a little carpentry work to subsidize their income.

The slender, blue-eyed bride of the saddlebag-clergyman from Georgia had only recently learned of her future blessing from the Lord, and she began to fear her husband's itchy feet. Mark had written that his employer's town was not known for its morality, especially during cattle season which lasted from late spring to mid-fall. Drovers from various parts of Texas and New Mexico would pass through town or nearby on their way to the cattle markets in Kansas. Few had any manners, most were vulgar in their speech and their actions. They slept wherever they wanted to, relieved themselves wherever they wanted to, and even shot each other over the silliest of arguments. . . whenever they wanted to. Mark had mentioned the feeling of dread due to the fact that there were always three or more fresh graves dug on Boot Hill awaiting the next victims of some cold-blooded killing.

"A fella can sure 'nough get hardened, here," wrote the young Christian cowpoke. "Seein' a man shot down over the turn of a card or a joke gone bad is nothing unusual."

"Despite the riff-raff and border hoodlums and women of the night who sometime live in this frontier trail-town," wrote the former plow-pusher from Georgia, "Franklinton is actually quiet in the daytime. The faint bawlin' of cows grazin' on Mr. Franklin's range is the most common sound. The only folks who walk the streets during the daylight hours are a few cowhands buyin' supplies or the dozen or so hard-workin' merchants who display their wares for the handful of townsfolk to gwak at. But come the first shades of twilight, the drunken fools and other low-lifes around the area come out of their holes, and the music in the saloons start up. Within an hour or so, tanked-up cowboys and soldiers roam the streets, shootin' at anythin' that catches their fancy as a target. The most minor brawl in a saloon might end up with somebody gettin' killed."

Grave diggers were kept busy, Mark had explained, mostly working at night when it was cooler to have graves ready for burying the next morning at sunrise. . . in a funeral procession where the unfortunate victim was carried through town on a plank followed by half-naked saloon girls enticing the spectators along the way.

Most of these women lived in the red light district just south of town dubbed "Heaven's Delight". Occasionally, a cowboy who showed one of the ladies too much gold might cross the little creek to never be heard from again. A large stone tied around his neck made for a watery grave and eliminated the necessity for a public burial.

Added to the repugnant actions of the traveling cowboys were the gamblers who rode into town set on taking the cowhands for every penny they had earned. Worst of all. . . there was no church, no preacher, no semblance of Christianity among any of the towns-folk or the pilgrims who stayed awhile. . . mostly out of fear of being run out of town on a rail. . . or being tarred and feathered. . . or both. . . or just shot.

Fact was. . . most of that part of the Panhandle that bordered the New Mexico territory was overflowing with cowhands and soldiers eager to drink and gamble away their pay. It was a place frequented by dishonest men of every kind and crudely attired "half-civilized" men and women who wore thick layers of dirt over their gaudy homespun outfits. In addition, there was very little law, except that enforced by the strongest ranchers in the area. And Franklinton was run by one man who dreamed of owning the biggest ranch in Texas. Willie Franklin wanted an open town where the social outcasts of the area could spend their money on bad whiskey and loose women so long as most of the profits from the entertainment centers came to him.

Tom and Sarah had prayed over the letter asking God's pro-tection for their young kinsman. They prayed that the Lord would send someone to the Godless, little frontier town. The tall, former hay-stacker had mentioned to his church his concern for the folks of Franklinton, too. And he had written his mentor, Brother Jeremiah, several times about the situation, hoping that the old frock-coat would have a simple solution to Mark's problem.

Sarah had noticed a look in her husband's eyes when they spoke about Mark and Franklinton's lack of spiritual leadership. Her sister, Ruth, had apparently noticed the same look in Sarah's eyes just before the slender blonde announced to her family that she was leaving Boston to tour the South with a traveling evangelistic team for a year. Ruth had tried to talk her younger sister out of making the trip, but Sarah had insisted that God was calling her to make the missionary journey.

That was over two years ago. The young songstress made the journey and eventually met Tom after singing at a revival in Shreveport. She had not returned to her hometown. The young preacher's wife knew that her circuit rider was struggling with a decision, but surely the Lord would not lead them away from their comfortable ministry in north Louisiana. . . especially now that she was with child.

****

Not many folks were up as the sun rose on the lone, young rider with the long black coat as his old Appaloosa topped the crest of the hill outside of a small farm community in central Texas. The rider, with reins in one hand and a worn-out Bible in the other, was headed back to his home base in Miller's Bluff after two weeks of riding from one small town to another preaching, singing, marrying folks, burying some others, and baptizing in creeks and streams wherever the need arose. The young preacher had not taken his Colt .45 with him, for the ways of the gun no longer intrigued this man of the cloth. Profane roustabouts fell into respectful silence when he approached.

Jesse Lane stood a man among men, kindly and gentle, yet if need be, his soft, blue eyes could turn to steel. Occasionally, the young Bible-expositor was forced to display his expertise with a six-gun. . . perform some "trick" that highlighted his skills of marksmanship, but he had not pulled a weapon on another man since that fateful night in November of 1878.

Over the last few months, Jesse's life had taken on a whole new sense of value from being a seeker of a reputation backed by a fast-draw to focusing on another world, a place where the souls of men could find peace and rest. The young Bible-beater was determined to live for that world now. Jesse spent two weeks each month in Miller's Bluff and two weeks ministering to folks in small towns scattered around Williamson and Bell Counties.

Down below, the young Scripture-proclaimer could see the outline of the tall, white steeple on the building in which many people had gained knowledge of Jesus Christ and His love. Sitting on the steps of the Philadelphia Church was the auburn-haired, green-eyed, schoolmarm wife of the young preacher waiting expectantly for the return of her circuit rider.

****

Chapter Nineteen

The Mission

Sarah McKelroy looked like death warmed over as she struggled to sit upright in the swaying wagon driven by her preacher husband, Tom. Her face was hidden by the shadow of the large calico sunbonnet tied tightly beneath her chin. She wore a plain dress of Puritan black which she had sewn together herself the day after her baby girl had been born dead.

The McKelroy's had traveled by stagecoach from Shreveport, Louisiana, as far as Salado, Texas, before Sarah had gone into labor, forcing the young missionary couple to put up at Stagecoach Inn. A doctor had been dispatched, but he had arrived too late to save the baby. Two days later, Tom McKelrory bought a wagon and a load of provisions, and with his weak, unrecooperated wife, set out to cover the twenty remaining miles left on their journey to find their old circuit riding friend, Brother Jeremiah, whom Tom hoped would help him establish a church in Franklinton, a city of pure cussedness in the Texas Panhandle. Tom had not had any return-correspondence with his aging mentor for several months nor had he heard of Brother Jeremiah having been shot down by the vengeful and murderous, Jeff Rutledge, the year before.

Tom McKelroy's eyes were shinning brightly as he drove the big prairie schooner to the white church building at the end of Miller's

Bluff's main street. Sarah breathed a silent prayer of thanksgiving that the jarring wagon ride was finally over. Tom paid no attention to the name on the sign in front of the one-room House of Worship known by all the townsfolk as Philadelphia Church. With one smooth move, the big man leaped to the ground and tied the lead mule to the closest hitchin' post. As Tom bounded onto the bottom steps, Jesse Lane, the second pastor of Philadelphia Church, and his young, pregnant wife, Gayle, stepped through the large, blue door onto the porch.

"Oh, excuse me, Sir," said a startled Tom, "is the preacher in?"

"I'm the preacher. Jesse Lane's the name," answered the young parson while extending his hand to Tom.

Tom shook Jesse's hand while looking at his wife, Sarah, still sitting on the wagon seat. Sarah, overhearing the conversation between the two men of God, closed her eyes and silently prayed that her beloved husband could still get his pastorate back at the two churches they had left in the hills of north Louisiana.

With a puzzled tone Tom inquired, "Where's Brother Jeremiah? I was under the impression that he was here in Miller's Bluff."

Both Jesse and Gayle dropped their heads. Then Jesse spoke as he glanced from Tom to Sarah. "You folks knew Brother Jeremiah did you?"

"Well, I do," answered Tom. "My wife there, Sarah, hasn't met him yet." Tom smiled his broadest, Georgian-country smile and added, "That old preacher sure changed my life."

"Jesse," said Gayle softly, "perhaps these folks would be more comfortable inside. . . out of the sun."

The young school teacher noticed the look of relief on the countenance of the stern-faced blonde lady perched in such a refined manner atop the wagon.

"Of course," said Jesse, "Pardon my lack of manners, Sir. Please, won't you and your wife come inside the parsonage here and sit a spell. You wouldn't by any chance be Tom McKelroy would you?"

"Why, yes, I am," answered Tom in his deep-southern drawl as he helped Sarah descend her wagon seat. An exhausted Sarah searched her husband's eyes for any sign of dread that the two had started their journey westward. She saw none.

"Come with me, Ma'am," said Gayle as she took Sarah's cold hands in hers. "You can wash up a bit inside. . . and rest a spell."

Sarah saw a genuine concern in the sparkling green eyes of the young woman who helped her walk the ten feet or so to a small, white house built by town folks as a parsonage for their young preacher and his new wife. Sarah paused momentarily to admire the flowers planted near the front porch. . . and the two rocking chairs sitting on either side of a small table to the left of the front door. She also noticed the delicate curtains framing the windows. At last she thought, they were back in civilization.

"I understand you and Brother Jeremiah crossed paths a few years back on a riverboat," ventured Jesse, testing the young man he escorted into his residence.

"Yes, Sir," stated Tom, "probably one of the best things that ever happened to me."

Tom began to relate the story of his meeting with Brother Jeremiah aboard the *Delta Queen* as the two young preachers followed their wives into the parsonage. Tom sat on the couch in the front room as Gayle excused herself and Sarah so that the frail-looking lady could refresh herself. Sarah had heard the story so many times, she could have told it.

Tom continued to explain how he had come to realize that there was more to life than card games and fancy dressed women. The former plowboy had given his life to Christ and traded his extravagant wardrobe for a broad-brimmed hat and a plain, black suit. He traded in his deck of 52 for a book of 66 and bid farewell to his famed *Delta Queen* for a horse on which he would eventually ride between two north Louisiana country churches. The only hold back to the "old days" was the massive gold watch he carried. The watch was a European-made Jurgensen that cost $1,000, with a one-carat diamond set in its stem. He had won the prize in his first all night poker game and considered it his good luck charm.

"I wrote Brother Jeremiah back almost a year ago tellin' him I had a favor to ask. I'd like him to help me start a church in Franklinton. So, if you could tell me where I might find him, I'd be much obliged," commented Tom.

Jesse swallowed hard and rubbed his chin before he answered slowly, "Brother Jeremiah was killed by a crazy man last Thanksgiving."

"Why?" asked a bewildered Tom.

Jesse related the story of Brother Jeremiah's conversion and his call to Miller's Bluff. His voice cracked several times as he told of the fire, Little Jimmy's murder, his own acceptance of Jesus, and the shootings in the church. Gayle and Sarah had returned to the little parlor about midway through Jesse's story. As her husband of ten months spoke of the old circuit rider's ministry in the small town, Gayle examined her young counterpart's reaction.

Neither Tom nor Jesse noticed, but Gayle could see the horror in Sarah's eyes. Sarah feared Tom going on to Franklinton without any help. She also feared that her own health might fail her on their hymn-singing, Bible-reading journey through the interior of Texas. Tom had often spoken of his dream of when the "church-goin' bell" would sound far and wide across the Texas prairie. Although Sarah and Tom had not been married much longer than Jesse and Gayle, she knew her husband well enough. Tom would go on to Franklinton without Brother Jeremiah. . . and she would follow him even to the edge of the world if need be.

The same evangelical instinct that had filled the being of the old Bible-thumper bloomed strong in the heart of Tom McKelroy. The tall preacher felt a sense of dreadful urgency to plant the Church's banner in the West Texas Panhandle and bring salvation to the lost souls of Franklinton. Tom perceived his and Sarah's mission as an opportunity to establish an oasis of civilization for future pioneers by preaching Christ and eventually introducing schools.

The immediate inspiration for Tom's trip, he explained to his new friends, was an impassioned letter from his cousin, Mark, who worked as a cowhand on the Flying F ranch owned by Willie Franklin. Mark, one of Tom's first converts, was the only Christian in the entire area as far as he knew. His younger cousin had described the violence, lust, and greedy inclinations of the men from the surrounding ranches that kept any real semblance of law from this Babylon-of-the-plains. Mark had developed a driving hunger for Christian fellowship and had written Tom begging him to come and start a church, bringing a touch of refinement to the community. Tom had written Mark to tell him that "big brother" and his new wife were on their way as soon as they could convince Brother Jeremiah to help.

Franklinton had been founded during 1868 to cater to the soldiers of nearby Fort Harrison and the cowboys who herded cattle on the open ranges along the Western Trail. The tiny community had first been named Longhorn City until a middle-age banker from New York named Willie Franklin acquired most of the acreage just a year after it had begun to rise from the barren prairie on the north bank of Muddy Creek. The sleepy little cow town had not grown much since the early days when about half a dozen framed buildings and perhaps twice as many tents dotted the landscape of the West Texas Panhandle, and nearly every structure still supported large hand lettered signs simply announcing "Saloon".

"Could I get you some coffee or water, Brother McKelroy?" asked Gayle.

"Water would do just fine, Ma'am," answered Tom.

"Sarah?" Gayle nodded towards the pretty, but pale, young, future missionary.

"Water, thank you," said Sarah with a smile, the first smile the former Bostonian had allowed to cross her lips in awhile. Both women sensed a common bond between them centered on their love for their husbands and their faith in their Lord.

"Tell me more about your mission," suggested Jesse.

As the former cardsharp-turned-preacher explained the letter from his cousin and his resignation from his churches in north central Louisiana, Sarah's mind drifted to the night she had first met Tom in Shreveport. Sarah had been a professional singer and a music teacher for a time back in Boston, but had joined an evangelistic team that had been touring the Northeast. The talented debutante journeyed with the team across the South, and they were to take a few weeks off after the two weeks at the tent revival sponsored by the First Baptist Church in Shreveport. Sarah had sung a beautiful new song written by Philip Bliss the night that Tom sat in the congregation. Her voice was a clear soprano of unusual quality and range, and she brought all movement within the tent that night to a complete standstill.

After the service, she and Tom were introduced by a mutual friend. The young, Georgian-born parson stared incredulously. Sarah, a blonde of sensuous features and slightly buxom figure was the prettiest woman he had ever seen. She fell in love with the charming former hay-stacker the moment she looked into his eyes. Tom had taken a little longer to realize that he wished to spend the rest of his life with the pretty lady from Massachusetts. . . at least an hour longer. They were married two weeks later, and after another two weeks, Tom was called to his first duel-pastorate in the hills of north Louisiana just ten miles south of the Arkansas line. The newlyweds had sent a telegram announcing their nuptials to Sarah's folks back in Boston.

Sarah had never really wanted to be a pastor's wife, much less a church-planter. The young blonde simply wanted to serve her Lord through song. In 1870, when she was but eleven, she made her first public appearance as a singer in her church in Boston. She had sung a duet with an older girl at a church affair on Christmas Eve. Sarah, though only a child and totally untrained, sang with ease and polish. After her first appearance, Sarah was much in demand and sang at church socials and other public gatherings. And the young Easterner was quite satisfied with her ministry of song. Then she met Tom McKelroy.

Sarah thought of her own problem-packed-pregnancy and miscarriage as she watched Gayle, who was obviously in the family way, move about the room. The young, blonde help-mate was heart-sore at parting from their new friends she had made in Louisiana. And though she was full of misgivings about what lay ahead, she knew that God was still in control. She would not murmur, nor would she give up. Like her Biblical namesake, Sarah would follow her husband wherever God led them. . . even if it meant establishing the first church in the hell-hole of Franklinton, Texas, where at least one murder was committed each week.

****

197

Chapter Twenty

The Preparation

Gayle Lane lay quietly in her bed beside her husband, listening to the gentle rhythm of an early autumn rain. She was much too excited to sleep as she ran over in her mind the final preparations that needed to be made before she and Jesse would leave Miller's Bluff with Tom and Sarah McKelroy for the West Texas plains. The four-some were scheduled to leave in just seven more days to start a church in the small cow town of Franklinton. A smile crossed the young woman's lips as she thought again of how she and Jesse had tried to out maneuver each other into considering the adventure.

"Gayle," Jesse had said at supper a couple of days after the arrival of the McKelroys, "God's been awfully good to us hasn't He?" The young preacher practiced his best nonchalant tone while he sopped his biscuits in the gravy from the beef stew Gayle had prepared that evening.

"Yes, He has," Gayle answered in her best imitation of Jesse's tone. "We owe Him a lot," she continued as she poured her husband another cup of coffee.

"I'm sure glad He gave me such a beautiful, loving, caring, soul-conscious wife," countered Jesse in a sincere, syrupy way.

"And I'm proud He gave me a husband who's not afraid to preach the Gospel to any man," countered Gayle. She had her head down slightly, and looked at Jesse with carefully raised eyebrows. Jesse blushed. The young Bible-thumper chewed thoughtfully for a few moments before continuing the conversation.

"You know, Gayle, the more I learn about the Lord, and the more I learn about people, the more convinced I am that man's biggest problem is simply not following God's leadership at the right time."

"I believe you're right, Jesse. And it really must be especially hard on the men folk. After all, God holds y'all responsible for leading us women," said Gayle coyly.

"It is frightening sometimes," Jesse added while taking another spoonful of his favorite dish. "Now you take Tom McKelroy for instance. God's called him to start a church in a pagan land far from friends and home, and yet, he's willing to go even without no help." Jesse mixed just the right amount of sincerity and concern with a factual tone.

"And Sarah's mighty courageous, too. She's not the strongest woman I've ever seen, but she's willing to follow Brother Mac," added Gayle.

"I wonder if we'd be willing to do as much," Jesse offered with just a hint of real questioning.

"Well, if the Lord ever told you to go to the wilderness to start a church, I'd go with you. . . with never a word of complaint," remarked Gayle.

The next few mouths full of food were filled with silence as the young couple tried to think of a way to let the other know what was really on their minds. Then, as if directed by an unseen Conductor, they said simultaneously, "Let's pray about going."

Gayle closed her eyes as tears of joy leaked from the corners. That time of prayer with Jesse was a spiritual renewing like she had not felt since Brother Jeremiah had first come to town. The young couple could hardly wait to share their experience and their decision with Tom and Sarah. The four chosen messengers of the Gospel would begin a 400 mile missionary adventure that would prove to be even more grueling than any of them imagined. None of them had ever been on such a journey, and they were thus not prepared for such trail activities as loading wagons and taking care of pack animals. While the women were both well trained in household duties, they really had no idea of what it would be like to prepare food on the trail in a torrential rainstorm after sitting five to eight hours a day in a slow moving prairie schooner traveling along bone-wrenching trails, shaken by fever and dizziness. Nothing would deter their God-appointed mission, not even Gayle being in the family way or the pale, humorless Sarah's own frailty.

The gentle rhythm of the rain continued on into the night, and Gayle Lane, excited by the prospect of what lay ahead, listened to every drop.

****

Tom and Jesse drove the McKelroy's wagon the 20 miles or so to the state capital of Austin to pick up a shipment of belongings that contained the few things collected by the young missionaries during their ministry in north Louisiana. The two men had left before sun rise, but the journey had been slow because of a rainstorm that at times made the trail disappear. Luckily, they didn't have to cross Brushy Creek or the Colorado River to get to the train station. They left as soon as the cargo was loaded into the big wagon for the return trip. The two protégés of Brother Jeremiah exchanged stories about their pastorates to help pass the time.

By mid-morning, the rain had slowed to a heavy mist. The young missionary men sat at a table in the back room of the Tay-Bel Spread with Miller's Bluff's leading men to discuss preparation for the Gospel adventure. Walter Bell and Isaiah Taylor each had different guide books and sets of directions that made Tom and Jesse's decisions about outfitting even more difficult. Tom and Jesse, themselves, had various, sometimes conflicting opinions.

"Pack animals would be much easier to handle on the journey, Brother Mac," suggested Walter Bell.

"Yes, but remember Gayle is going to have a baby, and I just feel like a wagon would be more comfortable for her," mentioned Jesse.

"I agree with Brother Lane. We'll need another good wagon, Mr. Bell," added Tom.

The big wagons were indeed more expensive and much slower than other forms of transportation available, but they provided more shelter and space. Of course there was always the danger that a top-heavy covered wagon might blow over in a prairie storm, or be overturned by rocks, or bog down to its hubs in soft sand unless the wheels were much wider than those on a farm wagon. The two missionaries considered these things and decided to take the chance.

"A new wagon'll cost maybe $75, Brother Mac," said Isaiah Taylor, "and we better figure on getting as many spare parts. . . like an extra wagon tongue. . . or a couple of wheels. . . and at least a spare axle or two. . . as many as you can afford in case of emergencies. We'd best try and get a good, used Studebaker. . . they're well built and durable."

Emergencies almost always arose during trips of any distance. Because of the high wheels needed for clearance, sharp turns were impossible. Wagon tongues often snapped in two when animals pulled too far right or left. The dry air of the West Texas plains could cause the spokes of the wooden wheels and rims to shrink, which in turn could cause the spokes and iron rims to just fall off, breaking the wheel. Neither Tom nor Jesse had even thought of those possibilities. They suddenly both thought of themselves as greenhorns.

"Be sure and get your women folk to waterproof the cover with linseed oil," instructed Walter Bell.

"Oh, Gayle's gone farther than that, Mr. Bell," answered Jesse. "She's done sewed little pockets and slings to the inner surface of the fabric on Brother Mac's wagon. . . for extra storage space."

The inside of a 10-by-4-foot covered wagon would not hold very much, so most pioneers piled their wagons high with every bit of food and clothes and furniture they reckoned essential. Supported by hickory bows, the cover of the wagon provided about five feet of headroom, and the pucker ropes at either end could be tightened to help keep out the weather.

"Now, you gonna buy horses, mules, or oxen to pull the wagons?" asked Isaiah Taylor while wetting his pencil with his tongue.

"Why cain't they just pile up everything in a wagon and head on out?" inquired Sheriff Owen.

"Owen," said Walter Bell, "you ever been outta Miller's Bluff?"

"No, Sir. . . least-wise not since I moved here a few years back. . . no. . . don't reckon I have," answered the town's law-enforcer after thinking really hard for a moment or two.

"Then why don't you go polish your badge!" replied Taylor and Bell simultaneously.

"Mules are best, Brother Mac," said Jesse. "I've worked with 'em before. They're sure-footed, smart, quick-moving, and durable."

"Well, now oxen can pull heavier loads," commented Walter Bell, "and they'll eat almost anything. 'Sides, they don't run away at night, and they's much cheaper than mules or horses."

"That's right," added Isaiah Taylor, "and in a pinch, oxen make good eatin'."

"Perhaps we should get both," said Tom. "Brother Lane and his wife can use the mules from our wagon, and Sarah and I will drive a team of oxen."

"Now, here's a list of extras that Mr. Bell and I are gonna throw in," said Isaiah Taylor as he handed the two church planters a penciled list that included pins and needles, brooms and brushes, ox and horse shoes, lasts and leather, pocket mirrors and pocket books, a juice-harp, and coffee.

"You'll need a milk cow, too," added Walter Bell. "Any extra milk could always be churned into butter if'n you hang it in pails beneath the wagon."

Mr. Bell and Mr. Taylor offered other bits of wisdom, like how to pack thick slabs of bacon in a barrel of bran to protect it from the heat of the plains, and how to pack eggs in corn meal for insulation. The more the men talked, the more Jesse wondered if Owen might have been right.

****

Gayle Lane had been busy for hours with the needle. She had already made two print dresses and was in the process of making an inflatable life preserver that might be needed for crossing streams along the trail. If time allowed, she planned on stitching a conical tent of striped bed ticking, oiled, of course, to make it water resistant. The missionary caravan had planned on traveling along the Chisholm Trail part of the way before turning northwestward just before reaching Ft. Worth, at least that was the plan they had decided on. And although this greatest of all the cattle trails north-ward to Kansas was well traveled in 1879, it was not without its perils. The trail crossed several treacherous rivers that had cost the lives of many a steer and many a cowboy.

The young school teacher was not frightened by the stories she had heard in town, and almost every person she met on the streets had one. Gayle believed that the Lord would be with them all the way. Still, common sense told her that crossing those streams and creeks and rivers would get their possessions wet, unless protected. So, she listened to the well-intentioned advice of everyone and did the best she could to get prepared for every emergency.

The auburn-haired, former school-marm had also packed several candles among the other treasures hidden within the other supplies. Brother Jeremiah had once told Jesse that candles were valuable on the trail. They not only provided light, but the wax could be used to start a fire with wood that was wet. The candle wax could be rubbed into the wood to make it easier to light, and the flame of the candle would beat using two dozen ordinary matches.

Gayle had also requested several of the townsfolk to give her self-addressed envelopes so that she could continue being close to her old home and friends. She had promised to keep everyone updated as much as possible about the success of their upcoming adventure.

****

Sarah McKelroy used most of her preparation time to rest and re-gain the strength she lost with her miscarriage. She was still heart-broken over the loss of her firstborn. Her physical frailty meant that Gayle had to do double work, but she, too had plans for the trip. Sarah knew that it would be hard for Gayle to turn her back on old friends and relatives. She knew, too, the difficulty in leaving behind furniture and small comforting treasures. Space in the wagons was at such a premium that it was all the men could do to find room for tents, weapons, tools, basic clothing, cooking utensils, medicine, and other supplies, not to mentioned the case of Bibles that Mr. Bell and Mr. Taylor provided. Knowing that they must take only the most necessary items, Sarah went to great lengths to tuck in special articles that helped a woman feel like a woman and a home look like a home: seeds from flowers and shrubs, little trinkets and wrappings for Christmas, a well-loved book, a few daguerreotypes of family. The pale, young, blue-eyed woman from Boston knew she might never see her family back east again, but she was confident that she could make a comfortable home for her beloved preacher-husband in the West Texas plains.

****

Jesse Lane had learned much about God's provisions from Brother Jeremiah as they visited folks all over the central Texas countryside near Miller's Bluff.

"God's never late, Boy," Brother Jeremiah had said, "and He never undersupplies our needs."

With just two days of preparation left before Jesse Lane and Tom McKelroy planned on starting a missionary adventure that would test their faith and strain their family relationships, an old, rough and rangy, bossy-lookin' trail veteran named Smilin' Jack Riley rode into Miller's Bluff on a speckled black-and-white mule.

Smilin' Jack had made his living driving stagecoaches and other heavy wagons with freight across the deserts to California after retiring from the Army as a scout some fifteen years prior. He looked like he'd been in the desert so long, he knew all the lizards by their first name. His face and forearms were burnt from the sun, and he squinted his blue eyes almost closed. . . partly because he had become used to doing that to help block out the sun and partly because he was just a mite far-sighted. His grey hair and beard were uncombed, and his clothes looked as if they hadn't been washed in a month of Sundays. His shirt sleeves were rolled up to his elbows, revealing his almost completely faded, red long johns. Jack wore both a belt and a pair of suspenders to keep up his khaki pants which were tucked inside his tall, unpolished boots. And he wore a .44 in a weather-beaten holster that flapped at his side as he walked.

The crusty old teamster searched out the two young preachers when he heard of their church planting mission. Smilin' Jack approached the small gate that led to the front porch of the church parsonage with a bit of uncertainty for he did not claim to be a Christian, though he had told folks on occasion that he did believe in God. He was more impressed with the courage of the two green-horns and their determination to follow God's call. The old mule-skinner figured that if he could talk these two young preachers into abandoning, or at least post-poning, their perceived mission, that just maybe they had not been listening to the right voice all along. Jack stood on the porch for just a few seconds before he knocked hard and loud.

Gayle excused herself from the small sitting room where Jesse and Tom were discussing the day's activities and their talks with Miller's Bluff's two most distinguished citizens to answer the knock at the door. Sarah McKelroy watched her every motion, envious of the special bundle Gayle carried inside her.

"Yes?" said Gayle as she peered into the craggy face of the old teamster standing hat in hand on her porch. The old man looked, to the young preacher's wife, as being out of place, uncomfortable, and rather thread-bare.

"Can I help you, Sir?" she asked with that same smile that had captured Jesse's heart so many years before.

Smilin' Jack tried smiling back at the pretty school-marm, but became suddenly a tad bit ashamed of his appearance. . . and his lack of teeth.

"'Scuse me, Ma'am," he finally muttered, "Ah'd like ta see those preacher fellas who wanta start a church in Franklinton. It's kinda important, Ma'am."

The old man tried not to stare at the young lady standing in front of him, but "sized her up" in his mind as being prettier than a bunch of blue-bonnets stuck in a cow's ear. Jack started to use his hat to knock some of the trail dust off of his torn and dirty vest.

"Certainly you can see them," replied Gayle. "Won't you come in and join our discussion about that very topic?" The young woman slid behind the door as she opened it widely to reveal their cozy little home.

"No, Ma'am," answered Smilin' Jack rather sheepishly, "I ain't dressed proper ta enter yore home. But Ah'd be much abliged if'n yew'd ask them fellars ta step out cheer on the porch fer jest a minute or two."

Gayle smiled again at the unexpected guest who stood as straight as he could, but didn't seem to want to match the young woman's gaze.

"I'll get them right away," she said.

Gayle left the door ajar just a bit and walked back into the sitting room to inform her husband and their new preaching partner of the request of their visitor. Jesse and Tom glanced at each other with their "who-could-this-man-be" look and excused themselves. Neither of the two men recognized the trail-dust-covered wrinkled wrangler waiting for them on the parsonage porch. Neither could they imagine what the old mule skinner would want to speak to them about. They didn't have to wait long for the answer to their second question.

"I don't know what yew two yayhoos heerd 'bout Franklinton, but I lived there a spell, and it ain't a place fittin' for good folks," he had said as he did his best to talk the two men into staying home.

"Sounds to me like the kind of place that really needs the Lord," said Jesse.

"Well the whole place is run by Willie Franklin," snarled the old teamster, "He's the tall hog at the trough, and he ain't a fella to be a messin' with. Why Ah'd wuldn't wanna be within rock-throwin' distance of a feller like him. Old Man Franklin owns most everythin' that kin be seed in everwhich direction. He's hopin' ta talk them boys down in Austin out of them three million acres theys set aside to sell fer thet new capitol buildin' theys a hankerin' fer. Franklin jest ain't gut the money theys a askin' yet. But he's gut a passel of fellers a workin' fer him. . . fellers hired as much fer their workin' of levers on a Winchester as their ability with a rope. Why most every one of 'em varmints is practically married to their gun. And Ah guarantee yew Franklin ain't gonna put up with a couple of wet-behind-the-ears

Psalm-singers comin' in and spoilin' things by startin' a church and bringin' civilization ta his town!"

"Surely Mr. Franklin would not mind that. . . us bringing a little civilization to his town," commented Tom, trying not to laugh at the old muleskinners remarks.

Smilin' Jack just shook his head and stomped his foot. For thirty minutes the grey-haired, heavy-bearded veteran of hundreds of western trips ranted and raved about the evils in Franklinton, all to no avail. So, he decided to change his tactics just a bit.

The crusty, old freight-hauler wrinkled his entire face and snorted, "Either of yew two pups know enythin' 'bout the Panhandle? Huh? No, I 'spec not! Why the weather there is crazy! Winter is bitter awful. . . yew cain't even 'magine how cold it gets when one of them Texas northers blows a blizzard down on ya. Blindin' snow. . . piled higher than the winders in a soddie. . . freezin' sleet. . . why yew cud freeze ta death just goin' ta. . . ta. . . relieve yersef out back."

Smilin' Jack looked at the two missionaries to see if what he said was causing them any consternation. It wasn't.

"Then thar's them gall-darned prairie fires," continued the veteran teamster. Land gets so parched from the heat in summer. . . spark frum a campfar or a bolt of lightnin' cud set the grass a burnin' fer days, and theys almost impossible to stop!"

The old muleskinner went on and on about the dust storms and the tornadoes that destroyed everything in their paths. Then he talked about attacks from renegade Comanches. Despite the horror stories Smilin' Jack told, the faith of the young preachers held firm. Finally, the trail-mappin' orator gave in. He looked first at one and then the other, wrinkled his whole face again, and snorted.

"Well, if'n I cain't stop ya, I'd best be goin' with ya. Yew two year-lins' probably git lost on the trail and end up in Floridy," he growled. "Ah gut my doubtfuls that yew'll even make it to Franklinton. Ain't seen such bull-headed stubbornness in all muh born put togethers!"

Then the old muleskinner turned and sauntered to where he tied his mule, all the time talking about the craziness of the two preachers' plans.

"Come on, yew ol' mountain canary, yew," he said to his mule, "Ah dun't want narry a bit of stubbornness outta yew! I had my fill of bull-headedness today!"

Jack grabbed the reins of his animal and walked down the street, leading his mule, and mumbling to himself while waving his left arm all about and spitting West Virginy coleslaw juice every few steps. Tom and Jesse just watched the bow-legged old man stomp onto the board-walk and enter Walter Bell's store, still too stunned to respond to Smilin' Jack's declarations.

Inside Bell's General Merchandise, the old bullwhacker filled a bag with cheese, crackers, and some tins of sardines and herring. Having seen the wives of the two young preachers, he felt the food along the way might leave a lot to be desired, and he wanted to be prepared.

"Both of them gals is mighty looksum, but thet don't mean they's can cook a possum stew!" he bellered at the shopkeeper's son as he filled his sack with his "just-in-case-provisions".

****

Finally the day arrived when the wagons had been given their last overhaul, the animals were sleek and healthy, and the weather was promising. Gayle and Sarah had spent the day before occupying themselves with washing, ironing, and sewing.

Smilin' Jack had given precise instructions to the group. "We cain't travel more'n a mile afore stoppin' fer awhile to let the oxen. . . uh. . . relieve themselves. At 'bout ten o'clock, we'll stop to let the oxen and mules graze while we eat our first meal and grease the wagon wheels. Then we'll start up agin after a coupla hours and ride til 'bout five or six. Then we'll camp fer the night. You'll need those last few hours of daylight to take care of the animals and do any repairs that might come along. 'Sides yew don't want to over-tire the animals. Ah've gut a route mapped out in muh hade. . . gonna avoid crossin' big rivers as much as possible. 'Course we's gut to cross about a million little streams. . . most of 'em drier than a Baptist picnic. . . rest of 'em only 'bout a foot or two wide and less'un a foot deep. Won't be no trouble. . . prob'bly. Jest yew two fellers

208

ought to best be a talkin' to yore Boss 'bout the rains. Sometimes it rains so hard the mud is belly-deep to a small cow!"

The curious foursome was excited about their journey but just a little reluctant to leave the many friends who had given so sacrificially. The members of Philadelphia Church had agreed to hold the pastor's position open for at least six months just in case Jesse and Gayle decided to come back home after getting the mission church going with the McKelroys.

"Preacher. . . uh. . . preachers," stuttered Walter Bell, "we ain't got no money to speak of, but we all want to be a part of your work. So, we brung you some stuff to help you along the way."

As the wagons began moving slowly down main street, Sarah recalled seeing the same folks who lined the boardwalk as the team left, before carrying ham, bacon, sacks of coffee, sugar, potatoes, dried apples and peaches, flour, meal, and beans to the little parsonage as a going away gift for the four evangelists.

Not one of the young marrieds thought about the hazards that might be ahead, hazards that Smilin' Jack was so gracious to point out.

"Yew folks' is crazy. Why there's liable to be dust storms, swollen rivers. . . mebbe a Texas-norther blowin' in a unseasonal blizzard. 'Sides that. . . yew likely as not to be 'tacked by bandits or wild Comanches. And there ain't a bit of privacy along the trail, Ladies. Too many things that'll scratch ya, bite ya, or sting ya out there in that God-forsaken country jest passed them hills yonder!!"

But the more the old wagoneer ranted about the hardships that would surely come, the more the four missionaries thought of evangelizing men bound for an eternity in Hell. This was God's mission; they were sure of that. And they were God's people; they were sure of that. And no fear or reluctance would block their exodus across the heart of Texas to that Babel of the plains, Franklinton; they were on a mission, and they were confident that they would not fail.

****

Chapter Twenty-one

The Journey

The seventh day of November in 1879 was a beautiful day to start an adventure. . . clear skies, cool, crisp air. The two young missionary couples, led by their sometimes humorous guide, Smilin' Jack Riley, tackled their Gospel spreading journey with a deep felt enthusiasm that caused even their worst fears to take a back seat.

"Ah knows a little short cut that'll mebbe save us a leedle dab of time," offered the old freight-hauler. "'Course it could get a bit rough every now and again, but we need to git to the Clear Fork of the Brazos before the fall rains gets too bad."

"What time are you figurin' that we'll get started?" asked Tom as he looked at his big European watch.

"Hmph," puffed the old muleskinner, "We'll leave at sun up, Sonny. Jest keep yore eyes on the heavens. . . theys the best time-keepin' device ever made. Watches wuz invinted for doctors and lawyers and. . . gambl'rs!"

Smilin' Jack spit his tar juice in the general direction of Tom's boots without hitting anything but dirt. The old bull-whacker just wanted the tall minister to understand that he was aware of Tom's background. Jack was indeed impressed with the two young couples' courage to carry out their plans despite their inattention to the dangers along the way as well as the dangers they would face after they got to their destination. Still, the veteran mule-skinner had asked around town about the character of his adopted wards in an effort to be prepared for the worst along the trail. . . if it came to that.

Sarah McKelroy, though full of a grim and resolute courage, was herself too physically weak to be traveling anywhere. The blonde, Yankee lady had given birth some two months prematurely to a still-born baby girl just ten days before the party's triumphant and enthusiastic departure from Miller's Bluff. Her pregnancy had not gone well from the beginning, and the trip westward from Shreveport, though partly by stagecoach and partly by train, across East Texas almost cost the woman her life. And although the young Bostonian was not fully recovered from her miscarriage, she was just as excited about the mission trip. She was also a bit more concerned than the others about the perils which she feared the foursome would face along the way to establishing a church on the edge of the frontier. Sarah tried not to show her concern for Gayle, but the timing of the trip to her own misfortune made the blonde-haired beauty empathize with her auburn-haired counterpart.

Tom was not unaware of his wife's physical condition, and had, in fact, tried to persuade Sarah to stay behind until she felt stronger. He had no desire to lose another wife.

"I'm deeply concerned for you, Darlin'" Tom had said the night before the four church planters had left Miller's Bluff. "Perhaps you should stay here with Miss Ida for a few weeks. I can send for you after we get settled in Franklinton. . . after you've had time to fully recover."

"My place is with my husband," she quickly declared. "Besides, I like the command just as it stands. . . 'go ye into all the world', and no exceptions for poor health. I'll be fine," she said bravely, trying to reassure her husband. . . and herself.

****

The first hour or so for the Bible-messengers out of Miller's Bluff was a time of getting acquainted with one another as well as learning something of the routine of the long ride ahead. The average speed of the wagons was only two to three miles per hour, which put their estimated arrival in the West Texas Panhandle about three weeks or so from their departure. The actual arrival, as Smilin' Jack continued to remind the four missionaries, depended a great deal on Nature. . . and the old muleskinner's version of Luck.

"Isn't the country beautiful?" asked Tom. "I don't think God made a more beautiful country. Not even the hills of Georgia can compare to this."

"Bet there ain't nuthin' like this up there in Boston, huh Mrs. Mac?" said Jesse leaning forward to see Tom and Sarah in the next wagon. The Chisholm Trail was wide enough for the two wagons to rattle along abreast, but soon the trail would narrow, and the wagons would have to trudge along single file as they would for most of the journey on Smilin' Jack's short-cut.

"We do have hills and trees, Brother Lane, but there is something about the vastness of the countryside that makes even far away seem up close." A slight smile crossed the lips of the thin and pale, blonde lady from the "far east". This was the second time Gayle had noticed her counterpart smile, even if it was only a slight smile.

"I do hope the journey won't be too much for you, Mrs. Lane," added Sarah after the McKelroy's wagon hit a rough spot in the trail.

"Oh, don't worry about me, Sister Sarah," answered Gayle. "Little Rufus and I will be just fine. Mary traveled over rougher country while carrying our Lord. . . I'll be fine."

Jesse glanced at Gayle and caught the sparkle of excitement in the green eyes of his helper. Gayle always seemed to look on the brighter side of life. From appearances, folks would think that the young school teacher had no fear of doing anything so long as Jesse was beside her. Her charm, her "fetchin' smile", as Smilin' Jack called it, and her own special brand of humor could make even the worst hardship bearable.

Actually Gayle tried not to think of days and nights ahead on steep roads or trails with little grading when the wagon might heave and plunge like a "storm-tossed ship" as Smilin' Jack had warned. Still she believed God would cause the journey to pass uneventfully. In fact, for the moment, the fairly level stretches north of Miller's Bluff made the trip almost lulling.

Though Sarah tried her best to not let her fears show, she was a bit apprehensive about what lay ahead for the traveling missionaries. And, of course, Sarah was deathly afraid of snakes. Smilin' Jack had painstakingly described the uncountable species of snakes that the foursome would come across on their journey. . . especially the varieties of poisonous snakes.

"Them ratt'lers is dangerous and sneaky," warned the old freight-hauler. "Them varments hide under rocks and in the brush. Sometimes they'll try to scare yew off with their noise makin'. . . sometimes them ornary critters will jest bite fer spite. And Gawd hep us ifn one of them sidewinders bites one of our animals! Mules have been known ta run lickety split fer a mile or so before keelin' over sudden like. Ah g'arantee the wagons won't be in grate shape afterwards!"

Then the crusty old trail-blazer kinda looked at his fellow travelers with a smirky grin and spurred his mule on ahead so that he couldn't be questioned.

While Smilin' Jack scouted ahead for forage for the mules and oxen as well as a good source of drinking water for his wards, the four missionaries engaged in fascinating conversation that was intended to combat the hours of boredom. Time was consumed by interesting stories from Tom and Jesse about past days of glory. When the storytelling paused, word games were played. Soon, even the word games gave way to silence, and the foursome began to dream of the day when the Gospel of Jesus would be proclaimed throughout the plains around Franklinton.

At about 11 a.m., Smilin' Jack signaled the noon halt. Each of the travelers quickly went about their assigned tasks for the noon meal. Tom inspected the wagons for any needed repairs, Jesse watered the stock, Sarah gathered some firewood for a campfire to cook the coffee, and Gayle set about preparing the short snack the foursome would enjoy before hitting the trail again.

Finally, after about ten hours of the methodical swaying of the wagons, the Pilgrims were instructed by their guide to stop and set up camp for the night. As soon as the wagons were unhitched and the animals hobbled, the weary men began hauling water, gathering fuel, and digging a trench in which to cook. Gayle had problems cooking over the open fire at first, and all, except Smilin' Jack, began to fear going hungry for awhile. The young, former-schoolmarm saw her suspended soup kettle upset four times as the fragile legs of a makeshift tripod kept giving way. But she was determined to have a soup and so re-hung the kettle five times. Finally, the starving foursome sat down to supper. . . or at least what was left of it.

Smilin' Jack still didn't trust the culinary efforts of the young school teacher, so he feasted on a pocketful of hardtack. He washed his meal down with a couple of swigs of whiskey. To the old mule-skinner, life in the West would just be unbearable without his coffee and an occasional "swaller" of home-brewed "snake medicine".

After the hot meal was eaten and final evening chores attended to for the night, the Gospel pilgrims relaxed. Stories that hadn't been shared before were told, with each of the young devil-dodgers trying to make the others laugh or realize some special Biblical truth. . . each that is, except Sarah who sat beside the campfire and stared at the slow burning limbs, thinking about how cozy her home was in Boston. Later, both women wrote about the day's travel and happenings in their journals. Had the casual reader happened upon these first-hand documents of personal history, they would have sworn that they were reading accounts from witnesses who had been on two different journeys.

****

For the first few days of the missionary adventure, the journey was accomplished with reasonable safety and few mishaps. The first real test along the way after leaving the Chisolm Trail on Smilin' Jack's short-cut was the crossing of the hills where grades in some areas were frequently brutal. The wagons in one place had to be partially unloaded, and both the teams were hitched together in order to get each one to the top. On the downward side, regular shoe brakes and chains locking the rear wheels were inadequate for braking the big wagons. To deal with the problem, Smilin' Jack instructed the two men to raise the rear axle. With the wagon's rear wheels jacked up, a log bore the weight of the rear of the vehicle and served as an effective drag as the wagon descended. At the bottom of the hill, the brake was simply discarded. It took the young missionaries three full days to get out of the rolling hills and back to level land.

Even though the rolling hills of northwestern Central Texas proved to be a formidable foe, the four messengers of God's grace still looked forward to their mission of planting a church in the worldly cow town of Franklinton. The weather had not discouraged them, either, nor had the humdrum of traveling across the vastness of what is Texas. . . yet. Grass was plentiful for their beasts of burden, and game was plentiful all along the way.

"Ah wuz proud of yew fellers," Smilin' Jack had said the first evening after the frontier ministers had crossed those rolling hills. "Y'all handled it purdy good, and Ah wuz as pleased as a rat in a grain bin. But we got a bigger problem comin' up. . . the Clear Fork of the Brazos. The place we gonna cross is wide and usually three or four feet deep with a bottom of gravel and sometimes quicksand. But thet there river changes all of the time, so's Ah ain't shure if'n yore animals won't be swimmin' and yore wagons a sinkin'. Mite be a purdy good idear fer yew boys ta do a little extra prayin' tanite."

Because of sudden rains in the late fall, streams and rivers often ran dangerously high. High water made the oxen and mules uneasy, and stumbling over an unseen rock could cause the wagon to flip over into swift water that often was much deeper just beyond the ford. Tom and Jesse knew that Smilin' Jack's suggestion was one to be considered.

Privacy was one of those things which the young newlyweds had taken for granted, even though their guide had warned both couples before leaving Miller's Bluff of that eventuality. On the trail, privacy was practically unheard of except when the two couples left in opposite directions for nightly prayer-time. Sometimes, even then, Smilin' Jack would wander onto one of the couples as they prayed or talked intimately. Sarah, the most nervous of the four, was the first of the group to be annoyed by the loss of privacy.

"Husband," she said one evening, "aren't we safe out here? We can see for miles. Surely heathen savages couldn't sneak up on us."

"Oh, Sarah, there probably aren't any Indians anywhere around here," the tall Georgian quipped. Tom had an urge to poke a little fun at his eastern wife, but decided against it.

"Then, couldn't we lag a day or so behind the others. . . we haven't had a moment alone since. . . Salado," responded the former Boston socialite with a definite crack in her voice.

"Sarah," Tom said softly, taking his wife's pale hands in his, "We're on a mission for God. We'll have lots of time to be alone later. I know things have been rough for you. I know how much you miss your family, and hopefully, in a couple of years, we can go back East for awhile and visit. Right now, we must concentrate on getting to Franklinton. The folks there need the Gospel."

Sarah looked deeply into her husband's eyes, sighed, and simply bowed her head.

****

Almost ten days into their journey to start a church in one of the most uncivilized towns on the Texas frontier, the young missionary team was surprised to discover that their guide, Smilin' Jack Riley, had actually led them into a small town. Callahan City was still a new settlement; most of the buildings still sported new lumber and there were tents housing some businesses, but it looked like St. Louis to the weary travelers.

"We's back on the Trail for a spell, Folks," said Smilin' Jack through his toothless grin. "This here's Calliehand City. . . on the Great Western Cattle trail to Dodge City! Ain't no herds comin' thru right now. . . but they's plenty of 'citement anyways. We'll camp outside uh town fer uh couple of days. . . rest the animals. . . ketch up on the news. . . and eat uh real home-cooked meal in the fanciest eatin' place west of Ft. Worth. No offense ma'am."

"None taken," answered Miss Gayle, her face beaming with the thought of not having to cook over a campfire if even for just a day.

"Look yonder, Gayle!" broke in Jesse, "this place even has a post office. You can mail all those letters you've been writin' to folks back home in Miller's Bluff." Both ladies seemed to have their spirits lifted by the thought of being back in civilization for awhile.

Tom and Jesse pulled up their respective wagons outside the tent housing the grocery store. Both men enjoyed a good venison steak, but since the bacon had long since been depleted, both of the young preachers had developed a hankerin' for some sow-belly and scrambled eggs for breakfast.

"We'll pick up a few things inside while you ladies visit the post office. Then we'll go down to the blacksmith's and have him look at the shoes on the mules. . . maybe inspect the wagons, too. . . look for problems that can be fixed now," offered Tom.

Even Sarah had a slight smile on her face as she surveyed the cow-town which had originally been designed just to be a supply stop for the trail-drivers, but had by 1879, become the "shoe-in" for county seat. . . or so everyone thought. The men helped their wives off the wagons, and the ladies hurried off to mail their own version of this missionary trip to concerned friends back home. Smilin' Jack had actually encouraged the ladies to write down their thoughts each day, hinting that there would be a post office somewhere along the way. Gayle and Sarah had pretty much given up hope of ever seeing a town again since Jack's "short cut" was designed to avoid river crossings as much as possible which also meant that small towns were also avoided. But here they were. . . in a hustling, bustling, little town on the Texas prairie. All the weary pilgrims could hardly wait to chin with the town folks.

For the most part, the citizens of Callahan City were friendly and supportive of the adventurous church-planters. The owner of the grocery store gave Tom and Jesse a box full of groceries; the black-smith replaced two shoes on the mules at no charge and inspected their wagons carefully, finding nothing desperately wrong; the local pastor, himself new to the town, and his wife shared their evening meal with the Gospel-preaching visitors, and even the local news-paper interviewed the foursome for an article that none of them would ever see. The newspaper was a weekly, and Smilin' Jack's "plan" only allowed for two nights in the little village.

"Time to get a move on, Folks," shouted Smilin' Jack, "we's burnin' daylight!" Of course, it was probably two hours before any daylight, but the old muleskinner was full of fat-back and beans from the Bluebonnet Café, and he was still concerned about the

217

place he had chosen to cross the Brazos. It should have been the most shallow place, but the old trail-driver had learned from the towns folk that the fall had been mighty wet. Every minute delayed here might become a longer delay later.

None of the missionaries were ready to continue, but they understood Jack's concerns. Reluctantly, the ladies began their routine chores of fixing biscuits with a piece of bacon and placing what they could of their supplies into the wagon while the men harnessed the teams and watered them. In less than an hour, the team was back on the trail to Franklinton.

By noon of the next day the church-planters had reached Clear Fork of the Brazos River in Shackelford County. This crossing was to be a "practice" experience for the two couples, according to Smilin' Jack. Clear Fork was deep in some places, but the spot the old trailblazer had chosen was less than a foot deep and less than 30 feet wide, but this spot ran rather swiftly. This spot was the best crossing for miles around because the banks of the river, at this spot, was not at all steep. Tom and Jesse approached the situation with the same courage and faith that had been their strength since they had started their journey some two weeks before. And sure enough, this test that Smilin' Jack had prepared boosted their ego and determination to continue onto the flat cattle lands of the Texas Panhandle.

Still, it had been another long day of jostling and bouncing along a trail that seemed to lead nowhere except to the next bump. And except for the river crossing, it had been another day of back-breaking monotony. . . a day that left the weary church pioneers exhausted after many hard hours on the trail.

The crossing, the cool weather, and the regular rigors of the journey had drained every last ounce of energy from the weary pilgrims. But their day was not over. They still had to make camp, fix supper and make what repairs might be necessary to keep their wagons moving. Just after dark, their cantankerous guide lifted the spirits of the two young Gospel-hounds.

"Yew fellas did gud," commented Smilin' Jack after supper that night. "Ah'm beginnin' to reckon yew jest mite make it to Franklinton. In two days, we'll be to the Brazos. . . that'll be the big test. Now if'n yew folks don't feel up to it, we kin bypass the Brazos altogether. . . but it'd prob'bly add another week or so to the trip. . . if'n every-thin' goes right." As the old man turned to walk away, he spit what seemed like a jug-full of his West Virginy coleslaw juice into the fire, which caused sparks to fly. Tom and Jesse turned their heads towards one another.

"Prayer time?" said Tom with a questioning tone.

"Prayer time," whispered Jesse. The young circuit rider poured the rest of the coffee onto the fire, and both men headed off to their wagons for some special prayer time with their wives and with their Lord.

****

Tom and Jesse discovered that their prayers for the Brazos had been too late. A late, fall storm up river had sent the waters flooding up and across the banks, totally erasing the trail. The two young Scripture-wranglers decided, with Smilin' Jack's help, to wait until morning to try and cross the swollen river. That decision would eventually cost the Bible-party some ten days after another unseasonal rainstorm came up during the night, forcing the church planters to remain stalled before the waters subsided sufficiently for them to cross. For awhile, their campsite would be their home.

Gayle and Sarah began to prepare the evening meal as usual. By this time, setting up the evening chuck had become routine. Sarah gathered a few twigs for firewood while Gayle prepared the grub and the coffee. Their men-folk were always hungry and ready to chow-down as soon as they had taken care of the animals. Smilin' Jack was a coffee addict, and he liked it almost boiling.

"Ah kin do without muh whiskey. . . but Ah cain't do without my Arbuckle's," he had told his fellow travelers the first night of the journey.

The picture set in Gayle's mind of the old muleskinner gulping his coffee always re-appeared in the pretty school-marm's mind every time she put the oversized pot next to the fire to make it piping hot. . . and the picture always made her smile no matter what kind of day she and fellow travelers had had.

"Surely you are not going to drink that coffee straight from the pot, Mr. Jack!" exclaimed Sarah one evening.

"Shur am, Honey. It cuts all the trail dust thet away," answered the old teamster with his broadest, snaggle-toothed grin.

With that, the veteran trail-driver gulped some coffee and wiped his unwashed face with the sleeve from his oily, buckskin jacket. . . and let out a deep sigh followed by a toothless grin and a little shake.

"Mitey fine. . ." he said, "Mitey fine. Whut's fer supper tanite, Missy? Ah'm hungrier 'n a woodpecker with a headache."

The old wrangler had finally tried Gayle's cooking and decided that it was much better than hardtack and venison-jerky. As far as Smilin' Jack was concerned, campin' out on the trail for the night was the best part of the day.

Sarah was still openly annoyed by the lack of finery the travelers were forced to endure. The ground or a large rock served as their table, and their table cloth was the same Indian rubber cloth used as Tom's rain coat. Their dishes were made of tin, and their spoons were wooden. Wooden basins, not pitchers, held their tea or milk and whatever meat was available from Smilin' Jack's frequent hunting and scouting trips during the day. And without chairs, they were forced to copy the Comanches by sitting cross-legged on the ground.

Life in camp was only tolerable during the ten days the two missionary couples waited for the Brazos River to lower its banks. At least the food was plentiful. Jesse and Tom went fishing most everyday, when they could, and usually brought back a mess of catfish or river bass for supper. Gayle became quite adept at making "son-of-a-gun" stew, as Smilin' Jack called it. The stew was a mixture of whatever the menfolk brought back to camp along with wild onions, berries, and acorns that the two women could gather. But on a couple of nights it was just beans and cornmeal.

The rains came almost every other night, sometimes torrential for a few minutes, sometimes just drizzly all night. Beds were made in the mud, and all of the travelers were out of humor about something at one time or another. Smilin' Jack scolded everybody, reminding them all that the whole idea was a bad one and hinting at every opportunity that it might be best if they turned back and headed to Miller's Bluff. Tom and Jesse were continuously soaking wet, looking sad and comfortless. Gayle was shut up in the wagon most of the time, trying not to worry about "Little Rufus", as Jesse referred to the baby. And Sarah hid from the others as much as she could, yearning for home and crying over her lost daughter. Worst of all was the awful, cold suppers when the men couldn't find enough dry wood to make a campfire. Jack shared his jerky with the others for as long as it held out. . . which wasn't long, and he complained about that.

For the moment, West Texas seemed like the edge of nowhere to the young Bostonian. Sarah was convinced that it was only pure pride that kept her husband and Jesse Lane focused on the mission, but the two preachers were beginning to question their decision to make the trip. Both men took to changing the subject of Smilin' Jack's daily rants about the futility of the endeavor. Even Gayle began to have doubts about traveling into that "dark region of savages", as Smilin' Jack frequently called the residents of Franklinton.

In her diary one cold night Gayle wrote, "It rained all night, again. Had a long bawl for no reason at all. . . just needed to cry some. Jesse seemed to pity me when he found out how bad I felt. Did we make the right choice? Is the Lord testing our resolve. . . or is He trying to tell us that we made a mistake?"

The biggest lesson the foursome had to learn was how to get along together during this break on their missionary trip. They were sometimes short-tempered and inconsiderate without meaning to be so. Actually the two couples had little in common other than their heartfelt desire to bring Christianity to the cowboys and soldiers around Franklinton, and, of course, their newlywed status. The two, young, itinerant preachers shared a vision, but both had their own ideas about how to accomplish that vision. Tom and Jesse shared preaching duties on Sundays on the trail. The former Georgia plowboy had a flamboyant style and frequently used humor to illustrate his stories. Jesse was more straight-forward, using a multitude of scriptures to prove his points.

The two women did not really like each other, but both had gained a deepening respect for the individuality of the other. Both had displayed unusual courage during the beginning of the odyssey that had uprooted their young homes and transplanted them, what seemed to each, a world apart from their friends. And all this during that crucial time period when both couples were still adjusting to the newness of married life.

To Gayle, Sarah was too stand-offish to be a pastor's wife. The prim and proper, former New England-socialite was totally opposite from the bouncy, whimsical Gayle. Most of the time, except for those rare occasions when she let her spirits sag a bit, Gayle sang or hummed, especially while working. When the former schoolmarm did feel bad, she simply hid herself from her fellow travelers. Sarah hardly ever sang anymore or hummed, despite that being her previous occupation and ministry. In fact, Sarah looked like someone had eaten her last biscuit most of the time. Although the blonde missionary lady complained very little to her husband, she found fault in almost everything around the travelers and expressed her discomfort in confidence to her younger counterpart while just the two of them did camp chores.

Gayle laughed out loud, sometimes, at what seemed to Sarah, the wrong times, like when Tom had come back from hunting with only a rattlesnake in hand. . . or at supper the week before when Jesse, with a heaping plate in one hand and a hot cup of coffee in the other, crossed his legs and dropped to the ground without spilling a bite of food or a drop of coffee. Then there was the afternoon when one of the wagons got stuck in the mud while crossing a shallow creek, and both Tom and Jesse fell into the slimy waters trying to pry the wagon out of the sink hole. Everybody laughed out loud at the sight of the two preachers covered from head to toe in mud. Everyone except Sarah. Sarah seldom even smiled anymore.

Both women, however, had an endearing faith in God and a never ending devotion to their husbands and their ministries. Gayle could sense this common ground and so had gone out of her way to be friends with the solemn Sarah.

****

"This here's the day," announced Smilin' Jack one cold and cloudy morning. "Brazos ain't gonna git much lower fer a long while yet, and Ah'm afeered thet winter's gonna be settin' in soon. Mite as well cross now."

"But can the wagons make it over?" asked a worried Jesse.

With each day, Gayle's midsection grew larger, and all four of the young church planters were beginning to worry about a miscarriage brought on by the hardships of the journey.

"Mebbe. Mebbe not. Ain't but one way to find out. Hitch 'em up, Preacher," barked the determined muleskinner.

Both couples prayed silently as they tied down barrels and jacked up the wagons to the highest level possible. Smilin' Jack forced the oxen and mules to swim through the swift current to the other side while Tom and Jesse rechecked the hitches on the wagons. The plan was to float the wagons across one at a time using the animals to pull the cargo through the waters, much like a ferry would do at a toll crossing. Gayle and Sarah would ride on the wagon box while Jesse and Tom stood on the wagon's seat, holding firmly to the heavy ropes while helping the animals pull the wagons to the far side of the river.

The first wagon, with the four missionaries aboard, plunged into the river, taking a diagonal course. The river was so deep in places that the water rushed through the wagon box, soaking the bottoms of the ladies' skirts and their goods. Anyone who might have overheard the noise of the crossing would have concluded that chaos attended the maneuver. Smilin' Jack's fiendish swearing, shouted in several languages, would have embarrassed even the strongest sailor. . . or the weakest Christian. Somehow, the four made the crossing safely.

It was during the middle of the second crossing that disaster struck. Smilin' Jack had instructed the men to stay on the north bank with their wives while he went back after the other wagon. Jack decided to just hitch up both teams to the remaining wagon, abandoning the experiment of the "ferry crossing".

Less than half way across, one of the wagon's wheels dislodged a rock which tilted the large, top heavy vehicle. The current continued pushing the wagon over on its side, and the swiftness of the flooded river quickly swept the prairie schooner down stream. The four Gospel-wranglers watched helplessly while the old wagoneer fought frantically to cut the animals free from the run away wagon. Unfortunately he was able to save the mules, but only one of the oxen. The two young preachers had to use all their strength to pull Smilin' Jack to safety. The larger of the two wagons, the one belonging to the McKelroys, and all the contents thereof, were lost. Sarah sank to the ground as if hit in the stomach by some unseen force. The last vestages of her former life were being carried away by the muddy waters of the Brazos River. Tom sat down beside his young wife and held her close as she sobbed.

Jesse and Gayle stood close by in a reassuring embrace. Smilin' Jack looked at the two couples and decided that this would be a good time to just rest for awhile. Without saying a word, he gathered a bit of firewood, started a fire, and sat close to the flames to dry off best he could. And as the missionary team sat staring at the fire, the clouds moved away allowing the sun to resume its majestic throne in the heavens. . . and a full rainbow like none of them had ever seen before appeared in the sky. And the birds in the trees started blending their voices into one harmonious melody.

As the church-planting team stared at the multi-colored arch in the heavens, Gayle sighed deeply and said, "Jesse. . . do you know what day it is? It's Thanksgiving!"

****

The young servants of God had been shattered by the accident, but not defeated. Their faith and courage were stretched, but not broken. With each sunrise came a new adventure. The journey became either too wet or too dry, too hot or too cold. Sometimes the young Bible pioneers would walk for miles in clouds of their own dust. Then the rains would come again, and the dust was turned into almost impassible mud.

Buffalo gnats, almost too small to see, worked their way into their ears. Rattlesnakes, abundant as the dust in West Texas, seemed to hide behind every rock with the intention of biting anything that moved. Jesse was able to practice his shooting almost every mile along the way, and each time he destroyed one of the rattlers, he'd be reminded of Brother Jeremiah sitting exhausted on the steps of the old, partially framed building that became a church back in Miller's Bluff.

For the women, even more disturbing were the onslaught of minor accidents, sudden fears, and the seemingly endless discomforts that gnawed at their faith. When the McKelroy's wagon tipped over, carefully rationed food supplies were lost. Sarah was appalled by the continuing threat of "wild beasts and other dangers." She grew increasingly depressed by the predictable monotony of the journey, always moving forward, but never arriving at their destination. Then there was the drudgery of camp work and a feeling of utter loneliness. Sometimes, because they had not seen another human being in such a long time, Sarah imagined that some great catastrophe had happened to the rest of the world, and only her four companions had survived. Often the former Easterner would help break camp, and then, walking ahead of the rest of the team, would throw herself down behind a large rock on the grassy plains and weep like a child for home and friends.

The journey was indeed rough for all, but their strong, unshakable faith in God forbade them to murmur out-loud against their fate. Each of the missionary party had fostered thoughts of giving up, but then something as simple as a squirrel or rabbit scurrying across their path and sitting up on their hind legs and stretching to view the weary pilgrims would brighten their day and strengthen their resolve. Though the hardships were many, the future rewards overshadowed their fears.

****

By the beginning of December, the worn-out missionary band found themselves three-fourths of the way to their destination in the West Texas Panhandle. The delays caused by the storms and the loss of the wagon created hardships that neither of the two couples or their guide, Smilin' Jack, had prepared for. Nevertheless, the pioneer church planters decided to go ahead on their one wagon caravan. They had come too far to turn back now.

Smilin' Jack steered his self-adopted wards to a small, one room store at a place called Espuela along the west bank of Duck

Creek. The little store, started three years earlier by John Henry Parrish, served the handful of travelers that passed that way as well as the cattlemen and buffalo hunters who roamed the plains. For the most part, the land around Parrish's small store was considered open-range, so cattle from some 30 small area ranches grazed the grasses from time to time.

"Yew fellers kin get some supplies here," said a very tired and haggard Jack. "And yew ladies kin rest uh spell, too."

The missionary team was indeed tired of the hazards they had faced and just a little disappointed that things hadn't gone more smoothly for them. Both the men and the women had begun to secretly question their decision to leave the ministries that they had back in central Texas and in north Louisiana for the desolation and pure cussedness of Franklinton. But each time they questioned their actions, the Lord brought them something to strengthen their belief in their mission. Espuela was that something this time. . . not a city or a town. . . just a dugout on a farm in the middle of nowhere. But it was a spot in the wilderness where supplies could be replaced and the mud could be washed off.

The four Psalm-singers would be refreshed physically, emotionally, and spiritually during the handful of hours they would spend at this isolated little store, partly because of what the store represented and partly because of what they overheard Smilin' Jack say to Parrish.

"We's gone through the mill, alright, Parrish," said Jack as he piled some blankets and canned goods on the wooden plank that served as a counter. "Been thru uh passel of troubles. Had uh bet on with muhself, and Ah lost! Thought fer shure them greenhorns woulda turned back by now! But them four tenderfoots didn't once get the give-ups. No sir! They seen the elephant and didn't shin out. They stuck to their 'riginal plan and didn't even once talk about lightin' a shuck! Why they's game as a banty rooster! Even thet thar pretty one thet's as big as a barn and 'bout to birth a young'un any day now."

The scruffy shopkeeper had tried to stop the old wagon-buster when he noticed that the four Scripture-beaters had entered his establishment, but his attempt was useless. The two ladies just stood in the doorway with their astonished husbands behind them. Then Smilin' Jack slowly turned around to look into the tear-filled eyes of the auburn-haired beauty he had just mentioned. The old teamster tried swallowing so that he could explain, but the lump in his throat was just too big. All four men knew how emotional ladies could get when they were in the family way. . . especially when things didn't seem to be going just right. The handful of seconds that passed seemed like hours to the befuddled men. Sarah just stood there with her mouth opened wide, in utter disbelief that she had heard what she had heard.

Gayle looked down at her bulging physique, and her bottom lip started to quiver. Then she looked at Smilin' Jack with the tears filling her eyes and said, "I can't see my toes. You're right, Jack. I am as big as a barn. . . and full of life. . . but I promise you I won't birth this young'un until we get to Franklinton!"

Then, Gayle started to smile. . . which led to a little giggle. . . which led to an all out laugh. . . which caused everyone to relax. . . and laugh. Everyone except Sarah. Her eyes welled up with tears as she once again thought of her miscarriage.

The Gospel heralds spent the night on the grassy plains of Espuela, and after an inspiring Bible lesson led by Jesse, turned in early, ready to finish their journey into the future led by their Lord and Savior, knowing that there might be some setbacks still ahead, but the victories would be even greater.

****

As Tom McKelroy drove the surviving wagon up a small draw, Smilin' Jack spotted three armed Comanches on horseback blocking the trail ahead. One of the Indians fired an arrow that stuck deep into the breast of the old bull whacker's mule, causing the animal to let out an agonizing wail. As the wounded animal fell, Smilin' Jack pulled his Navy Colt revolver and shot the leader. The two other renegades retreated, but they returned a few minutes later with a half dozen or more warriors armed with old muskets, bows, and arrows.

A long running battle began, with the wagon rolling full speed across the West Texas prairie, and the Comanches galloping behind on their ponies. Smilin' Jack rode one of the harnessed mules with Jesse spurring Homer, Brother Jeremiah's old Appaloosa, and firing over his shoulder while at a dead run. Tom handed the reins of the wagon to Gayle and climbed to the back of the wagon to shoot at the attackers who were in hot pursuit. Sarah hid behind a chest of drawers and prayed.

Finally, Gayle pulled the wagon close to a large rock where Jesse and Tom could put up a defense. The Indians attacked repeatedly with their usual hit and run tactics, but each time they were repulsed. Jesse aimed only to wound his adversaries, as did his Georgian counterpart. Smilin' Jack fired as fast as he could and actually hit no one. A shotgun is not very accurate unless the enemy gets close.

After one of the "retreats" to regroup, Gayle slapped the reins and the company of missionaries pulled out once again with the Indians pursing, despite their multiple wounds. The fighting lasted almost three miles before the Comanches took a brief intermission to try and out maneuver the wagon. The renegades learned quickly to stay within sight of the travelers, but out of range from Jesse's deadly six-shooter. Still, the prayer-warriors kept up a faster than normal pace.

By nightfall, the animals, as well as the defenders, were exhausted and frightened. A wide-eyed Sarah was shaking violently. Gayle was trying to keep a cool head as she bandaged Jesse's left wrist, which had been shattered by an Indian musket ball.

Tom sat beside the fevered Smilin' Jack, who was drinking his smuggled whiskey with abandon. The old teamster was carrying a Comanche arrowhead in his lower backside. Tom had been chosen to operate. The old muleskinner would take a long swig of his "Kansas sheep-dip" and sing a song with made up words. Tom looked at the old wagoneer and listened to the distinctive sounds coming from his mouth. The noise sounded like someone had forgotten to grease one of the wagon's wheels.

"I'm not sure I can do this," said Tom as he held the old muleskinner's Bowie knife over the fire to disinfect it.

"Yew got to, Mister," answered the old trail driver. "Yew iz the doctor now. Jest yew make shore thet frog sticker is sharp. . . and Ah'll jest glomb onto this here jug."

Smilin' Jack started grittin' what little teeth he had left like he could bite the sites clean off a six-gun.

"Now git it over with," whispered the old teamster.

Doctors weren't always available on the frontier when they were most needed, but they were responsible for bringing medical care to the West. Not that they were capable of doing much more than anyone with an average amount of common sense, but a doctor served as the beginning point for the modern medical man. Trouble was, Tom McKelroy was not a doctor.

It took over an hour for the former cardsharp to remove the arrowhead, mostly because Tom was so afraid of hurting the old mule-whacker. The old man had fainted from the pain early on and was still unconscious as Gayle applied toasted onion skins and plug tobacco wrapped in a warm cloth to the wound as Smilin' Jack had instructed her before Tom had started cutting.

As the old muleskinner rested, Tom and Jesse discussed plans for a diversionary tactic to confuse the Comanche warriors.

"If they come back with any more, I don't think we can hold off an attack," commented Tom.

"We've got to keep them busy. Maybe if we stake out the ox, they'll be satisfied," suggested Jesse.

"It's worth a try, Jesse. It's worth a try," agreed the former Georgia plow-pusher.

Long before sunrise, the missionary wagon slowly and quietly left what looked like a fortified campsite. The remaining ox was staked out in plain view. The idea must have worked, for the alert team saw no more Indians on their trip.

The Bible troop began to pray devoutly for the end of their long journey. The grinding discomfort of close quarters, hours of tedium and hours of terrifying peril, either natural or man-made, all began to take its toll on the young Pilgrims. Even Tom and Jesse began to view the magnitude of the evangelizing job that lay ahead with a grieved spirit. Things weren't going as they had dreamed.

Still, their faith in God and their desire to serve compelled them to continue the excursion into the wilderness of the Texas Panhandle. There was no voice for God in Franklinton, and the McKelroys and Lanes believed in their call to evangelize the ranch hands, soldiers, and scattered families of the area. The hardships actually made them more determined to see if their faith would carry them to the end of their journey.

"Ever trail's gut sum puddles," commented Smilin' Jack as the four missionaries pondered their journey. "There's no place 'round the campfire fer uh quitter's blanket. If'n yore Gawd is really behind this here plan of yourn. . . then I reckon yew'd be plum loco to go aginst 'im. 'Sides. . . we's almost there now."

The old man threw the last swallow of his coffee into the fire and placed his cup into the dishwashing bucket. Then he hobbled off to check on the mules like he did before turning in each night. Jesse and Tom looked at each other and grinned that special grin they had learned from Brother Jeremiah. Their journey would continue.

****

Chapter Twenty-two

The Labor

I t was the middle part of December, a Tuesday afternoon in the year 1879. Winter had become a cold fact in most regions of Texas, but none more prevalent than the plains of the Texas Panhandle. White Christmases were fairly commonplace for the area, and the signs from the clouds and temperature indicated that snow would be falling long before the "cows in the field" would start to "kneel in prayer" as was believed to happen on New Year's Eve. The cold wind howling along the treeless hillside made Gayle Lane pray harder for her husband's soon return to their camp with a doctor from nearby Franklinton. Gayle and her preacher husband, Jesse, had planned on spending Christmas Eve in a nice, warm, cozy house or hotel room along with their traveling companions and fellow church planters, Tom and Sarah McKelroy.

Seven long weeks before, these chosen messengers of the Gospel had joined together in the farm community of Miller's Bluff, Texas. Both couples were considered to be "newlyweds" even though Jesse and Gayle had been married for almost a year. Tom and Sarah had come to Miller's Bluff from Louisiana where they had been married in March of '78.

The younger of the two women approached the travail of child birth. Gayle's labor pains, aggravated by the rigors of the foursome's journey across the plains of Texas and the poor food along the way, were severe. Although the birth pangs experienced by the young, auburned-hair missionary had subsided momentarily, Gayle knew they would come again. She prayed more earnestly for Jesse's return from town with the doctor, for she was not looking forward to the moment of delivery with only Sarah at her side.

Gayle was positive that Sarah would need more courage than the frail Easterner had when the time came for "Little Rufus" to make his grand entrance into the world. Sarah, too, was a bit apprehensive of the moment as she suppressed the memory of the pain and emptiness of her own miscarriage just two months earlier. Neither woman displayed her fears, nor had either openly murmured much to their husbands during their trek into the wilderness that strained their faith in God.

"Ahh!" Gayle gasped in pain as the baby began to give indications that it might not wait for the arrival of the doctor.

"Shhh," whispered Sarah as she gripped Gayle's hand. "Stay calm. . . and breathe deeply, Gayle," coaxed the soon-to-be-midwife. Gayle's green eyes filled with tears as she gritted her teeth and threw back her head, her sweat-drenched hair pressing deep into the large feather pillow her Aunt Ida had given her as a wedding present the year before. The pain subsided, and the young school teacher's body relaxed though she still breathed heavily.

"Don't worry," said Sarah, forcing a smile as she wiped Gayle's forehead, still squeezing the young mother-to-be's hand. "Reverend Lane and Husband will be back soon. You just hold on there. Husband'll be here any minute."

Gayle gazed into the dark blue eyes of the woman who sat beside her now. Sarah was trying her best to comfort the frightened young preacher's wife even though she herself feared having to aid the delivery of the Lane's firstborn.

The circuit rider's young wife knew that her surrogate doctor empathized with her pains, and so allowed Sarah to stroke her wet forehead and squeeze her hand in an effort to give the blonde Bostonian an outlet for her own emotions; emotions which Gayle felt had been pent up way too long. As Sarah closed her eyes and began to pray silently for God to control the birth process for just a few hours, Gayle recognized that same worried look she had seen on Sarah's face the first day that Tom and his young bride had driven their prairie schooner down the main street of Miller's Bluff. Sarah prayed. . . and Gayle remembered.

The stress of the pioneering enterprise taxed the young missionaries' strength and considerably decayed their evangelical zeal. All were on the verge of giving up when Smilin' Jack squawked from the back of the lone, remaining wagon, "Yeh hoo! We's almost there! We's almost there!"

Tom and Jesse were stunned. There was no town in sight. There was but one continued plain, parched, whitened in some parts with alkali and altogether inhospitable, bleak, and desolate. Tom had complained the last couple of days of the perpetual alkali dust cloud that hung around the wagon. The dust penetrated the eyes, ears, nose, mouth, hair, and clothes. Its allies were thousands of little sand gnats that got under the clothes and bit harder than mosquitoes.

"See them there two peeks whar the sun's a settin? Thet means Franklinton's jest over the next little hill yonder!"

The joy of Smilin' Jack's revelation spread among the Bible-teachers faster than a prairie fire, for all were ready to reach their desired haven. Fatigue faded as both man and beast appeared alike driven by an unseen, powerful force, for the whole company galloped all the way to the top of the hill.

Exhausted, the young church-planters regained their beginning enthusiasm as they gazed with rapture at the scene below. Tom and Jesse decided to camp on the hill that night so that they could give thanks and plan their entry.

"Ahh!" The pains were back. Women who gave birth on the trail could rarely count on a doctor's help. Gayle grew more and more fearful of having only the assistance of Sarah. If only Jesse would return. Still, she recalled their arrival on the little hill.

Gayle and Sarah had been able to do the laundry in a small pond only the third time since they had left Miller's Bluff. Tom and Jesse spruced up and shaved. Smilin' Jack sat on a rock, smoking his pipe, and praised the life on the plains in a song for which he had a difficult time finding the right key.

"Yes, Sir. This is the life, Fellers. There's prairie chickens and quail everywhirs. And wild turkeys. . . plenty of jack rabbits, deer, antelope, and even a few bufflers all within shootin' range. Ain't nuthin' like a table full of good meat."

Sarah looked curiously at the old muleskinner at these last words, noting that the old man only had about half the normal amount of teeth in his mouth. She never could figure out how Jack ate that awful stuff he called jerky or how he could enjoy a "table full of good meat" with so few teeth.

Suddenly the young, green-eyed preacher's wife went into labor. Tom and Jesse carried Gayle to the wagon followed by a worried Sarah. Smilin' Jack told Jesse about the doctor in Franklinton. The problem was finding the right saloon that old Doc Talmadge used for an "office".

Generally, the frontier doctor spent most of his time removing bullets, mending fractures, and delivering babies. Occasionally, he would diagnose a disease. In other words, he spent most of his time working with the obvious. When a man has a broken bone, it is pretty easy to see what the trouble is. But when a person has a sharp pain in the back of his head, the diagnosis becomes more difficult and sophisticated. Smilin' Jack warned Jesse to not expect too much out of old Doc Talmadge.

Dr. Alexander Talmadge served as the town doctor as well as the town drunk for Franklinton. Although Doc had a housekeeper, he seldom changed his white coat or vest. Many of Franklinton's residents were not sure if his suit was white or grey. Rumor was that the town's medico seldom washed his hands and wore a dirty beard. Unless there was nothing else that could be done, folks who became sick didn't call him, fearing that his presence was more of a danger to the patient than whatever else ailed them.

But then there were others who said they didn't worry about germs on the old sawbones because old Doc was boiled most of the time. Bartenders joked that the town's physician probably graduated from medical school *magna cum loaded*, the way he drank. And his bedside manner was not much better. The old medicine-pusher had been punched several times by husbands who were angered by Doc's blatant disregard for common courtesy.

Once, when two gamblers got into a shooting scrape, Doc Talmadge was asked to treat one of the men who had a gun-shot hole in his leg. He put the man on a table, looked at the wound, pulled part of a dirty old handkerchief through it to "clean it", bandaged the wound, and collected his fee.

He regularly used only three prescriptions for everything: Iodex, a liniment, and a strong laxative. It is no wonder that Franklinton needed so much room on Boot Hill.

The young soul-wrangler and his Bible totin' colleague had hurriedly descended the hill on Homer and one of the mules to fetch Franklinton's doctor for Gayle. Her pregnancy had added to the crushing fatigues of the daily life on the trail which drained her physical resources dangerously low.

****

The pains began coming much more frequently. Both Sarah and Gayle prayed silently that their husbands would return in haste with the doctor in tow.

"Lord, help me!" groaned Gayle.

Strange thoughts began to flood her mind. She thought of Brother Jeremiah and Jesse kneeling in the early morning rain at Little Jimmy's grave. Then she thought of Jesse. The pain brought her so close to the jaws of death. What would her circuit rider do without her?

Outside, Smilin' Jack played with the coals of the camp fire. The old pathfinder had never been this close to a woman giving birth. True, he had attended the births of probably a hundred calves and at least a half-dozen horses and mules, but he had never witnessed the birth of a human being. This realization made the old freight-hauler rather uneasy.

"Mister," he said turning his eyes towards the stars twinkling in a clear sky. "Ain't talked to ya much lately. Mebbe Ah ain't got no right atalkin' now. But them two ladies in thar is in a heap of trouble. Theys both scar't plum out of thar wits. Preacher Tom and Preacher Jesse's gonna have a rough time findin' Doc Talmadge. Mite never find thet old drunk. Prob'ly be better if'n they don't. 'Course thet don't change whut Miss Gayle needs. Ah knows womens been ahavin' babies fer a long time now without no he'p sometimes, but Miss Gayle's special. She's a mitey brave lady. But she needs yore he'p somethin' fierce. Ah knows Ah ain't dun much anuthin' any count in muh life, and Ah've kilt my share o' men. Thet's why Ah ain't askin' nuthin' fer muhself. Now, Ah cain't make no promises, but if'n yew do he'p her. . . why, Ah'd be much a'bliged."

The old muleskinner continued staring at the fire before him, paying no attention to a lone coyote's melodious serenade. Sarah jumped at the howl, even though she had heard that noise numerous times in the past few weeks. Gayle heard, too, but her thoughts flashed to a book by Mark Twain she had read her class back in the little schoolhouse in Miller's Bluff.

"*This creature,*" wrote Twain, "*is so spineless and cowardly that even when his exposed teeth are pretending a threat, the rest of his face is apologizing for it.*"

The young schoolmarm enjoyed reading the works of Twain because he wrote like her Uncle Ethan talked. Another thought crossed her mind. Would she ever be able to read Twain again?

****

Willie Franklin had ridden into the grasslands of the Texas Panhandle during the late 1860's. After opening a dry goods store in Longhorn City, as it was then called, he dug a well near Marjoree Creek, built a small soddy and started rounding up strays. Soon he was selling cattle to England and making a fortune. Not long after that, the town was thriving, with a blacksmith, a brickyard, a lumberyard, and a bank. . . all either owned or run by Franklin. The town became headquarters of sorts for drovers and cowboys from New Mexico Territory on their way to Abilene or Dodge City, Kansas. The town, about 70 miles west of Tascosa, Texas, marked the edge of civilization of the Lone Star state's frontier. At best, the town's population ran under 100.

Old man Franklin didn't trust neighbors, and he hated Indians. His neighbors were driven off after the stockman had bought their land for a ridiculous price. And Indians, peaceful or not, were discouraged from crossing his land by well-placed rifle fire. Even small hunting parties disappeared if caught following tracks of buffalo onto his range.

In Franklinton, like many small, western cow towns, one of the most popular pastimes was getting drunk. It was a way to pass the time, meet new friends, and generally blot out the heat and stench of working cows for long stretches of time. And Franklinton had a number of saloons that sold cheap whiskey.

In fact, almost every third building in Franklinton was a saloon or at least sold strong drink to the cowboys and soldiers who frequented this small Panhandle town, and men were milling or staggering in and out of each one of them. Each of the rowdies who walked the streets was there for the express purpose of getting drunk and raising Cain. Some of the men were already so drunk, Tom noticed, they couldn't hit the ground with their hats in three tries.

"Ain't but one way to find that doctor, Tom," suggested Jesse. "You take one side of the street, and I'll take the other. We can meet back here."

"We'll find him, Jesse," said Tom in a reassuring tone. "The Lord will help us. Don't worry. God's still in control." Tom grinned at his young counterpart and wished that both of them had paid a little more attention to Smilin' Jack's description of the medicine man for whom they searched. All either of them could remember was that Doc Talmadge was old, overweight, unkept in appearance. . . and probably drunk.

As Jesse crossed the dusty street of Franklinton, his mind focused on Tom's last words to him. Jesse knew that the words of his former-cardsharp friend were truth. Brother Jeremiah had convinced them both of God's control and purpose. Both men were convinced that the Lord had led them to this sin-filled settlement. And both were convinced that God had protected them during the perils of the journey that tested their faith in some way or another each day over the past few weeks. Both men were convinced that their labor for Jesus would not be in vain. . . that the Lord of the Harvest would bring about a bountiful return on each seed planted in this spiritual wilderness. Jesse wasn't sure what God had planned, but he knew everything would be according to God's Will.

****

Chapter Twenty-three

The Full House

The Silver Mansion was most inappropriately named. Even by cow-town standards, the place was pitiful. The smoke-filled saloon in the middle of Franklinton was actually just a large, one-room structure. Moonlight flickered through chinks in the walls of the green lumber, and spider webs filled its rough-hewn rafters. The bar, which did not look very clean, was a 20 foot piece of rough lumber supported with barrels of rotgut whiskey and wine. Free food lay on the bar open to the filth and dust of the streets as well as the giant flies of northwest Texas. The place was foggy with smoke and smelled of sweating, unwashed bodies and cheap whiskey. The male customers who were chewing tobacco were remarkably bad marksmen, for the insides of the spittoons were left practically untouched. The floor was filthy, a combination of sawdust mixed with mud, tobacco juice, spilled beer. . . and, in spots, dried blood.

Most of the ranch hands that frequented the establishment wore blue jeans or buck-skin breeches stuffed into high-topped boots. Often protruding from one boot was a horn-handled fighting knife, and all carried a long-barreled Colt revolver in a belt holster strapped sometimes high and sometimes low on their hips.

The "Who-hit-John" served in this house of suds often led to trouble. Arguments over painted bar-maids or discussions at the gambling tables usually ended in someone being murdered. Sometimes house-employed musicians would be forced into performing a clog dance, and then shot when the audience became bored.

"Oh, merciful Father," said Jesse to himself, "how can anyone exist in this slime pit?" Jesse peeked into the Silver Mansion and shook his head.

"Come in or get out!" growled an overweight bartender. "Don't block my door, Mister! What'll you be havin'?"

Jesse reluctantly walked towards the bar. "Just some information, thanks," he said as he surveyed the patrons inside the Mansion.

"If'n it ain't about whiskey or cards, I cain't do you no good," growled the barkeeper.

"Do you know where I might find Doc Talmadge?" asked Jesse.

The bartender chewed his cigar a bit, raised his eyebrows, and answered with sarcasm, "You might find him in most any dark alley in town. . . or mebbe sleepin' off a drunk in the stables. But if'n you look right over yonder, you'll find him tryin' his best to get all roistered up on redeye and losin' the shirt off'n his back." The hefty saloon-keeper nodded towards Jesse's left.

Sitting in the corner, surrounded by five bearded cowboys, was a fat, red-nosed, man whose waistcoat was blotched with food stains hiding behind streaks of dirt. He swayed slightly from the effects of the whiskey he sipped while trying to focus his reddened eyes on the cards he held.

In those days, anyone who wanted to could hang out a sign with DOCTOR painted on it. Some who did were phony con-men from the east after a quick dollar. Others were fast-talking hawkers of patent medicines from New England. Some were merely reputation-seeking hospital attendants who had gained a smattering of medical knowledge.

Doc Talmadge did not have a fancy diploma from a prestigious medical school hanging on the wall of the small office in his house, which surprised no one. In fact, he had no diploma at all. The old sawbones had learned his trade first as a medical assistant during the War Between the States, and then had apprenticed himself to a lettered physician in the Indian Territory. As a young man, Doc had sincerely tried to learn the art of medicine, but had started hitting the "oh-be-joyful" soon after his wife died attempting to give birth some ten years earlier.

Still, in the West, a man was what he said he was until he was proven a liar. Thus, the hoaxes had their hay-day. Their knowledge of dispensing medicines usually consisted of quinine, laudanum, calomel, or gentian. Then to embellish these simple drugs, they placed various bottles of colored water and animal parts soaking in formaldehyde on their shelves. Their remedies were based on a mixture of superstition, black magic, and housewives' cures. In giving out prescriptions they might toss in a few Latin words, if they knew any, to impress their customers. Sometimes, they miraculously cured their patients. Sometimes they killed them with their cures.

It was obvious to the young cowboy-preacher that the town's sole medicine-man was drunker than a goat eating chinaberries. Had Gayle not needed a doctor so desperately, Jesse would have walked out of the sin nest. But the thought of his wife in pain gave the young missionary the extra strength he needed to confront the drunken physician at the poker table.

"Excuse me, Sir," said Jesse, "May I speak to you in private?"

"Not until I finish this hand, Son," answered the inebriated pill-pusher.

"But I need your services, Doctor. My wife is having a baby, and she's having problems," pleaded the young preacher.

"Lots of women have had babies without my assistance, Young Man," stated the filthy, cow-town bandage-roller rather matter-of-factly. "At the moment, I am more interested in helping this lady get a match. I'll take two," said Doc Talmadge to the man dealing the cards.

"Sir, I don't wish to use force, but I will if I must," insisted Jesse as he moved his hand towards the pistol hanging at his side.

Doc Talmadge finally looked up at the young, Bible-pioneer.

"Mister, these gentlemen sitting around here are all my friends. As you can see, I am quite busy. Should you persist in making a nuisance of yourself, I shall not be responsible for the actions of my friends. Now, kindly leave me alone. Three ladies," the sometimes surgeon said as he spread his poker hand for all to see.

A year or so before, Jesse would have been outraged at the lack of concern shown by the old doctor. Now he understood more of how Satan enslaved people with selfishness and blinded them to the needs of others. Jesse felt sorry for the lonely old man who drowned his fears in a bottle of "liquid courage".

"Sir," Jesse said calmly, "Do you ever think about Jesus Christ?"

"That's the last straw!" shouted the old medicine man as he slammed his cards to the table. "Jack, escort this loud-mouth, scourge of moral slackers from my presence!"

The squelch of chairs sliding heavily across the hard-wood floor was a cacophony of irritating noise as the five bearded cowboys jumped to their feet with guns drawn and cocked.

"Yew wanna walk out, Mister. . . or git carried out?" said the large bartender who pointed a cocked, double-barrel shotgun at the young frontier minister. "I reckon yew best skedaddle, Boy!" shouted the overweight barkeep, trying to make his point perfectly clear.

Jesse remembered something his mentor had once said, "Sometimes you gotta cut your loses and leave." Jesse sighed heavily.

"You've persuaded me to catch a breath of fresh air," stated the Bible-wrangler. The young preacher walked out of the grimy saloon with a prayer on his lips that Gayle would not become a widow and "Little Rufus" an orphan. He still needed the doctor, drunken or not, but he didn't know what else to do. Perhaps Tom would have an idea.

"I'm sorry, Jesse, I didn't find Doc Talmadge anywhere," said a worried Tom.

"I did, Tom. He's inside the Silver Mansion over there. . . drunk. . . playing cards. He's a loser, Tom. I'm not sure he could help Gayle anyway. Maybe we better just go back to camp," suggested the young Hallelujah-singer.

"Surely we can persuade him to come along," offered Tom. "He's bound to be of some help."

"The old man's wrapped up in his card playing. He only sees spades and clubs and diamonds and hearts. He only cares about himself. . . the cards in his hand and the drink on the table," mentioned Jesse.

"Maybe we can win him over to our side," said Tom with his own special little grin.

"How?" inquired the frustrated Psalm-singer. "The man is worthless. . . and would probably see two babies if he saw one!"

"I'll use tricks of the trade. Stay here and send up a prayer, Jesse. We'll be right out," stated Tom confidently with a wink.

****

Tom McKelroy strolled boldly into the cloudy bar room known as the Silver Mansion. His expert gambler's eye scoured the men sitting at the ragged card tables for the "loser" Jesse had described. As his gaze settled on the fat little man in the stained suit, his mind recalled the scene aboard the *Delta Queen* almost four years earlier. He had not played a hand of poker since that night and wondered if he still had the gift.

"Lord," he whispered to himself, "I need your help. Stretch this five dollars for Gayle's sake."

The clink of dice and the swish of dealt cards somehow stood out above the chatter of the cowboys occupying the hazy room. Tom approached the table where Doc Talmadge sat just as one of the men decided that he'd try one of the other entertainment centers of Franklinton.

"Mind if I join you folks?" asked Tom.

"Depends on if you want to talk or play cards," answered the scruffiest of the cowhands.

"Oh, to play cards, of course," grinned the unbeknownst preacher. "That is, if the stakes don't get too high. Can't afford to lose all my fortune before my partner and I start up our new business in town."

The rotund doctor and the other men grinned as if they had finally found a sure sucker. Strangers didn't normally take advantage of the fine entertainment and games of chance offered at the Silver Mansion. The reputation of that particular saloon and gambling house usually persuaded the occasional pilgrim passing through Franklinton to shy away from the regulars.

"Reckon we can keep it light, Mister," said Doc Talmadge.

For thirty minutes the group played poker. Tom was being set up, but he knew he had the game under control. Finally, he was able to make his move.

"How about we play one more hand," stated Tom. "No limit?"

"Sure," answered the old doctor with a grin and a twirl of his cigar. "Why not?"

Tom shuffled the cards with ease and then dealt five of the colored pasteboards to each man.

"Open fer five dollars," said the buck-toothed ranch hand on Tom's left.

"I'm in," said Talmadge. Two others folded before Tom tossed in his gold piece. Each man drew two cards.

"Five more," said the cowboy.

"See your five, and I'll raise you five," commented the doctor.

"Here's my ten," said Tom, "and I'll raise you fifty more."

"Cain't go that," answered the cowhand as he tossed his cards into the pot.

"Got too good a hand to let you win on a bluff, Sonny," said Doc Talmadge. "So, it'll cost you another twenty to stay in this game."

"I'll see your twenty," answered the former riverboat gambler without batting an eye, "and raise you another fifty."

"I don't have fifty," said the doctor soberly.

"But you have something better, Sir. Your services. My partner's wife is having a baby, and she needs a doctor. And although your blood might be a little thin with all the alcohol you've been con-suming, you, Sir, are the only doctor around. What do you say?"

"I ought to have you shot," answered the red-eyed physician. "But I admire your guts, Boy. What's the deal?"

"Simple," answered the former Georgia plowboy. " If you win, you get the pot. If I win, we leave here and go out to our camp just outside of town, and you get the honor of bringing a new citizen into this quaint, little village you call home."

The old doctor grinned widely. "Why not? Can you beat a full house. . . queens and tens?"

Tom looked at the cards spread on the table and then at the old medical practicner who had by this time leaned back in his chair and was grinning like a chessar cat.

"I hope the cold wind outside helps to sober you up, Doc. You'll need all your faculties. Full house. . . aces and kings," said Tom dryly.

"Well, if'n thet don't take the hide off'n the cow," said the cowboy who had stayed in the game the longest.

The intoxicated, scruffy physician pursed his lips, pushed back his chair and stood to his full 5 foot 7 inches while making an attempt to smooth out some of the wrinkles in his soiled jacket. "Shall we leave, Sir?"

Tom followed the doctor outside to where Jesse stood, still praying. "How'd you talk him into coming with us?" asked Jesse.

"The house was getting too full," said Doc Talmadge. "Besides, I needed the fresh air. Where's your camp, Gentlemen?"

****

By the time Jesse and Tom had arrived with Doc Talmadge, Gayle was entering the final stage of delivery. Sarah had already torn her petticoat into shreds as she prepared to do her best to play the role of mid-wife. Smilin' Jack had gathered enough wood for a small bonfire and started water boiling in a large pot. He didn't know why he was boiling the water, but he had always heard someone say that they'd need plenty of boiling water at times like this.

"Took ya long 'nugh! We'd done gived up on yuh!" said the old muleskinner. "Hurry up yersef in there, Doc."

"You gentlemen just stay here next to the fire. I'll be out in a little dab of time," said the doctor.

He looked into the wagon and saw, at least momentarily in his mind, his own wife and her struggles with giving birth. Although he viewed the situation through bloodshot eyes, he recalled his feeling of inadequacy and decided that he was not going to lose either patient. Then he looked at the terror on the face of the young blonde as well as the concern on the faces of all three men. And suddenly, the sarcastic medicine man's attitude changed into one of confidence.

"Do you folks have any soap?" asked the veteran of countless operations in a battlefield hospital. "I could use some hot water, too.

Don't worry, Gentlemen. . . this little lady and her soon-to-be family is gonna be just fine."

Doc Talmadge removed his coat and vest and thoroughly scrubbed his hands in hot water provided by the crusty, old mule-skinner. As he dried his hands on a clean towel provided by Sarah, he winked at the two future church-planters and nodded his head to reassure them that they had made the right decision in procuring his services.

The half-sober medico climbed onto the back of the wagon where Gayle lay anticipating the arrival of her first child. Doc surveyed the situation quickly and took a piece of a rattlesnake rattle from his little black bag and ground the rattle into a fine powder. Then he mixed the fine particles in a cup of water for the pretty woman from Miller's Bluff to drink. Delivery, without as much pain as before, came within ten minutes.

Each minute seemed like an hour to the three men outside the wagon, though. Tom thought of Sarah's miscarriage. Jesse thought of the endless night of the shooting in the church in Miller's Bluff. Smilin' Jack thought of the first day he met the whimsical Gayle and the tune she had been whistling as she opened the door of the parsonage. These thoughts brought some apprehension, some remorse, and some deeper understanding of God's direction in their lives. Each man thought of his boyhood and his folks and events long ago pushed into the annuals of the "good ol' days".

For some unknown reason, all three men suddenly turned their gaze on the camp fire, which was burning low because no one had put any wood on the fire in quite sometime. Then they looked up at each other and stated simultaneously, "Something's gone wrong. . . it's been too long!"

And so the pacing started. . . Jesse from the camp fire to the back of the wagon. . . Tom from left to right in front of the camp fire. . . Smilin' Jack from right to left behind the camp fire. None of them said another word to the other, but noticed the silence of the evening. . . no coyotes howled, no crickets chirped, no owls hooted, no night-critters broke a branch while moving from one locale to another. And no sounds from within the wagon. . . if you don't count the wails of anguish from Gayle and the moans of sympathy from

Sarah and the constant reassurance from the half-drunken doctor. The waiting for the men who had endured an arduous journey was sheer agony because each let his imagination run wild.

Suddenly the silence of the night air was split by the scream of a banshee, and then the cry of a baby. All three men stared wondering at the shadows on the canvas of the wagon. Sarah came to the back opening with a bundle in her arms.

"It's a boy, Reverend Lane!" Sarah said smiling broadly. "It's a boy!"

And then the scream again. Startled, Sarah turned to look behind her. Again a baby cried, and another huge smile crossed the lips of the previously sour-faced Sarah.

"It's another boy, Reverend! Another boy! You and Sister Gayle are really gonna have a full house now!"

****

Chapter Twenty-four

The New Beginning

New Year's Eve in 1879 ushered in more than the dawn of a new decade. So many fantastic and unusual events had taken place in the recent years in the United States that everyone looked forward to the 1880's with great expectations.

Mary Baker Eddy had chartered the First Church of Christ Scientist destined to enslave hundreds.

P. T. Barnum, called the Greatest Showman on Earth, was touring the country with a troupe comprised of 500 men and 200 horses.

Little Annie Oakley was dazzling audiences in small towns with her sharp shooter act as a part of Buffalo Bill's Wild West Show.

Educators and plain folks were reading and rereading Longfellow's story of Christianity entitled *Christus: a Mystery* or Mark Twain's *Adventures of Tom Sawyer* based on Twain's memories of his childhood in the sleepy river town of Hannibal, Missouri.

Hundreds of folks were enjoying the benefits of newly developed inventions like Bell's telephone, Edison's phonograph and light bulb, and Ritty's cash register.

H. J. Heinz was making a fortune in pickles while Proctor and Gamble in Cincinnati produced a bar of soap that floated.

And Aaron Montgomery Ward was making products affordable through his 72 page mail-order catalog. In addition, the Salvation

Army set up headquarters in Chicago to aid the unfortunate out-casts of society.

All across the nation, parents made plans for the future concerning their children. Jesse and Gayle Lane were busy making plans with their fellow missionaries, Tom and Sarah McKelroy in Franklinton, Texas.

In 1879 Franklinton was a raucous community just west of the Western Trail close to the New Mexico border in the Texas Panhandle. An amazing number of former gun fighters, trail tramps, and other shadowy characters drifted in and out of the small cow-town, mixing with immigrant sod-busters, local cowhands, and unwashed buffalo hunters like one skinner known, for obvious reasons, as Dirty Face Johnson, or just Dirty Slim. The adventures the greenhorn missionaries were about to experience would make the hardships of the trail seem like a Sunday School picnic.

"Lord, thank you for bringing us through the wilderness," prayed Gayle as she gently rocked the two cribs holding her twin sons. "I could hardly believe we made it two weeks ago after such a journey. But now we've found a home."

The cabin Gayle identified as home was a crude adobe containing a kitchen with a fireplace and two small bedrooms. It at one time had been owned by a merchant named Crooked Nose Benson. Benson sold farm supplies, but was given an offer that he couldn't refuse by Willie Franklin. So, Benson retired and moved to Austin some two years earlier. Smilin' Jack had suggested the empty little dirt shack as a possible place for the missionaries to reside. . . until they could build something better. Doc Talmadge had been given power of attorney over the selling or renting of the former business-man's property and allowed the church-planting group to stay in the house rent free.

The three-room, abandoned cabin that the Lanes and the McKelroys shared on the outskirts of town could hardly be described as a house, though, what with the dirt floors, broken window panes, and leaky roof, but the big fireplace and thick walls would provide a warm refuge from the winter snows for the two young sin-slaying couples. The land would not be hard to clear of the mesquite bushes that were mere apologies for trees. Compared to the rich forests of central Texas and north Louisiana, these "trees" made the general view more cheerless by their deformed and stunted growth.

Jesse and Tom had gone to town with Smilin' Jack to try and talk to the cowboys and soldiers that staggered from saloon to saloon celebrating the birth of the new decade. Franklinton was a typical trail town existing on the frontier. It did not have the stabilizing influence of farm families, so it became absolutely necessary to cater to the delights of the drovers. Willie Franklin, who owned the largest ranch in the area and most of the town, encouraged the trail bosses to use portions of his grazing lands for a fee and insisted that the cowboys they employed experience the hospitality of his town. There was no lawman in Franklinton to slow down the trail-hands who spent what little money they had foolishly trying to best the traveling gamblers who tended to follow the migrating herds or on the loose women who plied their trade in each saloon. Even the most casual observer would characterize this little settlement as a "sin hole".

"We'll find someone to listen to God's Word," Tom had said.

"Do be careful, Husband," cautioned a worried Sarah.

"Yew betcha we'll be keerful, ladies. But we's gut the Lord on our side. Not even old Go-lienth can stand 'gainst us," bragged Smilin' Jack.

Sarah had cried herself to sleep in the small room that she and Tom claimed as their own. Sarah was totally miserable, but she hid her emotions from husband Tom, relying on God's strength to pull her through. She thought often of the big house that her folks owned in Boston. . . so clean. . . and so many rooms. Thoughts of her former life with all the parties and the music was her mental escape from the little shack with the dirt floors. Still, it was the place where her husband dwelt, and she would dwell by his side. . . at least momentarily.

Gayle was content in the cozy little cabin and was as excited as ever about beginning a new life in the northern wilderness area of the Texas panhandle. She smiled broadly as she remembered their arrival in Franklinton when the group rattled into the sin-filled cow-town. The men in town, she thought, were disappointed that the women were missionaries, but were polite in their awe at the scene of the two lovely young women and the newborn babies. A group of the men, bold and reckless, even entertained them with "firin', drummin', singin', and dancin'" the first evening that the missionaries stayed in town at Doc Talmadge's house. Many of them staggered a might as they attempted to entertain the newcomers; quite as many swore lustily. The men had actually been "spies" from the town's saloons sent out to get a good look at the preaching team. It was quickly decided that a lesson would be given that would frighten these and all future aspirants away from Franklinton. Just how to do the deed had not been decided. . . perhaps the rail. . . perhaps a good neck-tie party.

"Funny," thought Gayle, "Sarah and I probably could have given a Bible to every cowboy in town if those we had brought with us hadn't been washed down the flooded Brazos. Perhaps, Lord, You will give such favor to Jesse and Tom."

And the Lord did give favor to Jesse and Tom. The spiritual battles were hard fought, and the Enemy attacked furiously on almost a day to day basis. Still, the victory came for the young missionary team. These church-planters would experience hardship, the tragedy of death, and even an occasional fight with thoughts of doubt. But each time the Devil attacked with viciousness, the missionary team would crop his horns and tie a knot in his tail. The church would become a centerpiece in the cultural development of this sin-filled cow town on the plains of the Texas Panhatndle because of a deep-rooted faith instilled in two young Bible-thumpers by one of the last of the old circuit riders.

****